Airplanes, Atlanta, & an Assassin

Mary Seifert

Books by Mary Seifert

Maverick, Movies, & Murder
Rescue, Rogues, & Renegade
Tinsel, Trials, & Traitors
Santa, Snowflakes, & Strychnine
Fishing, Festivities, & Fatalities
Diamonds, Diesel, & Doom
Creeps, Cache, & Corpses
Pranks, Payback & Poison
Juleps, Jockeys & Justice
Airplanes, Atlanta & an Assassin

Visit Mary's website and get a free recipe collection!
Scan the QR code

Airplanes, Atlanta, & an Assassin

Katie & Maverick Cozy Mysteries, Book 10

Mary Seifert

Secret Staircase Books

Airplanes, Atlanta, & an Assassin
Published by Secret Staircase Books, an imprint of
Columbine Publishing Group, LLC
PO Box 416, Angel Fire, NM 87710

Book layout and design by Secret Staircase Books
Cover images © Chernetskaya, Deeboldrick, Penywise, F11Photo,
Patrick Marcell Pelz
First trade paperback edition: July, 2025
First e-book edition: July, 2025

* * *

Publisher's Cataloging-in-Publication Data

Seifert, Mary
Airplanes, Atlanta, & an Assassin / by Mary Seifert.
p. cm.
ISBN 978-1649142245 (paperback)
ISBN 978-1649142252 (e-book)

1. Katie Wilk (Fictitious character). 2. Minnesota—Fiction. 3.
Amateur sleuths—Fiction. 4. Women sleuths—Fiction. 5. Dogs in
fiction. I. Title
Katie & Maverick Cozy Mystery Series : Book 10.
Siefert, Mary, Katie & Maverick cozy mysteries.

BISAC : FICTION / Mystery & Detective.
813/.54

For John and Thomas!

"Flying is learning how to throw yourself at the ground and miss."—Douglas Adams

"Aviation is proof that given the will, we have the capacity to achieve the impossible."—Eddie Rickenbacker

ONE

Carlee Parks-Bluestone made it to the head of the long line to receive her airline voucher when a black-haired, stout man with a beaky nose shoved his way in front of the registration desk and demanded, "How dare you bump me. Do you know who I am?"

The dolt accosting one of my students brought out the mama-bear in me. Carlee had never flown before, and feeling her anxiety, my protective instincts blazed. My nostrils flared. I stepped between them, into a cloud of cologne that made me want to sneeze, and turned to face the curious onlookers, mouths gaping in disbelief.

"Excuse me." I raised my hand to quiet the murmurings

and recited a line I'd held in reserve for just such an occasion. "Excuse me. Does anyone know this man? He seems to have forgotten his name."

I ignored the well-fitting, navy blue, Armani suit and tasseled, black shoes polished to a high shine, and focused on the twitch in his eye. My hand rested on my chest. "My name is Katie Wilk," I said slowly, as if speaking to a child. "Is there someone here with you, or someone we can call?"

His jaw dropped. A tall blond woman, following the exchange, covered her lips with long, slender fingers. The nails painted a glittery green matched her crinkling eyes. Her shoulders convulsed, smothering her laughter, and she gave me a thumbs up.

I turned to the agent before the self-centered man could sputter any other words of non-wisdom and said, "I'm sorry. I probably shouldn't have said that." The agent smirked and ushered us forward.

I'd already been put through the wringer. My patience had worn thin, and he'd stomped on my last nerve, but when Carlee gave me a high five, her accompanying grin and eye roll made it all worthwhile.

"Bet you never thought teaching would be so tough." Carlee tossed the curtain of straight black hair over her shoulder. Her silver-blue eyes lit with mischief.

Who would've guessed I'd end up in education, but when my life's goals spun off the rails, I needed to investigate a career other than mathematical cryptanalysis.

"How did you end up in Columbia, Minnesota? It's a long way from London," she teased gently.

"Just lucky. Columbia is the best place to be. How could I go wrong?"

I tried to mirror her laughter. I didn't tell her I applied for jobs all over the state and had only one interview. What do you do with a degree in the study of codes and algorithms when you no longer had the desire to study codes and algorithms? Research told me saying yes to extra duties might improve my chances and make me a more acceptable candidate. When they offered me the job to teach high school math—the only proposal I received—I signed on the dotted line.

"Let me assure you," she said. "We're the lucky ones. Look where you and Ms. Mackey got us today."

"Don't forget your amazing, sensational volunteer-attorney coach."

"Who could forget her?"

Our kids not only survived their first year of mock trial with three rookie coaches, they thrived and were the team representing the Gopher State, Minnesota, in Atlanta.

"Oh, Ms. Wilk," Carlee giggled as she pocketed her remuneration, and we headed to join our friends. "Another adventure."

I wanted to put as much distance as possible between the discourteous man and Carlee and me, but if I'd looked back over my shoulder, I probably would've been more vigilant.

Compartmentalizing the events leading to the encounter had ratcheted up my angst; I hoped the kids hadn't picked up on my fear. I hated flying, but I could hardly refuse the generous gift of airline tickets purchased for the students, coaches, and parent volunteers. I had, however, imagined all the ways we'd miss our flight and hadn't wanted to be late. The day began hours earlier when my co-chaperone and best friend, Jane Mackey, and I loaded our students onto the school van. They'd worked hard, and I wanted to provide a memorable experience. My job required escorting my team, smoothing out difficulties, and solving problems.

I allowed plenty of time to navigate the freeway in case unpredictable traffic or road construction hampered our arrival, and we'd reported to the Minneapolis-St. Paul International Airport three hours ahead of schedule. I'm glad we did.

Neither Jane nor any of my students set off any extraneous buzzing noises while we calmly checked in through TSA, and Jane shooed them ahead to the coffee shop to pick up light breakfast nibbles. Bringing up the rear, however, my pass through the security checkpoint triggered extra scrutiny.

"Step off to the side please," said a sour-faced, slight TSA agent. My heart thudded in my chest for no other reason than they'd singled me out, and I didn't have my trusted canine equalizer, Maverick, with me. "Stand with your feet on the white shoe prints and lift your hands over your head." She ran a wand up my right side and down the left, up my backside and down in front, while a male agent gently pawed through my bag.

He cast wary blue eyes my way and brought out the white gift box. I returned a strained smile. Carefully opening the lid, he peeled away the delicate blue and silver tissue paper studded with glossy stars—Columbia High School Cougar colors.

"What do we have here?" He folded back the padded cover and read the inscription, furrowing his brow. His eyes locked with mine, and he shook a head of short brown hair. "I take it you're not Brock Isaacson. Why do you have his diploma?" One of his eyebrows rose with suspicion. "Are you stealing someone's identity?"

"Do I look like a male high school graduate?" I chuckled.

The students in my charge and their parents trusted me. My head told me to take my responsibility seriously and not make waves with security. "Sorry. I'm a high school math teacher." I tried to swallow and stammered, tamping down an undeserved feeling of guilt. "I'm taking my students to

Atlanta for a competition."

I scoured the area for the royal-blue kerchiefs identifying my crew to support my explanation. The agent followed my frantic gaze and raised the other eyebrow skeptically. "You must've seen them. They were all wearing those Cougar scarves." I pointed to the blue fabric in the bin resting beneath my badly needed phone.

A single guffaw escaped from his female counterpart. "He's just joshing with you."

"It's one of the busiest times of the year. Gotta break up the day somehow." He conscientiously repackaged the carton, and his playful grin slowed my racing heart ... partway. Leery, I half expected him to further impede my exit with another infraction and didn't let my guard down until he tipped his head and slid my bag across the rolling surface. "Have a nice day, ma'am."

My carry-on snagged the edge of the counter. Flustered, I tied my kerchief around my neck, hefted my bag, and repeatedly yanked the handle, drawing undue attention from the other passengers. When the wheels clattered to the floor, I tugged the handle free, stared straight ahead, and ignoring the reserved whispers, bustled into the shopping area of the airport.

The fair-skinned figure with light brown hair and pale blue eyes looking back at me, distorted by the reflection in the glass windows of the stores I passed, gave me a jolt. I looked harried. I had to relax. Jane had the kids. They were fine. I'd catch up with them in a minute. Lowering my shoulders, I blinked my eyes, lifted my chin, and pasted on a smile. I almost pinched my cheeks for added color. I didn't want the kids to know how much I really hated everything to do with flying.

Weather delayed the incoming plane. We had boarded

thirty minutes behind schedule, and forty-two minutes later, after anxious bouts of fits and giggles checking watches and phone screens, we saw our pilot step out of the cockpit to make a brief announcement.

"Good morning, folks. Sorry for the delay, but due to mechanical issues, we've had to cancel our non-stop flight to Atlanta." As the air around me took on a rumble, he smiled uneasily and took a big breath. "We apologize for any inconvenience, and we'll do our best to accommodate you and get you to your final destination as quickly as possible. Please gather your belongings and check the seat pocket before disembarking. See the gate attendant for more details."

We exited the aircraft. Our students crowded around me, and I said decisively, "We'll catch another plane soon and still arrive in plenty of time to take advantage of everything we've planned before your competition begins in three days. Don't worry."

Famous last words. I hoped I wasn't constructing a false narrative for our future.

I massaged my temples as we waited our turn and inched our way to the desk for information. The smile glued to the young man's face never wavered as he checked our tickets. "It's a very busy Memorial weekend." His fingers flew over the keys. "It'll take a bit of maneuvering to get your entire group in the sky, but we'll get you on the next available flight, however …" He looked up at me, and one corner of his mouth turned down in a bit of alarm. "The operative word is *available*."

My heart leaped to my throat, and I gritted my teeth in frustration.

"And a nonstop will be impossible." His eyebrows, cheeks, and lips morphed into one big apology. "You'll be rerouted first through Detroit."

One could only take so much, but I forced my jaw to unclench. We would get to Atlanta.

Then, in a rehearsed facial transformation, he said. "And for your inconvenience, you've each earned five hundred dollars to use toward a ticket at a later date." With a flourish at a final key depression, he sent us on our way.

I led our entourage to obtain the vouchers. Unfortunately, I'd have to fly again in order to use mine. Carlee and I brought up the rear and were the last two of our party to receive the compensation for our trouble. I'd been at the end of my rope when we'd encountered the unknown entity suffering an identity crisis and lost what little cool I had remaining.

TWO

We had walked away from the vexatious passenger, still mute from my smart remark, and Carlee said, "Ms. Wilk, there's another one for our record book." She laughed off the confrontation. "You are keeping a journal for the trip, aren't you?"

"Of course," I said and mentally tapped my brain. I'd promised to keep track of our expedition, but I needed a notebook.

She read the consternation on my face. "You forgot, didn't you?"

"Yes, but I would've eventually remembered." I wore my most contrite expression while scouring the concourse for a gift shop. Barely visible through the sea of bobbing heads, three gates to the right, a bookstore offered its wares.

I pointed. "They'll have what I need."

I jogged against the swift-moving current of focused travelers and crews, dodging luggage rolling in all directions, and forging a diametrically opposed path. Ejected from the stream of bodies close enough to the entryway to spot the cloth-covered diaries, I purchased two and a new book on the history of cryptology. I rejoined our retinue and caught the tail end of Carlee's retelling the story of our encounter, making me look like a hero.

"You certainly gave him a piece of your mind," said Lorelei Calder.

"Be careful, Ms. Wilk," Jane said. "You don't have much mind in reserve."

Before I could cast her a seething glance, Lorelei laughed. Jane would get her comeuppance, but I forgave Lorelei her minor transgression. A junior, she performed brilliantly as the lead counsel on our team, and luckily, her parents consented to accompany us. Jane and Marietta, Lorelei's mom, both graduated from Emory and knew Atlanta and the surrounding area. Marietta spent much of our disrupted travel time mesmerizing the kids with tantalizing tales of the places we'd be visiting. Her phone screen lit up with a carousel of closeup shots of native animals in the wild, vivid birds of every color, fields filled with blankets of flowers, and tempting menus that listed recipes rarely found in Minnesota. "Georgia has its dangers, though, and I'll be sure to keep you apprised," she said.

"Hey, Ms. Wilk, where's Coach Dvorak?" Brock asked.

Patting the outside pocket of my bag, I ran my thumb around the edge of its rectangular contents and breathed a sigh of relief. Lorelei's boyfriend, Brock Isaacson, a senior, chose to attend Mock Trial America over his graduation ceremony, and our principal gave us permission to surprise him and bestow his diploma at the same time as his classmates. I inhaled deeply, erasing the nightmare of its possible confiscation when passing through airport security.

"She's already in Atlanta, taking some well-earned vacation days, and she'll check in with us on Monday."

Our attorney coach had flown down a day early to have what she called adult time before the students joined her. She and her law partner had blocked off two evenings for their social fraternization. We wouldn't be here without her. Dorene Dvorak's knowledge and guidance were of immeasurable help. Unbeknown to the kids, she had also arranged a tour of the Supreme Court of Georgia which included a private interview with one of the state supreme court justices.

When Marietta ran out of enticing things to talk about, I pulled out a deck of cards and taught the kids two new easy magic tricks. Lorelei explained how the tricks worked mathematically, and Brock gave his usual, "Of course," and hooted. "Way to spoil the mystique."

"That's my girl," said her dad.

Fifty-five minutes later, our team boarded our flight to Detroit with fingers crossed we'd make the connection to Georgia. With my attention focused on locating the heads of the kids scattered throughout the cabin as they took their seats, I wriggled down the aisle in first-class and bumped the elbow of the man who tried to budge in front of Carlee. He noisily waggled a glass of ice, and I attempted to slip by Mr. Buttinski, not wishing to antagonize him further. His glass stopped in mid-swing. Recognition dawned. The cubes clinked, and I cringed until I realized he addressed my partner.

"Janie?" When she didn't respond immediately, he put his empty hand out flat to stop her from continuing to her seat. The other hand went to his chest, spilling the remaining contents of the glass. As he swiped the ice away and dabbed at the front of his designer suit, he reported, full of self-importance, "Jane Mackey. It's me. Wendell."

She swept her curly blond locks behind her ear and stared with unblinking big brown eyes. "Wendell?" I didn't think it possible, but her eyes widened. "Wendell Gromm?"

The flight attendant urged us forward. "We have to clear the aisle and prepare for takeoff. Please find your seats."

Jane gave Wendell a two-finger salute, and we shambled to our places, two rows up from the restrooms. Jane rolled her eyes, and she plopped down onto her seat.

"You know him?" I asked, sitting next to her, fumbling my bag into the space beneath the seat in front of us.

At first, she avoided answering my question. "These accommodations are even a little tight for me," she said as she snuggled deeper into the upholstery. At just about five feet, depending on the footwear she chose, her comment emphasized the compact space. "I can't get comfortable." She pulled out her travel blanket and took a breath. "But that might be because of him."

"Wendell's the rude guy who cut in front of Carlee."

"Sounds about right." Jane sighed again. "Wendell Gromm and I attended the same elementary and high school. No matter what anyone said, he would debate the opposite and claim to have a better grasp of the data, and unfortunately, his arguments sounded reasonable. Even as a third grader. He cited well-known individuals like Albert Einstein or Steve Jobs or even Batman, but took the words completely out of context, adjusting them to fit his needs. I didn't bother to examine his sources until middle school, when he could no longer legitimately hold up his side of a disagreement. He became contentious, and we didn't spend much time together after ..." The words drifted off.

"Jane, you're clenching your fists."

"I never thought I'd ever have to see Wendell again."

"What happened?" I nodded my head encouragingly, hoping she'd resume her story.

"I'd rather not think of him. I'll just close my eyes and dream of my sexy husband-to-be, dismissing all thought of Wendell Gromm. Wake me when we're preparing for landing." She shrank into the seat, pulled the red fleece up to her chin, murmured, "Drew," and feigned immediate sleep.

Our plane prepared for take-off, but rather than relaxing for the trip ahead, I chewed the inside of my cheek. Having never flown before, not surprisingly, Carlee was the most overtly excited, and I couldn't differentiate her anxiety from elation. I'd flown before and had the same mixed feelings. I tapped the headrest in front of me.

"Having such a significant delay isn't usual, but the agent assured us the rest of our trip would pull off without a hitch. You doing okay, Carlee?"

She peeked between the seats. "This is great. Galen's a little scared though."

"Am not," a deep voice answered quickly.

Carlee's arm rose with his hand clenching hers. She giggled as he dragged their arms back down and admitted, "Maybe."

I tugged my new book from the carryall, but after rereading the first paragraph three times and not making any headway, I closed the cover and leaned back, letting good thoughts drift in and out of my consciousness.

I loved my first year teaching and everything that went with it. Of course, I'd had to deal with a few murders, but I'd made it through the first nine months and looked forward to year two.

The engines roared. We were finally on our way. My eyes

closed and my head fell back against the seat. I couldn't wait to see what other surprises our trip had in store for us.

Turns out, I could've waited after all.

THREE

We nearly struck out with the next curveball. Immediately upon exiting the plane at the Detroit Metropolitan Wayne County Airport after an uneventful one hour and forty-five-minute flight, we stood, dumbfounded, in front of the arrival and departure schedule board. Our connection had left the ground fifteen minutes before we landed.

"Why the long faces?" said Jane, nearly bursting with effervescence she could barely contain. "I've got this."

Jane's dad, and our team's benefactor, owned Sapphire Skyway in Georgia, a charter airline providing on-demand operations to the jet set. She knew airports and the right people and paraded us through the obstacle course of underling personnel and a considerable distance on the concourse to a secure section of the airport and an area of private offices.

Depositing us on plush chairs in an inviting waiting room with a wall of tall windows overlooking the bustling runways, she breezed past the desk and disappeared behind a pair of large wooden doors.

The friendly receptionist, wearing a white plastic name tag bearing the name Karly, came out from behind her desk with a tray, circled the room, offering bottles of soda, ice cold water, apples, bananas, and chewy granola bars while we waited. She towered over me, standing close to six feet, with sparkling eyes the color of a Brazil nut, curly dark-brown hair with a few strands of gray, and a gracious smile. "Jane Mackey is a fireball, isn't she?"

"How do you know Jane?" I said, grabbing a bottle of water and selecting a banana.

"She's been in and out of these offices for as long as I've been at this airport. Any friend of Jane's is welcome here. Can I get you anything else?" Karly's phone buzzed. "Excuse me." She resumed her place behind the desk and answered the summons. When she disconnected, she cast a gentle smile over our crew. "Mrs. Calder?" Lorelei's mother popped up. "Please go on in."

The ten-foot-high double doors swallowed Lorelei's mom like the yawning maw of the Grand Canyon. The doors closed behind her with the hint of a click, and I couldn't bring myself to make eye contact with the kids lest my unease show. I had promises to keep.

We sat in silence, sipping beverages and finishing our snacks, until Marietta and Jane exited the executive office ten minutes later. Glancing back over her shoulder, Jane laughingly promised someone behind the door, deep in the recesses of the room, to "catch up soon."

"Let's get a move on." Marietta raised her hands, fluttering her fingertips to rally our band of confused scholars, and hustled us back the way we'd come. "We have nine seats on a commercial flight boarding in twenty minutes, and if we hurry, we'll have just enough time to freshen up."

Marietta trooped through the airport, shepherding our convoy, encouraging haste. Brock's head swiveled back and forth as he jogged along next to Jane and whispered his concern. "Ms. Mackey, how's this going to work? I'm sure you noticed there are eleven of us."

"We need Mr. Calder to take charge of the males on the trip, and Mrs. Calder's psychology skills always come in handy. In addition, Ms. Lavigne is already booked on the same flight, so Ms. Wilk and I will take the next available seats."

Brock grunted and hustled ahead to join his friends.

My eyes opened wide, and I swallowed hard. Our principal, Mr. Phil Ganka, had recruited a fellow math teacher, ZaZa Lavigne, to assist in supervising our kids for our long trip and provide an extra pair of hands in Atlanta, but she'd taken care to settle her own travel plans and accommodations. It seemed the less she and I interacted, the better. Once upon a time, ZaZa and I had been friends while attending school at the Royal Holloway in London and getting a degree in mathematical cryptanalysis, until the man she secretly had her heart set on fell in love with me.

"Jane, do you think this is the best course of action?" I whispered. Even though I was happy to avoid taking the same flight as ZaZa, I had a few misgivings. I didn't expect much from her. She'd given our kids bad advice the first time she supervised their performance. They didn't totally trust her judgement, and neither did I.

"I had a three-way conversation with Mr. Ganka and ZaZa. She promised to do her job and is perfectly willing and able to be the teacher contact until we get to Atlanta. She'll connect our kids with the real brains behind this group. You and I know Dorene is the most important adult mentor in our equation."

I nodded. "She groomed the kids to be the winners they are, knowing the ups and downs, the ins and outs of any legal issue. We have the best attorney coach in the nation, and she's already got her fancy footwear on the ground in Atlanta. We, my friend, are merely window dressing."

"Fairly swanky window dressing, you have to admit." Jane framed her beautiful face with her elegant fingers and batted her eyelashes. "And we shouldn't get in too far behind their landing time. There's even a slight chance we might land before them. Don't worry. Between the Calders and Dorene, they won't even miss us."

I thought I'd remind her about our earliest beginnings and give credence to the work she and I had done during the year leading up to the competition, but at this point, the students were so proficient, all we did was escort them to and from the various competitions and take care of paperwork.

"How are we getting there?"

"One of my dad's newly minted commercial pilots is making a return trip to Atlanta. We can hitch a ride, but the plane isn't big enough for all of us."

I started to nod my head.

She continued, "I wouldn't want the kids to ride along in case something should happen to put them in jeopardy, however unlikely."

My head stopped mid-nod. She continued, "And our permission slips only cover transportation explicitly spelled out prior to our leaving Columbia." I chewed on the inside of my cheek. The timing issue left us with few options, but my mind reeled, and a chill darted up my spine as I tried to settle the restlessness fluttering around in my own stomach. I wished our original travel plans had worked out.

The kids and the Calders had minutes to spare and stopped briefly at the restrooms across from the gate. Emerging, I found every seat in the waiting area full and spotted ZaZa (she was hard to miss). I gave a tentative wave. She sashayed to the edge of her row of seats, rhythmically clacking her black Louboutin stilettos, taking stock of the kids, and greeting Jane. One corner of her mouth inched its way into a smirk, and she said in her heavy French accent, "Here you are needing my help again, Katie. I promise I will take terrific care of the team."

"Thank you." My heart pounded in my chest. She had a weird way of dredging up mixed emotions. "You remember Mrs. Calder, Lorelei's mom? She and her husband are the parent chaperones." ZaZa politely extended her hand, and they shook. "And Dorene Dvorak will meet you at the airport." ZaZa's grin turned upside down, and she pouted. Dorene did not appreciate any of the talent ZaZa saw in herself. I'd warned Marietta, and it would take some of her best work to keep them from setting each other off. "Jane doesn't think we'll be far behind. We'll keep you posted when we land."

Passengers began boarding. Marietta performed her motherly duties when their rows were called, counted heads, nodded at Jane and me, and directed her charges toward the attendant to have their tickets scanned.

"Be on your best behavior for the Calders," I called over the heads of the other travelers surging toward the gate. "And remember, Ms. Lavigne will be watching. You know she'll report the smallest infraction." I worked a smile onto my face, but I heard my kids moan, and I tried not to sound deflated. "See you in a few hours," I said to their retreating backs as they disappeared down the jetway.

"They'll be fine, and we'll be in the air shortly," said Jane, nudging my elbow. "Our flying chariot awaits. Let's go meet the crew."

I trudged lamely after my best friend, towing my carry-on, following the signs for the terminal-to-terminal shuttle to general aviation. After a short wait, we squeezed onto the wobbling transport, taking the last two standing-room-only spots and hanging on for dear life.

Eight miles later, the shuttle jerked to a stop, and we hopped off. Jane slung her designer bag over her shoulder, threaded her arm through mine and said, "We're off to see—"

"Janie?" a strident voice called from behind us.

FOUR

J ane's fists bunched at her hips. She scowled. "Are you following me, Wendell?"

He jogged next to her, and apparently winded with his minor exertion, bent at the waist and clasped his hands over his knees. "All the remaining seats to Atlanta have been taken by some school group from Minnesota. Why they gave them preferential treatment, I'll never know," he huffed, disgruntled. "I was going to arrange private transportation, but saw you, and I'm assuming you're headed for Atlanta. Could I catch a ride on one of the Sapphire planes?" When she didn't answer, he said, "I'll take any destination away from here." He stood up and took a deep breath before adding, "And you know you owe me."

Jane's usually expressive warm brown eyes cooled and

projected nothing, and as she hid her true feelings, I realized they ran very deep.

"Sorry, I shouldn't have brought that up." Wendell's tone didn't fit his words nor the eager look on his face. "It's imperative I reach Atlanta as quickly as possible, and you do have the means at your disposal." He snagged a linen handkerchief embroidered with a scripted red F from the rear pocket of his khakis and swiped at the nape of his neck. "I can pay."

Jane looked down the concourse. "Of course you can ride with us. As you said, we have the accommodations, and more passengers will help Dad make better use of those resources." She reached up and rubbed her first two fingers up and down her forehead. "You don't have to pay."

"Thanks. You're a champ." As if he'd just registered another person standing next to Jane, he said, "And you are?"

"This is my friend, Katie," said Jane.

I felt his dark eyes bore into me. "Do I know you?" he said as he tilted his head to get a better look.

Jane read her phone screen and redirected his train of thought. "They're preparing for takeoff. We'd better head to gate—"

"I know the way." Wendell gripped the handle on his extra-large suitcase and tipped it onto the rollers, setting off at a brisk pace. He skirted the other passengers and crews making their way down the concourse. "Come on," he called over his shoulder.

Jane lowered her head and shook it from side to side. When she raised her eyes, she plastered a smile on her face. "I guess we'd better catch up. Our flight crew might not believe Wendell." Her eyes creased at the corners. "Although that might not be all that bad."

A runner, yoga teacher, exercise guru, and Tough Mudder

competitor, Jane's uncharacteristic methodical and slow exacting pace surprisingly allowed Wendell to reach a set of double doors about a hundred yards ahead of us. He initiated a conversation with a man in uniform. Wendell shifted from foot to foot as the exchange became more animated, and he raised his unencumbered hand in exasperation, beckoning us not to tarry. By the time Jane and I drew level, the heated conversation had exacted a bright red hue on Wendell's face.

"Tell him, Janie," Wendell said in the same whiny, entitled tenor he had when he'd budged in line in front of Carlee.

Jane ignored him and reached out a hand to the tall, dark, handsome man sporting four stripes on his epaulets. "Hello, Captain. We haven't been properly introduced yet, but I'm Jane Mackey. I believe my dad contacted you about perhaps fixing our transportation dilemma. We'd very much like to fly with you to Atlanta, if that meets with your approval."

He accepted her hand, but before the pilot had a chance to answer, Wendell's mouth dropped open in disbelief, and he released another moronic query. "Who's the boss, anyway? Just tell them where you want to go," he said, lifting his chin, displaying his arrogance.

Jane turned and faced him. Her back went rigid, and she looked much taller than her almost five feet would allow.

"Mr. Gromm," I warned. "I'd listen carefully if I were you."

With fire in her eyes, steel in her voice, and something akin to ice in her veins, Jane stuck a finger at him and said, "Prioritizing the safety of the passengers and crew is paramount to Sapphire Skyway. The flights are planned with diligence. They don't just pop into the sky willy nilly. The crews are professionals. Wendell, if you want the privilege of attaining a seat on this airplane, you will be civil, you will mind every written and unwritten suggestion in the code of sky travel ethics, exceeding the industry standards, and you will be polite. I will not tolerate distractions to the crew, or a disruption of Sapphire Skyway's service nor mistreatment of the employees or other passengers or …" Her voice took on a razor-sharp edge and she took one step closer to him. Nose to nose, she said, "You will walk to Atlanta. Am I making myself clear?"

I thought I detected smoke billowing out of his ears, but he silently acquiesced and tipped his head forward one time. He stepped back, and I almost laughed.

Jane forced a smile and turned to the wide-eyed pilot. "Well, what do you say?"

"*The* Jane Mackey," he replied enthusiastically, removed his cap, and bowed at the waist. He came up with shining hazelnut eyes, and cheeks trying to tame a huge grin. His broad shoulders jiggled a bit, restraining his laughter. "We've heard about you, and we'd love to have you fly with us, Ms. Mackey. I'm Richard."

"Please, call me Jane. This is my friend, Katie Wilk." Her smile tightened almost imperceptibly, and she pointed her thumb at him. "And he's Wendell Gromm. Just tell us when and where you want us, and we'll try to stay out of your way so you can get this show on the road, or rather, in the sky."

Richard's smile dropped from his lips, and he stammered, "I am the captain, and I have about two dozen more trips than my co-pilot, but I'm sure your dad shared this is only my second lead flight from Detroit to Atlanta."

"I also know you're a qualified pilot or you wouldn't be in my father's employ."

Richard finger-combed through his very short hair. He secured a captain's cap on his head, nodded, and unlocked the door opening into the bright sunshine. The three of us followed him down the ramp and onto the tarmac. He passed a grounds crew delivering boxes of cargo and stopped at the base of a set of stairs to a white, black, and silver plane with sapphire-blue highlights. He pivoted to face us and beamed.

A genuine smile opened in Jane's face, and she announced, appreciatively, "Cessna Citation Sovereign Plus." She laid her open palm on the fuselage and recited, "Sixty-three feet six inches long, twenty feet four inches high, with a range of almost three thousand nautical miles and a true air speed of four hundred sixty knots. Pratt and Whitney 306D engines. This baby's spectacular."

Richard nodded his head and gestured for us to ascend the stairs. Wendell tramped up first. We followed and were greeted at the top of the stairs by an attractive flight attendant with surprise in her blue eyes. She tugged at the collar of her crisp white shirt and adjusted her skirt while scrutinizing our disparate threesome. "What's going on?"

There must be something in the water. She was the second woman in less than an hour to exceed five-feet-ten-inches. In the flight attendant's three-inch heels, she hovered nearly a foot above Jane. Her intense eyes looked past us and sought some kind of confirmation from Richard who gave it. I couldn't tell if she was pleased or unhappy.

"We're waiting for the first officer, but I'll begin the pre-flight check if you can get our passengers situated," said Richard as he headed toward the front of the Citation.

"Late as usual," she said, forcing a smile. Her curly light brown hair bounced as she greeted us. "Welcome. We weren't expecting any passengers, so our provisions are limited and definitely not up to Sapphire Skyway standards." She checked the watch on her wrist. "I have just enough time to run and procure something if you've a special requirement."

Jane squelched the peep forming on Wendall's tongue, speaking for all of us. "Whatever you have will be perfectly fine. I'm Jane Mackey."

A glint shown in the attendant's eyes and a huge smile graced her face. "I've heard so much about you. What an opportunity. Welcome aboard."

It seemed everyone related to Sapphire Skyway knew of Jane. Maybe I'd learn more about her. I'd certainly take the opportunity to ask questions and listen.

Wendell clenched his jaw, barreling past the flight attendant and onto the plane. He tossed a worn backpack into the front closet and proceeded to thump his huge suitcase over the metal threshold, banging the sides of his case against the interior wall. The attendant raised her eyebrows.

Jane said, "Don't worry. I'll figure out where we'll secure his bag."

The attendant shrugged a what-can-you-do and said, "I'm Dianne." She stepped back to let Jane and me enter, and I couldn't believe my eyes.

FIVE

The breathtaking opulence and brilliant illumination stopped me cold. Luxurious, broad, creamy streamlined leather seats in ecru, trimmed with a light tan, lined both sides of a wide plush carpeted aisle. Lights shone from everywhere—recessed in the ceiling and on the floor, embedded in the walls, affixed under the counters—and emphasized the gleaming polished brass fixtures.

Wendell unfolded a nice-sized collapsible table and tossed his briefcase on top. Oblivious to his surroundings, ignoring them at any rate, he unloaded the contents. Jane nudged his suitcase out of the aisle with her knee, aiming for the rear of the cabin.

"Hey, what do you think you're doing?" By the time he finished his question, he'd choked back his anger.

Jane narrowed her eyes. "Your job. I'm stowing your luggage." She gave the hard-sided gray bag one final shove into the internally accessible baggage compartment and slammed the door.

I still hadn't moved from the entry, drinking in the warm wood accents in a walnut veneer and reveling in the classical music playing softly in the background. Dianne took my carry-on and set it in the front storage unit. As I stepped inside the spacious cabin, I ducked, not quite certain my head wouldn't bump the ceiling, and ambled past a buffed white marble-topped counter accommodating a glistening La Spaziale espresso machine, a Plexor rapid cook microwave, and a tall, fully stocked fridge with sparkling glass doors. The interior lights on the upper cabinet illuminated crystal glassware, alphabetized bottles of high-end liquor, and canned and bottled beverages lined up in order by height.

I'd never seen anything like the aircraft and carefully followed the row of lights in the sunken floor, sliding onto a heavenly cushioned chair. The comfortable seat gently swiveled and the button on the side allowed me to recline at an infinite number of angles.

Dianne watched my reaction with a gleam in her eye. I intended to give her effusive praise, but my phone rang. I read the screen and answered with a twinge of apprehension.

"Marietta?"

"Katie, we're all fine and about to take off. I primed the kids in a role-playing game to make Ms. Lavigne feel like she's in charge, but it was a tough sell." She chortled. "I can see why."

"I never would have thought of that tactic, but as you know, they are very talented actors. I think that's what contributed to getting them where they are today. Thank you."

"No problem. Do you have your flying orders yet?"

"I am sitting in one of Sapphire Skyway's Citations."

"Oooh. I've been researching Jane's dad's company. Not too shabby. My husband is jealous."

"It is nice. Jane has complete confidence in the pilot, and I met him, but I'm sure the other parents will be happiest and less nervous knowing their children are flying with a well-established crew. We shouldn't be far behind you."

"Fair skies, Katie."

"Thanks. And to you, Marietta."

No sooner had we disconnected, when Pete called. "Hi, Beautiful. Everything okay?"

My face warmed. "Hey, there." Dr. Pete Erickson's calm, mellow voice had a soothing effect, and some of my stress evaporated. I gave him a short version of our trip highlights and delighted in admitting to traveling in Sapphire Skyway elegance. "Can you believe our luck?"

"I'm not sure your students will think being saddled with the sage on the stage is lucky. Is everything working out?"

"Hold on. I'm converting to screen so you can take in the sights too." When Pete's handsome face filled the display, I almost forgot why I wanted to switch over. The twinkle in his chocolate-brown eyes made my heart flip. I mentally shook my head and reluctantly turned the camera away from his chiseled chin and broad grin to view my surroundings, alighting on the galley, the seats, the ceiling and floor, the bright lights, skimming by the stooped figure of Wendell, and landing on Jane. I noticed her googly eyes and the phone in her hand as she waved and determined she must be talking to her fiancé, Drew.

Pete chuckled. "Flying in style, I see, and you'll get a few hours reprieve before you have to take over your role as guide on the side."

I heard a voice from behind him. "Dr. Erickson, you're wanted in Triage Three."

Nurse Susie Teasdale, nee Kelton, and I had a tumultuous history, but her now happily married and very pregnant form waddled into the foreground. "Hi, Katie. I'm keeping him occupied." She waved and left the room.

"That she is." He shook his head of dark curls. "Wish I was with you, but I've got to go. Talk to you soon."

Richard stepped through the entry and into the cockpit, busy checking gauges and flipping switches. I sat quietly with my phone in my hand until Wendell broke into my cheerful thoughts. "What are you so happy about?"

My eyebrow arched, but my grin stayed locked in place as I shook my head and reached for a brochure in the side pocket. I thumbed through the scant manual explaining the interactive state-of-the-art controller built to operate the WIFI, cabin lights, window treatments, temperature, and LCD map display, and tapped the corresponding icons on the screen to examine the activation mechanism.

Wendell's phone trilled, and his answer could be heard all the way back to Minnesota. "It's certainly taken you long enough." I peeked at Wendell as he checked his nails. "I know I'm not there yet." He grumbled about our delays. "I'm catching a ride with Janie." He exhaled. "Yes, Jane Mackey." He drummed his fingers on the table. "No, I don't want to go there."

Jane leaned close and whispered, "Thanks for being a good sport. I'm sorry about …" She jerked her head in the direction of Wendell. "I don't know why I capitulated. I guess I feel sorry for him, but it's obvious he hasn't changed."

"I'm just happy we have a ride to Atlanta." I waggled my eyebrows. "In perfect style. This is great."

"Felicity," Wendell growled. "Just be at the airport in time to pick me up. We'll talk about it then. The plane should be on the ground in less than an hour and a half. Don't be late." He disconnected and tossed his phone onto the seat next to him.

"You finally made an honest woman out of Felicity, Wendell. Well done," Jane said.

"We have not tied the knot, not that it's any concern of yours."

Jane snuck a look at me and made a silent 'oh' with her lips. She leaned close and said, "I'm surprised. Felicity has the characteristics which have always attracted Wendell—money and looks. They've been together since high school. He's lucky to have her, but I've always wondered what she sees in him. She's the CEO of a successful business she took over from her mother, designer perfumes."

We turned toward the heavy footsteps tromping up the metal stairs.

"Dianne," crooned a smarmy voice. A redhead sporting tiny coils popped into the entry and presented Dianne with an ornate crystal bottle of light brown liquid.

The man dipped his head to the pilot. "Richard," he said, and hung a beat-up leather bomber jacket in the front closet. When he glanced into the cabin, the first look I read on the man's face was one of surprise, then what might have been a hint of anger, followed immediately by recognition, disappointment, and finally resolution.

"Well, if it isn't the boss's daughter. To what do we owe the pleasure of your company, Jane Mackey?"

Jane grinned in recognition and locked eyes with the newcomer. "Nice to see you too, Noah."

Wendell's head came up from the papers on the table, and he cleared his throat. Noah swung his gaze and glared. "And Wendy Gromm."

"It's Wendell," Gromm said through gritted teeth. "You still have that ratty old jacket, I see."

Noah's eyes narrowed for an instant. I thought he might have a few choice words for Wendell, but he threw back his head and laughed. "Hail, hail, the gang's all here."

"The three of you know each other?" I said in wonder. My voice cooled their brewing resentment.

Noticing me for the first time, Noah plastered on a Cheshire cat grin. "And who is this lovely lady?"

"This is my friend, Katie Wilk. Katie, Noah Lexington."

"Very pleased to meet you, Katie." Noah reached for my hand, so I lifted it toward him. He clasped it tightly within his strong paws, rotated it ninety degrees, and kissed the back.

I hadn't meant to, but my insides curdled. *Ew, who does that?*

"Same old Casanova. You haven't changed a bit," Wendell said with reluctance and perhaps a bit of envy. "Smuggled any forbidden fruit lately?"

"Jealous much?" Noah strolled to the closet in the back and deposited a travel bag, then ambled past Wendell, mirroring his look of entitlement.

"Noah," Richard said from the cockpit. "Get moving. I've completed my pre-flight checklist, and you've got work to do."

Dianne flattened herself against the counter to allow Noah to walk through and into the cockpit. He drew the curtain closed. She shook her shoulders and straightened before busying herself by removing a green bottle from the fridge and arranging an array of flutes on a silver tray. She popped the cork and dispensed the golden bubbly within. As she delivered the sparkling beverage and a cup of ginormous chocolate-covered strawberries to each of us, she said reassuringly, "It won't be long now. Enjoy and let me know if

I can be of further assistance. Ms. Mackey—"

"Please, Dianne, I'm Jane."

She smiled broadly. "We're flying into DeKalb Peachtree Airport, and we've arranged a private car to transport you to your hotel."

Wendell overheard her. "I'd like a ride to—"

"There are cabs, Ubers, and Lyfts available for your employment," Jane said with grace and finality. "Thanks, Dianne."

Wendell tossed back the flute, guzzling the contents in one swift motion, and held the glass out for more. Dianne returned with the bottle and poured.

Jane and I clinked glasses. The first tiny ambrosial sip slid down with a tickle. I justified the indulgence by following it with a bite of healthy fruit and had to swipe away the luscious strawberry juice trickling down my chin.

"What is this, Dianne?" I said appreciatively, lifting the flute.

"This is our house favorite, a 2015 Louis Roederer Cristal Brut."

Wendell held out for more. Dianne furrowed her brow, looking for consent. Jane raised one finger. Dianne poured again.

I hesitated before savoring another wee dram of liquid courage. "Jane, how do you know Noah? Was he a classmate too?"

She gazed deeply through the fizzing and set the glass on the table. I reluctantly followed suit. "We began ATP flight school together."

SIX

Began, as in …?" I hoped to elicit a bit more information. Wendell's husky voice answered instead. "Began as in Noah had to stop and start again in order to work and pay for the classes because he didn't have a father with bottomless pockets of money like some people we know." His sour tone grated on the few gossamer threads remaining of my nerves. "And I decided I didn't want daily reminders of my family's losses, so I attended a different location. It worked out though, and we were still able to follow in the footsteps of our ancestors—Noah's WWI bomber forefather. My dad. Jane's dad. Now, if you two chatterboxes would keep it down, I've got work to finish."

Jane gritted her teeth and lowered her eyes like *el toro* aiming to charge an unaware matador, but before she could make her retort, a rich baritone came over the sound system. "This is your captain, Richard Krizmanich. Please fasten your seat belts, folks. Prepare the cabin for departure. Dianne will give a quick refresher, though we shouldn't require any of the safety instructions. We're cleared for departure and have approximately one hour and five minutes of flight time ahead of us. Sit back, relax, and enjoy the ride. I certainly will."

The muscles on Jane's face softened as we listened to the familiar words of air travel safety. When Dianne completed her spiel, Jane took in a lungful of air. Her head dropped back, and she bit her lip.

"Are you okay?" I whispered.

She nodded and we settled in for takeoff. I glanced out the window and noticed the dazzling sun lowering in the sky.

As soon as the jet reached its cruising altitude and the lights on the fasten seat belt signs turned off, Wendell rose and wobbled to the luggage compartment. He staggered a bit but extracted a suitcase and began to rummage through.

I didn't want to look or act like Wendell, so I pushed my glass to the center of the table. Jane gestured and Dianne removed our crystal flutes, but I retained control of the berries. I popped a smaller one in my mouth and hummed in satisfaction. Wendell plodded to his seat and tottered into it. He painstakingly arranged his tabletop, a tablet, loose papers, and a pen, adjusting the precise placement of the items, and began a loud dissertation into a wafer-thin device.

"Don't mind him. He's dictated his notes for as long as I've known him." Jane lowered her voice, "Which, I've decided, has been too long. You took forever to join us for breakfast. What happened?"

I gave her the less than amusing rundown of my TSA encounter.

"Brock's in for a surprise." She swiped a chuckle from her lips and said, "Can we make another pass through our itinerary?"

I knew how to distract like the best of them and leaned forward to share my excitement for the week ahead. "We haven't yet missed anything we purchased tickets for. Had we arrived when expected, we were scheduled to partake in a curated walking tour sponsored by the local bar association. They sent a map with the registration material highlighting alternate routes near our hotel in different colors for varying distances to walk, and we can do it at any time. The ticketed events begin on Sunday. Our competition orientation starts Tuesday afternoon. The first head-to-head occurs bright and early Wednesday morning, but the *pièce de résistance* is the Brock edition of the Columbia graduation ceremony slated for a lavish French dinner Thursday at *La Petite Salle à Manger*."

Pretending Wendell wasn't three feet away making an obnoxious recording, we quietly discussed our tournament prognosis and ambitious ideas for summer. When I quizzed her about the wedding plans, Jane glowed.

"We're shooting for October when we have a four-day break. You've done so much to help, but I don't think I can get ready any sooner. Drew has already asked for vacation, and he's planned our honeymoon. It's a surprise." She wrinkled her nose and squinted her eyes, and I could almost see her trying to guess where the two of them might spend their first few days of marital bliss. Her eyes flashed wide. "It's a good time for Dad to take off, too."

We talked dresses, showers, registries, music, gifts, and venues. Time raced by.

Relaxing into the seat, she looked out the window longingly. "Sometimes, I miss it, just a little bit."

"Flying?"

Jane smiled wistfully. "Flying. And working with Dad. I know he wanted me to join him, but I love teaching." She gave a contented sigh and raised her controller for the cabin management system to lower our window shade and block out the blindingly brilliant yellow and orange of the sun about to make its descent behind an enormous bank of dark clouds. The ping before the announcement startled me.

A slightly more tenor voice came through the speakers. "This is Noah. Sorry to break in on you, but we are going to take a little jaunt to the east to skirt a pocket of storms brewing which will add a few minutes to our overall flight time. Just didn't want anyone to worry. It might get a bit bumpy, so I've turned on the seat belt sign." The sound in the background included a pop and a whiz, followed by Noah clearing his throat. "The next thing you know we'll be landing."

We secured our belts as Dianne made another pass to distribute bottles of water and snacks. I chose an apple from the wicker basket and stared at it, seeing nothing, pondering the whereabouts and safety of our kids. Dianne settled into her jump seat. I turned on the map and noticed we passed over Knoxville, entering airspace above a vast green expanse.

Seconds later, although predicted, the bump caught me unprepared. Jane leaned forward, grinned, and patted my knee. I acted as if it was no big deal until we felt another jolt, and my fingers seized the armrests in a death grip.

Wendell sniggered. "If this is the best Sapphire Skyway can do, I'm glad things worked out the way they did. These guys are bums."

The jet lurched a third time, and Jane unbuckled her seat belt. She floundered as the plane rolled a bit, and Dianne said, "Jane, you should return to your seat."

Jane nodded an affirmation but stumbled and reached for the heavy drape separating the cockpit from the cabin. As she teased it back, she said, "Hey guys, can I do anything to help up here?"

The jet banked hard to the left. Still clamped in Jane's grip, the curtain separated from the rod holding it.

She tripped forward. "Richard, what's going on?" She prodded him, and he toppled to his left. "Richard! Noah?" She grappled with Noah's arm and had the same lack of response. She buried her mouth and nose in the crook of her arm, and I heard a muffled, "Wendell, get in here. I need help."

I whipped my head around to make sure he'd heard her. He hiccupped, and his face turned a pale shade of olive. He cowered behind clenched eyes, hunching his shoulders and hiding his face. "Wendell?"

"I lied," he whispered. "I couldn't cut it. I quit. I never got a pilot's license. I can't help." His lips quivered as he drew a pair of thick, black-framed glasses from his inside pocket.

Jane leaned over and steadied the aircraft. I unhooked my belt and rushed to her side.

She raised her blue Cougar kerchief, wrapping the bottom half of her face, and said in a rush, "Careful. Cover up, and don't inhale that stuff." She pointed to a light dusting of white powder on the instrument panel. "I don't know what it is, but it can't be good." She sprinkled water from a bottle and resumed collecting the residue in a piece of light-colored fabric, folding it over on itself, trapping the contents inside. I hid my face behind the scarf, feeling like a bandit in an old Western.

She braced herself against the center pedestal and grunted as she tried to drag Richard's limp form out of the pilot's seat. I reached in and grabbed his arms as soon as I could get hold of him. I whispered, "Wendell's scared stiff. He can't move and won't be any use to you. Tell me what you need me to do."

Jane called over her shoulder, "Dianne, help Katie get Richard strapped in." Dianne and I inched him towards the first open seat. Jane swayed, laying first one palm against the wall of the small space and then the other. She scrambled into the seat vacated by Richard. "Katie, get Noah out of here."

"Wendell," I yelled. "Help us." He didn't budge, so Dianne and I tugged at Noah's belt, arms, and shirt, bumped him across the floor, wrestling the dead weight, and hauled him into the seat across from Wendell. If Wendell hadn't pressed his face into his fists, he'd certainly have cringed at my look of repulsion.

Jane accessed the intercom, and her clipped words filled the sound system. "Dianne, get your seatbelt on. Katie, I need you up here."

I lurched into the cockpit and fell into the recently vacated seat next to Jane. "Have you ever flown one of these before?"

She shook her head. The shiny black instrument panel caught the reflection of her ultra serious face. She touched a screen and frowned, muttering, "Terrain. Obstacles. Balance. There's a caution light. I don't know how, but the gauge reads low fuel." She struck the screen again and toggled some switches, grappling to operate the guidance system. "We're not moving well. The GPS is disconnected. Comms are down." Her brow scrunched. "The transponder isn't functioning."

She strong-armed the controls, and as the plane pitched, three notecards fluttered to the floor. I collected them one by one and read the headings for taxi, visual, and departure checklists. Precisely squaring up the corners, I secured them in a stretchy net pack adjacent to my seat. A strange pattern covered the backs. Always searching for a message and unable to decipher any significance in these symbols, my forehead crinkled.

Jane shook her head. "I've never had an actual forced landing, but I've done a number of simulations and reproduced several successful events."

I gave up on the characters and silently screamed in my mind, "What!"

"Our light's fading fast, and we've got to find some place to land. We're over the national forest, lots and lots of trees, so keep your eyes peeled for any open area."

The glowing colors and gauges on the control panel and the multiple LCD screens in front of me were mesmerizing, but the frozen images confused me. I bit down hard to keep my teeth from chattering and tightened my hold on the armrests, then breathed deeply through the cotton fabric mask as she recited measurements from memory, "Take off distance three thousand five hundred thirty feet. Landing distance two thousand six hundred feet. There's not enough." Her head swung from side to side, taking in as much information as possible. "Not enough. I don't know, Katie. This is one of the preeminent short-field runway performance crafts out there, and we'll have to take her down. We'll have to do the best we can." She scoured the displays in front of her and peered through the windows at what little we could see outside.

I followed her instructions and hurriedly scanned everything around me. Above us, a wide band of thunderheads erupted in intense electric pulsing. A few drops of rain streaked across the windscreen, warping our view. Below us, I caught occasional pinpoints of yellow dotting the ground amid swaths of what looked like a very dark textured carpet.

"I think these are the last details Richard and Noah had. See this? Incoming weather." Jane pointed to a stationary shot of a yellow, green, and red blob on the monitor in front of her. She glanced out at the lightning throbbing in the distant thunderheads. "It's almost on us." She mouthed words and numbers in front of her but looked up as the world lit in another flash. "Look for a field. Something flat-ish anyway."

Flat-ish? I stretched a crooked, shaky finger toward a break in the landscape.

"Good job. That's it—an open tract between the foliage, a dark path in the middle, maybe an old logging road or backroads pass. Hold on. We've got to land while we can still see and before the tempest catches up to us. We're aiming …" She pointed and repeated. "There. With your help, we'll land this little lady. Watch that gauge. Let me know when it changes. Just tap its frame." She nodded, appearing to read through another checklist. "Glide speed. Check. Suitable landing area. Check. Gear extension. Check. Flaps." Her head made a jerky rectangle as she searched. "Flaps. Check."

She called over the sound system and her words sizzled with energy, "Prepare for impact." She glanced at me and said with conviction, "Buckle up, girlfriend. Today is not our day to die."

SEVEN

Jane eased back the throttle and the aircraft's forward movement appeared to slow, but our rate of descent increased as we fell from the sky. I left my eyebrows and my stomach in the clouds and mouthed a quick prayer. Lights flashed. The ground rushed up to meet us, setting off the proximity warning system. A gauntlet of invisible talons scraped and scratched the hull. A loud crack preceded a jarring spin, and I squeezed my eyes shut against the dizzying whirl of my surroundings.

After what felt like hours but in reality, was mere seconds, we came to a dead stop. Poor choice of words, I realized, but I didn't know how we could still be in one piece and alive. I listened to the strange sounds and slowly peeled open my eyes, one at a time, to strobing red and white light. Shaking my head didn't clear my vision of the slightly canted world outside.

I focused, tested my limbs, and found no major damage. Nothing hurt until a blood curdling scream erupted and assaulted my ears.

Thankfully, it wasn't me.

Dull lights dimly illuminated the interior. I unbuckled my belt and toppled toward my friend, searching her pale face and whispering her name, "Jane?" She didn't move. I gently nudged her and said more loudly. "Jane?" Nothing. My chest tightened and I prodded her with more force. Her eyes fluttered open. I released the breath I'd been holding. "Are you okay?"

She tried to lean forward and moaned. "I'll be fine, but I wrenched my left arm, and my ankle is killing me." She flexed the fingers of her right hand and groaned but sat up straighter. "How are the others?"

I glanced over my shoulder. The yelling had stopped, but nothing moved. How would I report that? "I'll check."

Dianne stirred so I crawled to her first. She touched her knuckle to her forehead. It came away stained dark—probably blood. "Dianne, you're hurt." Her head bobbled on her neck, and as she opened her eyes, even in the faint light, I could see her pupils were two different sizes. Confusion and fear closed over her features. I called to Jane, "Dianne has symptoms of a possible head injury."

"The passengers," Dianne murmured.

When she tried twice to rise against her belt without releasing it, I ordered her to be still. "I'll take care of them. You take care of you."

The yelling started up again. Wendell's hands covered his splotchy face, and he wailed repeatedly, "We're all going to die."

"Wendell. Get a hold of yourself. We've landed. We're safe."

His yelping died down, but he droned the same message, "We're going to die."

My last milliliter of patience vaporized, and I spat, "Stay in your seat. You're going to be just fine." I worried about Jane and Dianne and Richard and Noah and wouldn't continue to listen to Wendell spouting his thoughtless, self-serving words.

I checked Richard's airway and breathing, but didn't see any sign of his reviving soon. His head lolled heavily, chin on his chest, and I couldn't rouse him. I dragged myself up the incline and did the same with Noah. He wrenched away when I touched his hand, and even though he hadn't awakened, the small movement gave me hope.

I couldn't begin to imagine what had happened to the pilots and the electronic systems and crawled back to Jane, working against gravity.

She lay against the headrest. Her usually sun-kissed skin had taken on an unhealthy yellowish hue and she sat as still as stone, with her eyes closed. If I hadn't seen her chest rise and fall, I would have assumed she was unconscious, or worse. I gently touched her arm. She recoiled and said, "Status report."

"Richard and Noah are still out cold. Wendell's a mess, and Dianne is going to need medical attention." I bent down to pick up one more notecard filled with the peculiar linear symbols inside half inch circles, and a groan escaped Jane's lips. I shoved the errant card in my pocket and leaned close to her.

"Sabotage," she hissed. "I think Richard and Noah may have been drugged by an aerosol dispensed in the cockpit, but I can't quite put my finger on it." She indicated the spray pattern near an open can of an energy drink nestled unassumingly in one of the cupholders. "This had to be done on purpose, otherwise I can't explain it." She lowered her voice although I think I was the only one who could hear her. "It looks like everything stopped working when we altered the flight path. I'm not sure when we last connected with air traffic control. With the storm raging, if we're outside radio coverage or the sector handoff didn't happen properly, ATC might not recognize we're in trouble. We didn't exactly crash. I landed the plane well enough that we might not have triggered the emergency locator transmitter." My jaw dropped. "We're in the middle of nowhere, in and out of satellite range, and I don't know how soon anyone will come looking for us."

Her breath caught on a painful inhalation. "I don't think I can walk." She slapped her cell phone against her thigh. "No connection. According to the last waypoint, we're in the Nantahala National Forest. Katie, you'll have to go for help. You're our best hope. I know it'll be pitch dark soon, but I'm fairly sure you'll find Maglites, a topographical map, and an emergency kit …" She struggled to get the words out over her thickening tongue. "In the storage closet."

Thunder boomed. A bolt of lightning ripped across the sky. The strike point made contact, and a tree exploded. Sparks flew and ignited the groundcover too close for comfort.

"We should get out of the plane, but right now inside seems the safest place to be."

Yellow tongues of flame danced across Wendell's flabbergasted face as he snuck a peek out the window next to him, but before he could holler again, Jane hit a release, and the airstairs started to unfold. It was as if I could read her mind. I glared at Wendell, daring him to open his mouth. I ripped the fire extinguisher from its base on the wall, and dashed to the doorway but was stymied by the clunking, squeaking sounds coming from the mechanism groaning in an attempt to lower the stairs.

I drove my foot at the door and threw my shoulder into it. It separated a bit from the frame with a sound of crunching metal. I repeatedly kicked and thrust until it hung free a few more inches, providing enough room for me to slither through. I swung out and dropped into the unknown.

Colliding with the hard ground jarred my knees, and I staggered before catching my balance. I slogged through dense scrub and brambles, lumbering close enough to the end of the wing to witness the individual flames, cracking and snapping. I silently recited the instructions I knew by heart, recounting the acronym—PASS. I pulled the pin on the extinguisher, aimed the nozzle, squeezed the lever, and swept the spray from side to side. More than half the time I tried to cook at home, I set off a fire alarm in my kitchen, so I was acutely familiar with the operation of an extinguisher. For once my penchant for poor meal preparation paid off, and I properly dispensed the fire-stopping chemical.

My breath caught as a figure appeared next to me. Hefting a second extinguisher, Noah splattered the surrounding grass with white spume. After a few extra squirts to squelch the floating cinders, I breathed more easily. The foam smothered the fire, and I almost commended the fine job we'd done until I noticed Noah falter. I lent an arm to steady him as tiny cold splatters dribbled off the end of my nose. Rain. Before we could move, the sky opened up and gushed. At least the water would make the vegetation less likely to catch fire from another lightning discharge, I hoped.

When the heavens lit up with a throbbing glow, we scrambled to the airstairs, grappling with the breach and yanking on the door. Standing in lightning could be life threatening, and we'd already had enough of that. Noah stretched and crawled partway inside. Weakening, he lingered at the entry only long enough for me to give him a nudge. I slid my fingers into the indentation on the panel and hooked my fingers around the handle. With the momentum gained by my third hop, I swung my leg up on the staircase and hauled my sopping body inside.

His knees buckled, and Noah collapsed into an empty seat, falling back into unconsciousness, his face ashen and his breathing laborious. He wouldn't be moving again anytime soon.

Water plastered my hair to my head, and I shook to get rid of the excess, but the suffocating quiet brought me up short. Gusty, lashing rain and resounding thunder were the only sounds I heard. I clambered next to Jane and almost tossed her from the seat with my shaking.

"Easy, Katie. Easy," she said with her eyes closed.

"I thought … I don't know what I thought."

"It's pouring, I know, but you have to go now. We're depending on you. I don't know what happened to the pilots, but we can't—" Lightning lit up the windshield and thunder boomed. Her brown eyes slowly opened and filled me with purpose. She took a deep breath and grabbed my hand. "*I'm* depending on you. Help me get to the cabin."

She leaned on me and hobbled past Dianne, settling into a rear-facing seat. I retrieved bottles of water, fruit, and granola bars, piling them next to Jane along with a large first aid kit.

I hesitated to remove the journals—my tie to the kids—but at this rate, I'd probably need two more before the week ended. I emptied my bag and refilled it with the items I collected under Jane's supervision—the map, the flashlights, a secondary first aid kit, and emergency supplies.

"There should be rain gear in the external luggage compartment." She explained how to access the space, squeezed my hand, and laid an orienteering compass on my palm, saying softly, "Take Wendell with you."

"But …"

"You can't go by yourself, and no one else is in any shape to make the trip. Besides, he's better than nothing." Her head dropped back onto the seat, and her eyes closed. "Maybe."

"Wendell." Jane forced out the name. He recoiled. "Pull together what you need. You're going with Katie to get help."

"Are you crazy? We can't go out in this weather. We should wait until morning. The storm'll make it impossible—"

"Stop your fulminating," Jane said harshly, and silenced the bellyaching Wendell. Her eyes opened wide. Then she stopped all movement as if considering the words she'd just said, and a chortle escaped before being stifled by pain. "What am I going to do, Katie? It sounds like my sesquipedalian Drew is rubbing off on me."

"That's not necessarily a bad thing." I nodded and read the engraving on the compass. "May Faith and Love Be Your Guide."

She curled her fingers around mine. "It was his engagement gift to me." She grimaced. "Get the gear."

Dianne began to sob.

"Hurry. Go now." Jane gently prodded me with her elbow. "And be careful, my friend."

I hugged her with such intensity, she grunted. "Sorry. I forgot." I released her, grabbed my bag, and used every gymnastic skill I owned to maneuver out the less-than-ideal opening, vaulting to the ground.

Wendell's bulky backpack landed with a thud. After a few more crashes and creaks, the doorway widened a fraction. He shimmied and oomphed and jumped down behind me. "I know who you are," he said with a quiet undercurrent of threat.

"I know who I am too," I said, wishing I could dodge the conversation, as dodging raindrops wouldn't be successful.

"Very funny. Your kids took my seat on the flight to Atlanta and now look where I am."

I ignored him, headed toward the rear of the aircraft, and grappled with the portal. It opened begrudgingly, squawking as I pulled. I flipped on the flashlight and shined it over the interior in search of the slickers and went rigid.

"What's the hold up? I'm not getting any drier standing out here. Can't you hurry?"

But I couldn't move.

"Come on, already. Get the rain jackets." Wendell shuffled me out of his way. He set his ponderous pack on the ground and stood. He grasped the metal edges of the entrance, and before he could haul himself inside, he said, "Incredible."

EIGHT

Wendell climbed into the jam-packed cargo hold and brushed aside wires hanging from the ceiling. Glass shards crunched beneath his feet. He scanned the disorder and muttered something unintelligible.

"What did you say?" I lost track of him in the tangle of hardware and heard a moan. "Wendell?"

I scrambled into the cramped compartment and combed through the electronic equipment in search of the source of the sound.

"Hacked," he said, as he knelt on top of the jumbled components in a refrigerator-sized plywood replica of the console in the cockpit fastened to the cargo bay by mesh straps. He lifted the limp hand of a woman lying face down on the floor and let it drop. "Out cold. Help me get her trussed up." He yanked the cables from the apparatus and wound them around her hands.

I gasped. "Wendell, can't you see she needs help?" In my haste to get to her aid, I tripped on some of the gear and came face to face with the blond woman. Her hair tangled in a set of headphones, and she lay amid the broken screen of a computer smeared with what looked like blood, breathing shallowly, as Wendell wrapped her legs in plastic-coated wires.

He slid her to the rear of the space and out of my reach. "Maybe I couldn't cut it as a pilot, but I know enough to understand why the aircraft behaved the way it did."

"What do you mean?" Clearing the jungle binding my shoe and pushing off the ground, I fixed Wendell with a glacial stare.

"Whoever she is, she managed the Citation controls by remote, but not so distantly there could be any disruption from outside signals." He stepped over the woman. "I'm thinking with all this equipment, she was prepared to land the plane. We have to make sure she doesn't get away when she comes around." Wendell fished through the pockets of her heavy coat.

"What do you think you're doing?" I used my most successful teacher voice.

"I'm looking for ID."

"Even if everything you say is true, you shouldn't move her around like that. We have to help her. I'll get one of the crew. They'll know what this is." My forefinger did a helicopter rotator motion, circling the area. "Just wait."

He shook his head in disbelief and rolled her unceremoniously onto her back, tightly wrapping her feet. "Wait for whom? None of them are in a position to give any assistance."

I narrowed my eyes, trying to recall where I'd seen the

familiar female face.

"She's an assassin," he said.

Wendell's unbelievable comment knocked me for a loop. "She's a what?" I drew a big circle with my chin, emphasizing my skepticism. "Who do you think she was here to kill?"

He stood straight, and his imperious look gave me his answer. "Who do you think?" He bent and picked up some of the items scattered across the floor. "She came for me."

"Right," I said with as much incredulity in my voice as I could summon. "Why would anyone want to kill you?"

"They've been after me since I left Wayzata."

"Minnesota?" I scrutinized the victim's face and recognized the blond hair. My fingers covered my lips. The fancy painted nails clinched it, even though I couldn't see the sparkly green eyes. My hand dropped to my side. "She stood behind you at the Minneapolis-St. Paul airport when you tried to budge in line."

His eyes grew big and round. "Because she was there to kill me." He hitched the tie around her hands snugly and stood.

He rooted around inside the confined space until he located the box he wanted. Three fluorescent yellow raincoats flew to the floor. He extracted a couple of dark-colored slickers, threw them over his shoulder, and shambled back to the opening. "I need to get out of here, and you're coming with me."

"I. Will. Not. Go. Anywhere with you. I'm getting help." I jumped to the ground and slipped on the slick, wet grasses. The flashlight slammed into the soft earth, and I ended up on my hands and knees. My nails sank into the muddy ground, but I rose with as much dignity as I could muster and headed back to the airstairs for two reasons. Jane needed to know what we'd found so we could decide what to do next, and I wanted to get as far away from Wendell-the-crazy-person as I could.

"No need to tell Janie," Wendell said in a sing-song voice. "She has her hands full with Richard, Dianne, and Noah."

I continued toward the entryway, but Wendell's sharp, low, menacing words stopped me in my tracks.

"Turn around slowly, Katie, or you may never see your friend again." I swiveled deliberately and found myself looking down a long gun barrel.

"How did you get a gun on the plane?"

"I didn't have to." He cocked his head at the woman. "She did." A distant crackling sounded from inside the luggage compartment. "She's still getting some reception." He crab-walked to the console and yanked all the wires. "This whole thing was too well-planned, and her associates are probably not far away."

"That's good." I took a tentative step toward the airstair. "Maybe they can help Jane and the others."

"Stop where you are. This has nothing to do with Jane. You don't understand. They're going to kill me."

"Why would you even think that? And how would they have the time to assemble and outfit this … whatever it is?"

"We were on the ground for almost an hour before take-off. This is what they do." His contagious paranoia sent shivers up my arms.

"Who are these people? What have you done?"

He ignored my question. "This is a portable simulator outfitted with working devices, ready at a moment's notice, as you can see." His hand directed my attention to the rigging, and I still couldn't see. "Wasn't there residue from an aerosol in the cockpit?"

I nodded reluctantly. "Jane had us cover our noses and mouths. She didn't know what it was, but it looked like it had spewed from an energy drink."

"Jane's right. Sabotage. That woman works for a tech company excelling in guidance systems and secure communications. After she incapacitated Lexington and Krizmanich, it looks like she took control of the aircraft from back here. But she didn't know about Jane. Jane manually wrested control and landed. The assassin failed in her mission, but she wouldn't have been alone."

"Jane needs to know." I inched away from the hold.

"You haven't been hearing me. They'll all be fine. It's me. These people want to get rid of me. I can't be here when they arrive." The woman began to stir. "Let's get moving."

"What if they hurt Jane or the others?"

"They're after me. Me alone. And you're coming with me."

"You don't need me."

"You know too much."

"I don't know anything." I recalled the Wendell from the landing and realized he was terrified.

His voice rose, and he threw me a rain slicker. "Unless you're willing to bear the elements, put that on. You're going with me."

"Wendell, what have you done to warrant someone wanting to kill you?"

He didn't answer, but the end of the gun waved twice away from the Skyway jet. "Get out that compass. We're leaving now."

"Where are we going?" I thrust my arms into the jacket, pulled up the hood, and hitched my backpack over my shoulders.

"Right before we lost control, the LCD readout provided a fair account of our flight path, but I had a feeling something like this might happen—"

"And you didn't warn anybody?" My voice rose an octave.

He blew me off again and extracted some paper from his inside pocket, shaking it into a small map, messily folding away the unnecessary portion, and using the front flap of his jacket to protect it from the elements.

"Who even has a map?"

Noting the confusion on my face, he jerked his head behind him and said, "I confiscated the map and this ..." he waved the firearm, "... from the floor of the luggage compartment. I'd been monitoring our flight path. We should be about here." I squinted in the dim, strobing light from the aircraft as he pointed to a squiggly line. "They'll never expect us to locate this isolated fire watch tower." He pointed to a symbol that looked like a house on stilts.

"Who are *they*?" Wendell didn't answer. "How do you know what's there?"

"It's on the legend." He gave me a look of disbelief. "From there, I'll coordinate my transportation, and you can get Jane and the others the help they need. Otherwise ..." He let his comment hang and my imagination to run wild. "We're heading south."

I took plodding steps meant to either irritate Wendell enough to leave me behind or give someone in the Citation time to look out and see what might be going on. Neither intention worked the way it should have. He pressed the cold hard metal against my back. "Walk faster ... carefully."

I swung the Maglite from side to side, and Wendell responded with another poke to my ribs. "Turn it off, unless I tell you otherwise."

I did what I was told. The complete cloud cover blotted out any bit of skylight and shrouded everything in darkness. I lifted my hand and made out a faint outline of what should have been my five fingers before having to swipe the rainwater from my face. "How do you expect me to follow the road or read this compass in the dark?"

"There's a light on the compass. Depress the crown twice. It'll illuminate a small circle for you to hike by."

Sure enough, a soft green glow allowed me to see the compass rose. We headed south. In the muted rays emanating from the treasure in my hand, I could make out signs of tall vegetation bordering the lane. If we stayed on the muddy path there was a destination in front of us and a trail leading back the way we'd come.

"March. I don't want to be here when they track down the aircraft. We've got to be long gone."

The storm intensified. Although the pounding thunder and lightning seemed more distant, the rain came in buckets. Considering the weather and terrain, we moved quickly down the seldom traveled pass for what seemed like an eternity, and I continually accessed the compass light. The day had taken its toll. My arms and legs ached, and I stumbled on the uneven path. "How far do we have to go?"

"You'll see when we arrive at the ranger station."

Paper rattled behind me. A light turned on and was immediately dimmed. I glanced over my shoulder and saw Wendell juggling the gun, the map, his cumbersome pack, and his phone, stepping in the tracks I'd left. I had little confidence he knew where we were headed and no confidence he knew how to handle the firearm.

I stopped, stretched, and patted my back pants pocket. I still had my device too. Although the phones hadn't connected where the Citation had gone down, mine just might link up when we hit higher ground, if I could just keep it hidden from Wendell.

NINE

The rain muffled our steps. I trudged forward, dragging my feet, trying to stay off Wendell's radar, leaving footprints melting in the squishy earth. Hampered by the weight of my wet clothes, I was chilled to the core and fearful of what lay in store. Shivering, I occasionally flashed the compass light to make sure we continued to walk on the weathered track while my other hand nestled in the flannel-lined pocket, testing the numb, wrinkly, paper-thin skin of my fingertips.

"The road splits just ahead," said the voice from behind me. "We could go one of two ways, but we'll use the low maintenance gravel road, a more direct route through the forest to the tower if we maintain a south-southeasterly bearing and cut off the lengthy switchback. Our followers need transportation to get to the aircraft. They'll choose the fork to the west that can handle motorized vehicles first. They won't find us, and they'll have to decide where to look next and hike in. We'll get to that ranger lookout before they figure out where we've gone. We'll be way ahead of them."

"How do you know you'll be able to get help at the fire tower?"

"Communication connection. That's my ticket out of here."

"And are you sure you know where we are?"

"We don't have time to argue. Get going. To the left."

The world around us was so overrun with foliage, calling the deer path low maintenance was being generous.

A bit later, Wendell said, "Wilk, get over here and shine that compass light." He pulled out the map and traced a few paths with his forefinger. "We leave the trail here."

"And go where?" Anger inched its way into my words.

"Shortcut."

My first step off the trail landed me in a trench and, with water collecting in my shoes, I hoped Wendell would get close enough for me to, if not overpower him, at least get rid of the gun. He didn't. He stayed at least eight feet away, close enough to see yet too far to catch unaware.

I blundered forward. Twigs and branches tugged at my jacket and my hair and scratched my face and hands. Maybe if I held onto one of the branches and released it to smack into Wendell, I could make a run for it. But he stayed far enough behind that none of the limbs would have caught him.

Not long after leaving the path, the ground rose abruptly. Slogging uphill, my legs ached. I grasped the scrubby, sturdy brush and hauled myself up, cracking and breaking my nails. My hands slipped on tiny barbs, impaling the delicate wrinkly ends of my fingers.

When Wendell sucked in air, I lowered my voice and said,

"We need to take a break. I need to drink some water, and it sounds like you need to breathe."

Wendell nodded. I found a downed tree trunk on which to sit. I opened my pack and took out a bottle of water, unscrewed the cap, and tipped the beverage over my parched lips, trying to figure out how they could be so dry while I traipsed through the rain-drenched countryside.

Wendell dropped onto another fallen log and reached out his hand.

"What?" As much as I didn't want to believe it, I had a pretty good shot at reading his face and thought I knew, but I'd make Wendell ask for it anyway.

"Water."

"Why? What's in your pack? It's so full, you can barely lift it."

"I brought what I needed," he said in a huff. "I knew you brought the safety equipment and supplies Jane recommended." With the gun in his hand, he gestured a 'give-it-here.'

I handed him one of my extra bottles, maintaining my hold on the neck, while I dispensed my two cents. "Don't drink it all. It might have to last you a while." He snorted. "In fact, we should probably refill with rainwater. When it stops raining, we won't have another source. I separated everything I found in the galley for all of us, and if you didn't bring a portion from what I laid out, we are divvying up my one-sixth share of the supplies."

He guzzled the water, not listening to anything I said, draining his bottle. I sipped, constantly cupping my hand and funneling the precipitation to refill mine.

"Got anything to eat?" Wendell said, holding out an open palm. He knew I did. He'd watched me bundle the supplies.

I dug in my pack and pulled out two protein bars. I passed one to my captor and ripped the end away from the other. If he got to eat, so did I, but I hoped we'd arrive soon wherever Wendell wanted to be, and I could get back to Jane, so we could join the kids.

I took a small bite, and my throat closed up. Our kids—brilliant, fun, high school students—had worked diligently and beaten the odds. If I'd worn anything with buttons, they would have popped at the memory of the last nine months. I'd do whatever Wendell required of me in order to watch them complete a fantastic year and compete against the best in the country in their *Titanic* trial. The kids and I had grown up together, me as a first-year teacher and advisor to the mock trial team and science club, the students as self-sufficient, well-mannered, intelligent, inquisitive, first-time mock trial team participants.

I'd need all the energy I could muster, so I chomped on the rest of the chalky white chocolate, cranberry, and oatmeal cake, swallowing each dry bite as if it were my last, which could very well be the case.

Wendell licked his fingers, teased the map out of his back pocket, and flattened it against his knee. "We've got a few miles in front of us. Let's go."

I rose and stretched, burrowed the water bottle in the deep compartment of the rain jacket, and hefted my bag over my shoulder. The precipitation let up a bit, and I narrowed my eyes at the narcissistic man across from me. "Now where?"

"We keep going straight south until we come across a hiking trail. It's marked well on the map." He clamped his hands on his knees and heaved his bulky frame to standing.

"Is it okay if I turn on the flashlight? No one should be able to see the beam this far in. It should be safe enough."

"Yeah, go ahead, but don't try any funny business."

Though we seemed to be following a neglected wild game trail, the bright light beam showed just how impenetrable and forbidding the vast forest around us was, and because I needed two hands to pull myself along the incline, I stuffed the flashlight into my pocket. The bright shaft pointed up and bounced against the canopy of tender leaves accompanied by Wendell's wheezing as we trekked through the woods.

Our pace slowed when the path clogged with new growth such that even a mouse would have had trouble getting through. Often, we climbed the same muddy route after slipping down. At times, we could only go south by backtracking north, and at this rate, the 'couple of miles' could take hours. I panted, but Wendell carried a greater load, and his shoulders sagged under the weight of his pack.

"Do you need a rest?"

He grunted and used the gun to signal 'keep going.'

The small mountains turned into bigger mountains, but the rain let up, and we climbed more steadily. Cresting one particularly steep gradient, it seemed we'd hit a summit. The elevation tapered off. Tree limbs broke a distant artificial light into fragments.

"I told you. There's the ranger station. Get a move on," Wendell said, picking up his pace. "The sooner we get there, the better."

He dashed around me and grabbed at my sleeve, aiming to drag me with him. The space didn't feel right. The dense woods had opened slightly, and the thick earthy scent in the air lightened. I batted his hand away and stood still, breathing deeply. He turned back to hurry me along as I pulled the flashlight out of my pocket and shined the light on our surroundings.

"It's right there," Wendell said irately, pointing. He stepped, lost his balance, and tripped under the substantial weight he carried. He toppled forward and grunted. I followed his momentum with the light beam, which found his head hanging out over the precipice at the top of the mountain. His fingertips clenched the edge of the cliff above a drop into the rocky abyss.

This time I was in perfect synchronicity with Wendell's scream.

TEN

The pack slid off one shoulder and tumbled over Wendell's head. Loose stones and gravel fell and echoed from the dangerous dark depths. He stuck out the hand holding the gun, twisted his wrist, and tangled it up in the straps. He hung on, crying out, and the weight threatened to tow him past the point of no return.

"Let it go," I cried, latching onto his shoe. "The pack's too heavy. It's dragging you over the edge."

"No." Wendell clung to the backpack with one hand, trying to slither back from the rim and yelling, "Help me."

"I am." Shrieking, I planted my heels and stretched, reaching past his ankle and clutching the fabric of his pants when Jane's compass skittered from my pocket and rolled across the ground. I watched its trajectory as it hit a small stone, bounced once, became airborne, and plummeted into the void, ricocheting into rocks again and again as it caromed off the escarpment, taking much of my courage with it. What would I tell Jane when I saw her again? Would I ever see her again?

My fingers tightened and the fabric in my hand ripped at the same time Wendell gave a frightful heave, and the pack flew at me, jerking him with it. We collapsed in a heap.

He stood, and after readjusting his backpack, stared at me. "Why didn't you let me go?"

Seriously. I shook my head. "I wouldn't do that." *Yet.*

"Let's go."

I met his glare head on. "I can't. I'm still shaking. What's the matter with you? If those people who are after you don't kill you, at the rate you're going, you'll do the honors yourself."

I unsteadily rose to my feet. My fists landed on my hips, and I blurted out, "What do you have in your bag that's so important you'd risk your life?"

When would I ever learn?

Ignoring my question, he grabbed the Maglite from where it had fallen and stepped away from the steep rock face, slowly sweeping the outcropping to assess where we should go next. He navigated to a patch of grasses growing on a narrow ledge. "There. That looks like an animal trail."

As if.

He carelessly brandished the end of the gun, backing me away from his pack, and he bent down over it. I raised up on my toes and craned my neck, curious to see what was inside, but he straddled the carryall and blocked my view. Wendell unzipped his bag, and my tension eased until he turned around, holding a length of flat nylon webbing with a clasp at one end like a leash. Visions of my own dog danced before my eyes.

"Clip this around your waist. I'll lead, but I wouldn't want you to roam too far." The light danced forbiddingly across the branches and limbs as he swung the Maglite to make his point. "And, ya know, fall or get hurt."

"For my protection." *Right.* "You can't be serious." I crossed my arms, indicating my stubborn unwillingness to cooperate.

"We're almost there. Hurry up." He tossed me the end of the gray strapping, emphasizing his earnestness with his gun hand, and used my heart against me. "Jane needs you."

I begrudgingly wrapped the cable around my midsection and secured the end. Now I was leashed to an armed idiot bent on lugging a reluctant millstone. I'll admit, he no longer rushed headlong into the trees, but rather painstakingly decided where his next step should be. Nevertheless, when he released the cedar branch which smacked me in the face leaving a welt covered in sap, I knew I would have done better.

We lumbered on with intent, but the forest was so incredibly impassable, in no time we lost sight of the ranger outpost. Without the compass and attempting to navigate with total cloud coverage, Wendell directed us by what he described as gut instinct.

He took each step with deliberation, checking his footing on the wet ground before proceeding. When Wendell slipped on stone fragments, he yanked me forward, but I grabbed the nearest stable, attached branch and stopped us from forward momentum into the unknown—again. With his face pale and drawn, he said. "Let's take a break."

"Yes, let's. If we wait until we can see something, we'll be better off."

He dropped to the ground. I reached to untether myself and he said, "Leave it. I wouldn't want you wandering off."

He nestled against the trunk of a wide old oak, crossing his arms, leaving the firearm on top. I wriggled into a cavity at the base of a hickory tree. I closed my eyes and before I could even hope to sleep, I was off to Neverland.

When I woke, millions of sparkling stars splattered the clear, dark sky, and if I reached up, I felt my hand would come away sprinkled with glitter. The light of the crescent moon cast Wendell's form in an eerie yellow-green glow, and shadows stretched across our rest area.

I kept still, listening, and heard night sounds dancing on the wind. Concentrating, I attempted to differentiate the origins—a distant high-pitched careening of a bird, the occasional bellow of a moose, a small rodent's chirping, the hoot of an owl, the piercing yowl of a young fox, ferocious cricking of bats swooping overhead, and squeaking branches, heavy from rain. Soon an overlay of myriad bugs clicking caused me to squirm. I sighed, not hearing help on the way.

Wendell barely moved. I reached for the clip at my waist, not knowing what I would do once freed. My thumb quietly drew back the spring-loaded clasp.

Without opening his eyes, Wendell's gruff voice said, "Don't."

No longer intent on being civil, I said, "I am going to relieve myself all alone. Get over it. Where would I run to? I have no idea where we are." *And neither do you*, I thought.

I noisily unhooked the restraint and took indignant pounding steps around the tree. When I returned, I found Wendell digging in my bag.

"What do you think you're doing?"

He didn't even have the sense to look sheepish. "Breakfast. I think it's getting lighter, and we should be able to move more easily. We've got to be close."

I wanted to scream. *We could be anywhere.*

He pivoted on the balls of his feet. He'd extracted two apples and held one out as a peace offering. My mouth watered, and my stomach growled. He lifted it closer, and I snatched it off his palm. We munched the sweet fruit in silence, and in the time it took to devour the apple to its core, the multitude of stars faded, leaving mere pinpricks against a slightly less than indigo sky.

He coiled the nylon binding and tucked it back in the bag. His fingers brushed against his pants leg, wiping dirt onto the grimier, dark material. He stood and muscled his arms through the straps of his sack. "The faster we get going, the sooner you're rid of me."

With its weight lessened by even the slightest amount, I turned on the light and hefted my bag more easily. We began our steady tramp across undulating terrain, rising and falling, seldom tapering off. I couldn't fathom how many steps we'd taken. It had been less than half a day, and it felt as if we'd walked forever. A short sip of water quenched my thirst, but I wondered just what getting rid of him meant. After all, I'd been kidnapped at gunpoint.

ELEVEN

The dark diminished with every step we took. Morning dawned, and birdsong poured in from every direction—whistling, cooing, tweeting, and a percussive repetitive bleating. I might've heard a wren and a dove but promised myself I'd definitely learn to match the calls with their crooner—when I got out of this mess.

"What is that?" Wendell spun on his heels, feverishly waving the gun, pointing in every direction. "Dowse the light," he hissed.

I fumbled and finally found the switch.

"Do you hear that? Twigs breaking, and they don't care if they are heard."

"Calm down. The woods are waking. Birds and animals. That's it."

He breathed in and out and nodded to go ahead. When we could clearly make out the shapes on the ground in front of us, Wendell picked up our pace. I longed for the rays of sunshine to burn off the ever-present damp chill, but the sheer landscape restricted access to direct sunlight until we stepped into a clearing. The rain had scrubbed the sky deep blue. Atop a small rise, buzzing bees darted from yellow-and-white daisies to small bouquets of tiny pink blossoms clustered together on tall green shrubbery. Fluttering butterfly wings glittered in the sunlight like animated confetti.

On the opposite side of the unspoiled expanse, a white-tailed doe and her spotted fawn perked up, became alert, and eyed our approach. We spooked them, and they bounded gracefully out of sight, fluffy white tails bouncing as they retreated.

A pair of bright red cardinals swooped and rolled overhead. I recognized the short, rapid wing beats and the black and white markings of a chickadee flitting among the trees. Instead of enjoying the sights, however, I examined the ground for blights and traps rather than blessings and treasures.

Here and there, pink bleeding hearts bloomed on long stems of pale green. I spied a patch of orchids and searched my memory for words of advice from Marietta. Many of the flowers found in the wild of the Southeast have been used for both medicinal and toxic purposes. I didn't have any idea which plant was which, so I held my hands away to avoid contact. The melody of "We're Off to See the Wizard" came to mind, and I had a vision of Dorothy and her cohorts sagging to the ground after running through a field of poisonous poppies.

"Get it off me. Get it off me," Wendell screeched, dragging me out of my reverie.

I couldn't see anything. "What's the matter?"

"There's something crawling on my neck. Take it away." His voice wobbled, and he swatted awkwardly at a place behind his ear, jumping from foot to foot.

"Don't move."

He stopped moving but shuddered uncontrollably. "Help me."

He recklessly clanked the firearm against his head when he pulled his crown forward to expose his neck. I shoved the gun hand away and peered above his collar, plucking off a tiny wingless bug.

"What is it?" he bellowed.

I deposited it on a rock. "It's a tick."

"Bloodsucker. Now I'll get Lyme disease." He rubbed the back of his neck, then grabbed another rock and crushed the tick with more vehemence than I'd ever seen in him. "I feel like they're crawling all over me. Let's move."

His head swiveled impatiently, scanning the edge of the forest, as I removed my raincoat and balled it up, squashing it into my pack. He said, "South," and stomped through the lush field. I suddenly felt a similar creeping of unseen critters, brushed at my cheek, and stepped lively to keep up.

The spectacular panorama I viewed through the opening in the trees looked out over miles and miles of rugged geography painted in shades of green, carved up by ribbons of silver, and sprinkled with pools reflecting sky-blue. If I'd witness this bucolic scene with anybody but Wendell, it would've been glorious. Tears clouded my eyes.

"What's wrong with you?"

"Wrong with me? What's wrong with me?" My voice intensified. "You made me abandon my best friend in a downed plane, hurting. My students are going to knock the socks off their competitors, and we wanted to witness their national debut, but I don't see any way for that to happen now." I sniffled. "We're lost, in the middle of nowhere, and you're pointing a gun at me."

Wendell grunted. "I know precisely where we are. We've been going downhill for a while. Pretty soon we'll have to head up and arrive at the lookout. Keep moving."

I hoped he was right. Back in the shade of the cool woods, the terrain seemed to take us more down than up. Maybe Wendell knew what he was doing after all. My concentration wavered. I missed my footing, collapsing on my right leg, and let out a pain-filled groan.

"Now what?"

My teeth clenched, and I seethed. "I turned my knee." I hated being with Wendell. Not knowing what the future would bring, I said, "Leave me here. You can send someone to find me when you're safe. Just go."

"Not happening. You can't stay here."

My stomach rumbled. My knee throbbed. I pounded my fist against my thigh. "Why not?" Hurt, angry, and tired, my innermost thoughts blasted free. "You're probably just going to shoot me anyway."

He backed up a step and had the audacity to look affronted. He straightened his right arm, pointed the gun to the sky, and pulled the trigger. I shrank from the expected crack that never happened.

"What can I say? I don't like guns, but I needed you. The bullets are here." He patted his breast pocket. "I wouldn't hurt you. You didn't let me fall. I can't leave you alone in the wild." His manic eyes darkened.

I stared at him and shook with rage. "Why would you be so cruel?" My vain attempts to stand on my injured leg and make a dignified getaway didn't fare well. I crumpled to the ground.

Surrounded by detritus of fallen timber and old trees, Wendell located a branch with a 'y' shaped end. As he tore away the little twigs, he said, "We should be safe soon, where your phone will connect, and you can call for help."

He'd known about my phone all along.

He handed me a crutch. "Here, use this."

I couldn't bring myself to thank him. The staff stood a bit too tall but allowed me to hobble and hop behind him. We hiked around a particularly tight grove of trees, and the sound of rushing water greeted us. It thundered and boomed as it descended from a rocky ledge in a lacy veil to a pool below. I peered through the mist created by a gorgeous cascade at the sunlight forming a double rainbow against the cerulean sky directly overhead. Momentarily disregarding Wendell, I stopped in my tracks, awestruck.

A noisy river otter stood on its hind legs staring at us, chuckling and hissing, looking like he was ready to take a plunge. It ignored Wendell's attempts to scare it away, so Wendell walked down the riverbank.

Upon his return, he yelled over the continuous rush of the waterfall, "It looks as if this is calmer than any other place along the river. I think we can wade through here to get to the other side if we avoid that … animal." He cocked his head, and the otter chirruped.

Wendell's somber words deflated my optimism. In reality, rushing water poured into the pond next to us, and plumes pounded the base of the falls, feeding the swiftly moving water in front of us. It burbled over substantial boulders and rocks and looked no less intimidating than any other spot.

Wendell removed his shoes, stuffed his socks inside, tied the laces, and hung them around his neck. He rolled up his pants legs and nodded. "You might want to do the same."

The last remnants of the rainwater had evaporated from

my clothes, and I couldn't imagine getting wet all over again. I reluctantly removed my shoes and socks, crusty with dried mud, leaves, and burrs.

Wendell pocketed the gun, descended to the water's edge, and stepped from the shore to the nearest flat stone, teetered, then caught his balance. He took another step. And another. The words he called over his shoulder were almost lost in the cacophony surrounding us. "It's fine."

I had few options. I tied the laces of my shoes together in front of me around the straps of my backpack to help keep it secure and took a deep breath. The staff acted like a third leg, and the first steps were easy, but the chilly splashes caused me to shiver, and midway across, I slid on a stone, slimy with lichen, dropped the stick, and pitched into the unexpectedly deep torrent of water.

My body slammed into the ice-cold river, forcing the air from my lungs. I couldn't get my footing and fought to take a breath as the strong current carried me along and quickly swept me downstream, away from Wendell. I bounced against hard, stationary items submerged below the surface, pummeled from side to side, and could almost hear dinging as if hitting the bumpers on a pinball machine. The turbulence in the water increased, rippling and foamy. The surge dragged me under. I came up sputtering and inhaled a mouthful of water before the world around me spun out of control.

I couldn't catch my breath. From deep in my subconscious came words I learned from CJ Bluestone, Carlee's dad and Maverick's search-and-rescue trainer. "Stay calm, no matter what the problem." I had a problem—a big problem.

My heavy pack continued to pull me under. No matter how much I wriggled and writhed, I couldn't shrug it loose. I thrashed and my shoes thumped my chest. Then I remembered the ties, but my numb fingers didn't have the dexterity to undo the knots. The river quickly turned to rapids, more froth, faster moving, more stones, and an increase in the roar of spilling water. Whatever waited for me wouldn't be gentle, and my efforts to steer toward shore made no headway. I watched a huge log a few hundred yards in front of me rise up and plummet out of sight. Kicking and flailing had little impact on my trajectory. My strength declined. My head filled with a million thoughts, some welcome memories and some regrets, when I realized, I wasn't going to make it.

TWELVE

My eyes drifted closed. With nothing left to give, I relaxed my arms and let the cold wash over me. Dad joined my dear friend and landlady, Ida Clemashevski, in a kaleidoscope of familiar faces, streaking through what was left of my consciousness. I regretted that my loss would make them sad. Maverick grinned sloppily and his wagging tail swept away the scene. It filled with the visages of my mock trial team, then morphed into other smiling countenances from my year in Columbia.

A page seemed to turn, and I had a picture in my mind of Jane dressed in an exquisite white Cinderella gown, carrying roses and daisies, walking gracefully down an aisle on her father's arm. My heart thumped as my view shifted to the best man. Pete's handsome face and sparkling eyes infused me with a burst of vigor to resist the powerful force dragging me away. For an instant I thought I'd win, but my remaining energy diminished rapidly, and I realized I wouldn't ever get another delicious kiss.

I'm so sorry, Pete. I love you.

As if from a very far distance, I floated above the scene and caught a vision of Drew standing at the front of a church, mouth agape, struck speechless for the first time since I'd met him, his eyes gazing at his beautiful bride. As I delighted in his wordlessness, he transformed into dashing and debonair Charles with his mischievous blue eyes, thick blond hair, and affable smile. The pins and needles piercing my ice-cold hands and feet dulled. Welcome warmth embraced me.

Charles and I were married for only seventeen days before he was taken from me. Dad, Charles and I enjoyed biking the trails circling my hometown, but the final time, when Dad spotted the glint of a gun, he and Charles formed a human shield. Dad's traumatic brain injury still wielded its limitations. Charles died. Sometimes I wished it had been me. We never found the shooter.

"Promise me you'll live a good life," he'd said as his blood poured from his wound. This time I heard, "Promise me you'll live. Stay calm."

However, 'stay calm' weren't Charles's words. As I focused on the voice, Charles said again, "Live," and began to fade.

My heart thumped wildly in my chest. "Thank you," I said. I fought to keep his mien before me as CJ's direction returned to haunt me. "Stay calm."

But the instruction was no longer solely in my mind. Somebody repeated the words aloud. My ears perked up. Buffeted against jagged boulders, I blended all the loves in my life and summoned one last smidgeon of fury. I kicked hard and broke the surface, coughing and gasping. I couldn't identify the source of the words, but scanned the shoreline distorted by the crystal lenses of moving water. A huge splash drenched my face and blinded me. Panicked, I dropped again like a lead weight and struggled to find any direction away from the river bottom.

Something sharp caught my shoulder and yanked me to the surface. As it dragged me closer to where the timber took a nosedive, I bucked in fear but couldn't break free of the vise-grip. When I realized I could harness the power of the current, I stopped thrashing unproductively. Instead of fighting, I kicked in sync with the pull and surged toward the water's edge.

Strong hands dragged me from the depths, bumped my body over the rugged ground, and turned me on my side. I spewed water, then inhaled and sputtered again. I wiped my mouth with the back of my hand and spat, but recoiled as droplets of freezing water splattered my face. My thoughts whirled. A smooth tongue on my cheek made me gag. I didn't want help or anything else from Wendell.

Warm hands caressed my face and tenderly, but firmly, embraced it. A mellifluous voice said, "Katie? Open your eyes. It's me."

When the world came into focus, I knew I'd died and gone to heaven—though it felt like I'd gone through the other place to get there. Warm chocolate eyes blocked out everything else. I leaned away, still not believing what might be before me. Words sprang from my gravelly throat. "Pete. What? How?"

"Sh. I'll tell you everything, but first we need to get you out of here."

I clutched his arm, and my throat tightened. "Jane?"

"She's safe. She wouldn't let Drew transport her to the hospital until we found you, but she's being taken care of as we speak. The crew is all okay."

My stomach flopped, and I gripped his arm tighter. "He has a gun."

"That guy with you?"

I nodded. "But it might not be loaded."

Pete jerked his head, addressing the people milling around us. "Gromm might be armed. Fan out and keep your eyes peeled." When the uniforms registered in my muddled brain, I recognized them as belonging to some type of law enforcement. Pete focused on me again. "We haven't seen him, and I'll guarantee his fire power couldn't rival ours. Are you okay?"

"I think so."

No sooner had the words left my lips when we were assaulted with another barrage of cold droplets accompanied by a long rattle. Pete chuckled as he cradled me, shielding me a bit from the icy prickling onslaught. I ducked under his arm and saw my dog. Not to be denied, Maverick pranced close, tongue hanging out, panting, waiting for an acknowledgment. Pete dragged him into our embrace, smiling at my yip of surprise. Water drenched Maverick from tip to tail.

Pete bowed his head and said, "We let the dogs loose, and they found you, but Maverick was magnificent. You should have seen him soar over the raging river. Then he chomped on your shoulder, probably not too gently, and pulled you to safety. I should take a look at that."

"My heroes," I said, on a long exhale.

Pete searched my face. My heart somersaulted. Then he leaned down and gently kissed me. My arm crept over his shoulder, and my fingers caressed his neck. His enchanting curls tickled the back of my hand, and when we came up for air, my eyes closed, and I smacked my lips. "Delicious." Pete chuckled, and a cough came from someone else I couldn't see. I smiled shyly. "How did you even know where I was?"

Pete tilted his head and began palpating my shoulder. "It seems not long after you left Jane, the communications system reengaged, and she was able to forward information about the downed plane. She complained about not being able to call you or the guy she sent with you, so the groggy copilot helped Jane hobble out to check the plane. They discovered a woman tied up in the cargo hold, thrashing around. Jane regretted removing the gag."

I flinched. He massaged my shoulder. "Jane determined the mishmash of equipment surrounding the woman could have been used to control the plane and decided the woman was a threat. You should have heard her. Jane was furious, and she didn't know if anyone else was involved. She worried about your safety, but it's probably a good thing she couldn't walk, or you'd all have been out lost in the wilderness." Pete deftly released my pack and slid it from my arms.

"How did you get here?"

"Once Jane reported you were missing, Mr. Mackey arranged our immediate flight to Franklin and CJ—"

"CJ's here too?" I rubbernecked around Pete. Tall, broad, stalwart CJ Bluestone stood under the canopy of leaves with Renegade standing guard at his side. CJ cleared his throat again and nodded once. Tears filled my eyes. "But how did you know where to look?"

"While we were in the air, Jane tracked your exceedingly sporadic phone signal."

I reached into one pocket and withdrew a dripping, soggy, dead device.

"Over objections from your students, as a precaution and to make parents feel more comfortable, remember Jane had you all turn on the Find Me feature, and it looks like this time it paid off." Pete's eyebrows rose. "Your position indicator would come and go as you crested each promontory. She never took her eyes from her screen. Good thing she caught it when she did. When she shared the data, the rangers knew of only one destination on this path—an isolated and abandoned fire tower, so we headed this way and got close enough for the dogs to trail you. Maverick and Renegade in action are a sight to behold."

"Come here, Maverick." I held out my hand. He stepped under my fingers for a scratch but couldn't sit. His tail hung limp and flaccid.

"He's hurt. What's the matter?" My anxiety gene ratcheted up a notch.

"Swimmer's tail," CJ said. "Over exertion. He worked hard to find you and then dove into the cold water, paddling against the current to haul you to safety. He will need to rest, but his tail will be fine."

My forehead knotted up. "Oh, Maverick." I buried my face in his chest. Pete crushed us both against him. "And you came," I said, nestling against his chest. His warm, soft lips found my forehead.

Smelling his cologne made my heart squishy, but I looked up to watch his reaction when I asked, "Are the kids okay? Have you heard from Marietta Calder?"

The enigmatic smile was open to interpretation. "They are anxiously awaiting both you and Jane." With a serious tone to his voice, he said, "What happened, Katie?"

I cringed. "After the pilot and first officer lost consciousness, Jane performed like an accomplished aviator. Pete, you should've seen her. She was amazing." I worked on fully remembering what had occurred while running my fingers over the ridges on my dog's head. He dropped and rolled onto his back so I could rub his belly. "She took over the controls, but she couldn't connect with anyone, and a bunch of stuff was going wrong—fuel, GPS." I tried to recall everything Jane had told me. "Jane and the flight attendant got banged up, but Wendell and I weren't injured."

"The Gromm guy?"

I nodded. "Jane sent us to get help. Gromm rightfully determined we'd been hijacked and declared we needed to get out of there before the rest of her team arrived."

Pete's eyes popped. "More of them?"

I shrugged. "He disconnected the connections to the hacking paraphernalia and probably allowed the communications to reengage."

Pete nodded. "Why did you go with him?"

"I thought he had a loaded gun."

His fingers lightly stroked my cheekbone, and they came away sticky.

"He'll be lucky we don't find him." A rare moment of anger flared, and for an instant, Pete's eyes gleamed the color of onyx.

He hauled me off the ground. I hopped on my good leg. He furrowed his brow. "I fell." He supported me for an instant before scooping me up and carrying me to the rumbling four-wheeler, with CJ in the driver's seat, and Maverick and Renegade sharing the bench as passengers.

The paved road accommodated our vehicle, as well as hikers and bikers enjoying the outdoors on a gorgeous, warm spring afternoon, on their way to the spot Wendell had seen on the map. We'd have been overrun with people if we'd stayed on the trail.

I trembled and wondered if any of them partnered with the woman we'd left in the cargo hold. Maybe taking the shortcut had saved Wendell's life. And mine.

THIRTEEN

We filled Jane's hospital room, and the gratifying squeeze I received from her left welcome marks on my back and arms. In answer to my grunt, she said, "This hug is from your dad and Ida and so many more. We'll get real live ones from the kids when we get to Atlanta," and crashed back onto the bed.

The remarkable stereo laughter burbling from the doorway came from Pete and Drew. What a twosome. They were both smart, tall, kind, intense, and loyal, but that's where the similarities ended. I loved the way Pete's dark brown hair flopped over his forehead and gently curled around his collar and my heart did a happy dance, excited I'd still get to see where *we* would go. Drew's short white-blond hair gave him the military bearing he earned being an agent for the

Minnesota Bureau of Criminal Apprehension. Drew's blue eyes were shielded by black horn-rimmed glasses. Pete's warm, dark eyes winked behind long lashes. Pete's lithe biker body exuded speed, whereas Drew's solid form promised brawn.

"Any word on Wendell or what could have made him a target?" Jane asked.

Drew's laugh halted, and his mouth twitched in indecision. He stepped into the room and beckoned to Pete, who closed the door behind them.

"What is it, Drew? We've got a right to know. We could've been killed." Jane furrowed her brow, and her lower lip protruded.

Drew relented. "Wendell Gromm stole some proprietary blueprints from a very private, select company with government ties and an influential CEO. Wendell is in deep doodoo, and not only will he be charged with theft, he'll face kidnapping charges when he's found. The sheriff and the FBI are both on the lookout for him."

Jane's mouth opened, but no sound emerged.

Final test results on the pilots were pending, but Dianne, Noah, and Richard had been released with orders to consult their primary care physicians. I'd been given the okay, but my knee ached, and bruises in varying shades of black-and-blue covered my body, so I gingerly took a seat on the plastic molded visitor's chair and remembered the strange exchanges between Wendell and Jane. "Jane, you've known Wendell a while. What happened between the two of you?"

Drew's head turned to carefully watch Jane answer my question.

She inhaled. "I almost feel sorry for him." Her eyes locked on her fingers, lacing and unlacing them. She raised her eyes and said, "Almost. Wendell's Dad and mine were partners in an aviation start up. You've met my dad. He's driven and no slacker. He's honest as the day is long." Her voice quieted. "Wendell's mom ran away about the same time my mom died."

The bed squeaked when Drew sat next to Jane. He wrapped his arm around her shoulder, and she snuffled. "I stuck up for him when the bullies teased him. We formed an alliance for a brief time in elementary school until he discovered teachers applauded his ability to successfully win an argument with words instead of a physical confrontation. They encouraged him. I watched out for him, but I didn't worry about him until he began to tell big stories to win his debates. I called him on it. He laughed at my concern, and I quit listening, quit supporting him. Maybe that's when he needed a friend most."

"Friendship is a two-way street." I glanced at the roomful of people I loved and thought how lucky I was. Friends understood failures. If there ever was a right time to tell Jane I lost her engagement gift, it had to be now. "Jane? I lost your compass."

Her expression froze. I thought I'd failed her until she said, "Thank goodness. I don't know what convinced my handsome fiancé I'd ever hike that far away from civilization. And besides, I sent you out into the wild with a crazy man. A crazy man whose dad lost their home to gambling. Wendell told bigger and bigger stories. Convincing, but lies all the same. My dad worked his tail off. He supported Wendell's dad, lent him money for rent and food, kept their business in the black. But when Wendell's dad flew while intoxicated, he lost his license. He could no longer hold up his end of the partnership, nor did he wish to. My dad bought him out at a more than fair market value. Wendell hated what happened and let everyone believe he was victimized."

"The 'poor me' kid," said Drew.

"After years of intensely applying all his business acumen to his love of flying, Dad created Sapphire Skyway, one of the hallmarks in the industry. He loves his career and has earned his success. As you know, he's financially sound."

The euphemism elicited a huff from Drew, and Jane let out a tiny laugh, too, before pursing her lips. "Wendell blames my dad, and his rants go all over the place. He believes he was robbed of his legacy. He inferred his mom and my dad had a fling, and that's what drove his dad to drink and her to leave, but I saw her bruises." Jane shook her head. "Wendell's dad hit her, and sometimes my dad blames himself for not being more forceful when he first saw what was going on, but he couldn't have changed anything. Wendell's dad barely tolerated him. I don't think his dad ever cared for anyone but himself."

"That's why you treat Wendell with deference. Because you and your dad thrived, you feel sorry for him."

"I did." Jane's voice took on an edge. "But not anymore. He burned that bridge. He's a leech just like his dad, and it's time he was stopped. I only hope law enforcement catches up with him before I do."

The room went silent as we pondered the implications. Pete sat on the arm of my chair. "Drew, have they identified the woman?"

Jane's eyebrows arched in her pained face.

Drew sucked the air out of the room and looked to the ceiling for guidance. When he exhaled, he glanced at Pete. "Until she stopped talking, Natalianna Kuznetsov maintained she was the victim of a kidnapping gone wrong. She kept referring to the awful little man who tied her up. She used her superficial wounds to support her claim. However, Kuznetsov's been on a watch list for years. Although she can't be tied definitively to any other crimes, the agency we contacted asserted she might be a gun for hire. She may very well have been assigned to take possession of the plane and dispose of Gromm. She hasn't said another word, so we might never find out who hired her, if anyone."

He gently stroked Jane's nervous fingers. "A sophisticated hacking system was found in the hold. Although she claimed it was a job, she tried to control the plane and failed. If she had a gun, it might have been the link the agency needed to nail her, but it appears her weapon was carted off by Wendell and used to take Katie into the Nantahala National Forest."

Jane's chin dropped to her chest. "Why would she attempt something so dangerous?"

Drew said, "You landed the plane, love. And saved six lives."

"And I, for one, am truly grateful. You were magnificent." I pushed my sore bones out of the chair. My limp was barely noticeable. I went to Jane's other side, sat on the thin, uncomfortable mattress, and gave her another hug. "I owe you my life."

"The feeling is mutual." One corner of Jane's mouth crept into a smile. "Please, get the doctor, Drew. I'd like to get out of here so we can do what we set out to do. If I'm not mistaken, it's only about an hour flight from here, so we'll still be able to get in some recreational time with the kids." Drew jumped up and headed toward the door, but before he could complete his mission, Jane said, "Can you come with us?"

"I'm in. I'm off through Thursday," Drew said and disappeared down the hallway.

"Me, too." Pete stood and extended his arms over his head. "I've always wanted to take a tour of Atlanta, and I'd love to see the students compete."

The three of us turned at the decisive rap on the door frame.

FOURTEEN

"Dad." Jane's face lit up. She threw her booted foot off the bed, and I tiptoed next to Pete.

Mr. Mackey looked his daughter up and down. "I'm going to fire those incompetent—"

"Dad, you can't. It wasn't their fault. Someone was after Wendell and hijacked the Citation with very sophisticated hardware and software."

"Yes, my dear daughter. I've seen it. It's incredible and, unfortunately, took no time to hack into our guidance system, electronics, and communications. We're going to have to do something about that, but what possessed you to offer Wendell transportation to Atlanta in the first place?"

Before I could question how everything could have fallen into place with such little advanced warning, Mr. Mackey strode to Jane's side. "You've known what trouble he can cause. And now stealing on top of everything else. The apple didn't fall far from that tree."

"Da-ad." He bowed his head, admonished by her tone. "What if he'd found another ride, one that didn't have me around to save the day?"

He embraced her with the ferocity of a bear. When he broke the connection, he reached into his breast pocket, removed a phone, and held it out to me. "It's good to see you again, Ms. Wilk. This is a replacement. It doesn't come anywhere near balancing your level of involvement in the safe return of my aircraft, my crew, and my daughter, although I'll admit, they're all pretty banged up." His lively eyes sparkled.

"Thank you for everything, Mr. Mackey. You didn't have to get me a phone, but I appreciate it very much." It was powered on and charged up. "And please, call me Katie."

"And you can call me Hendrix. Katie, I only do things I want to do."

"Da-ad," Jane said again. "Your name is Mitchell."

"Yes, well." His daughter might be the only person in the world who could get Mitchell Mackey to blush such a shocking pink. "Your chariot awaits, as do your students. You should be in Atlanta in time for bed check. Dr. Bluestone and the pups are already at the airport. We just have a few details to iron out."

The next hour whizzed by. Mitchell, the magician, furnished clean, fashionable clothes—approved by Jane, of course—and made certain I checked in with my dad and Marietta Calder. Along with my phone, he supplied a new roller pack with shoulder straps into which my few meager belongings had been transferred, including the journals and my new book.

A deputy from the sheriff's department took our

statements. She handed us each a pen and indicated a line at the bottom of the page. "I have all your pertinent contact information. Sign here, please." As she collected the pages, she said, "You are free to leave." She kept her eyes glued to Jane and me. "However, scuttlebutt around the office has you sleuthing back in Minnesota. We in North Carolina would appreciate you leaving the investigation to the professionals."

Her remark hit close to home, and I'd have liked nothing better than to leave it to law enforcement. Jane at first looked confused. "Where did you hear that?" Her eyes scoured the ward and alighted on the only familiar face, Drew. Although he looked just out of earshot, his face and ears had turned an unhealthy, blotchy red.

Jane smiled and said sweetly, matching the deputy's soothing drawl, "You won't have to worry about us, sugar." Some of her Midwest vocals crept into the next words. "But *he* certainly should."

Drew had the wherewithal to look penitent, but his shoulders stopped mid-shrug, and he turned to the commotion at the elevator bay.

"Where is she? Where is that conniving boyfriend stealer?" A feisty woman pointed her finger at Jane. "You. What did you do with my Wendell?" She rearranged her buxom cleavage and stomped past Drew. "Well, what do you have to say?"

Jane's head dropped back, and she blew out one word. "Felicity."

"Don't you dare Felicity me, you hussy. I waited and waited for his arrival, just like he asked, but he didn't answer my calls. If I hadn't found out you appropriated the plane, I'd still be waiting. It's all your fault. You're the same as ever, I see. Always get what you want." The woman shook her straight blond hair with teal, hot pink, and orange highlights, as if it was a cape draped over her shoulders. "I have proof you've been seeing him behind my back. I won't let you get away with it. Where is he? What have you done with him?"

Drew strolled to Jane's side and nodded to the deputy who circled behind Felicity.

Jane said, "Wendell flew on the Sapphire Skyway Citation. On our way to Atlanta, we lost our pilots, and I was forced to land in the Nantahala National Forest. He is now wanted by the sheriff's department and the FBI for kidnapping."

"Then he's not hurt?"

I couldn't read her tone of voice well. She almost sounded disappointed.

"I need to talk to him." She also sounded whiny. Her finger brushed a spot at the base of her cheek.

Jane's left eyebrow raised, the way it did when she talked to a recalcitrant history student. "I have no idea where he is, nor do I want to."

Felicity sneered. "Like I believe that. He told me you always wanted what you couldn't have, and you can't have Wendell."

Drew cleared his throat, and Jane took that moment to introduce them. "Felicity, this is my *fiancé*, Bureau of Criminal Apprehension Agent, Drew Kidd. If you have anything more to say, perhaps you'd like to tell it to the sheriff's deputy as she escorts you out of here." Jane nodded to the woman behind Felicity.

The deputy extended a hand to take Felicity's arm, but Felicity wrenched it out of reach. "This isn't over," she said as she marched to the elevator under our watchful eyes.

"Oh, it's over," Drew sighed and stepped away to make a call.

Mitchell stepped off and held the elevator, tipping an imaginary hat. Felicity brushed by him, grunted in disgust, and tramped on. Mitchell shook his head as the door closed.

"She still isn't a fan of yours, is she, my dear? Has she never gotten over you winning the chemistry scholarship she expected to win at graduation? I suppose it didn't help, at that age you were so much more alike, teachers often confused the two of you."

I shot a surprised look at Jane. No one would ever mistake one for the other now.

Jane shook her head sadly. "I don't know what she sees in Wendell. She could do so much better."

"Let's get you out of here," said her dad.

Mitchell arranged a last-minute physical check and quick release by the attending physician who conspired with Pete to keep an eye on Jane and me, monitor our recovery, and make sure we rehydrated well. Although she complained, Mitchell insisted Jane follow orders explicitly, and we accompanied a surly patient as her nurse wheeled her to the exit. The hospital glass doors whooshed apart, and a glossy black Rolls Royce stretch limousine purred under the porte-cochère. I stopped at the entry and gaped at the uniformed driver opening the car door.

Jane shook her head. "Don't get used to this, Wilk. We live in West Central Minnesota. We don't even have a steady ride-hailing service yet."

I walked under the large overhang, slipped inside the automobile, and blissfully sank into the pillowy seats.

Mitchell and Jane spoke softly while Drew, Pete, and I gawked at the buildings blurring as we drove by and applauded the beautiful landscapes.

Jane chuckled, and her dad asked, "You've never been to

North Carolina before?"

"I haven't," I said. "There's such an eclectic mix of architecture and geography. It's mind-boggling."

Mitchell nodded approvingly at Jane. "You won't mind, then," she said, "if we set a date to return?"

"I'm all in." I pulled down my sleeve, cupped my palm inside the cuff, and swiped a big circle on the window, removing the telltale nose prints left by my fascination. "I've always wanted to hike a tiny slice of the Appalachian Trail."

Pete and Drew gave each other a knowing glance.

"What did I say?"

"You already have," Mitchell said.

I contemplated the events of the last thirty-six hours before saying, "But I wasn't paying attention. I didn't see anything." My peripheral vision caught a stunning view from the car window, and I whirled in my seat, trying to capture it all.

Mitchell watched my reaction as he said, "We're passing through the foothills of the Blue Ridge Mountains. And behind you loom the Great Smokey Mountains. When next you visit, plan a more extensive trip—with time to experience the sights."

Road traffic increased as we neared the airport, and I craned my neck to catch the sleek silver aircraft dotting the sky. We glided to the gate where Mitchell slid his plastic ID through a card reader and the white guard arm crept up to admit us. The limo sailed across the tarmac and stopped at the foot of the airstairs, leading up to a second aircraft wearing the colors and insignia of Sapphire Skyway.

I knew, in all likelihood, we would not encounter another forced landing. Nevertheless, I had a difficult time getting my feet to move up the steps, and I breathed deeply in my lame attempt to tamp down my feelings and seek rational thoughts.

Pete read my mind. He took my hand and lightly stroked my fingers. Trust took up more space than the fear. I got lost in the emotional support from his warm brown eyes and returned his reassuring smile. The next thing I knew, I found myself seated in a large comfortable chair among wonderful friends, slathered in messy dog kisses. When Maverick settled, he skipped the sitting and dropped to the floor at my feet, with his head on his paws, his furtive eyes scrutinizing every move in the cabin, and the tip of his tail swishing guardedly.

"Still sore, Mav?" I said, rustling his silky ears.

A tall blond flight attendant stepped cautiously around my good boy and offered champagne or iced tea. Feeling the need to be ready for any eventuality for the rest of our trip, I accepted the latter.

"My name is Jack. If there's anything you need, let me know. Mr. Mackey has ordered Beef Wellington for his guests, unless you'd like something else."

Jack's blue eyes twinkled as I vigorously nodded my head, again flummoxed by the lavish ministrations. "Beef Wellington would be sensational."

Mitchell sat next to CJ, facing Jane and Drew, with a look of pride. He clinked a bubbling champagne flute with Drew and tipped it my way in a gesture of welcome.

My new phone rang. "Lorelei?"

"Ms. Wilk, thank goodness. We were so worried. Mr. Mackey has been updating us. Do you know when you'll get to Atlanta?"

"We're on the plane, and I've been told we'll arrive in plenty of time for a bed check."

"Very funny." She giggled. "We can't wait until you and Ms. Mackey get here."

"We're eager to get there too. What's on the agenda for this evening?"

"Mr. Mackey got us early reservations at a restaurant—a Michelin restaurant. My mom told Ms. Lavigne we'd take advantage of the once in a lifetime opportunity, with or without her. We just finished the bougie experience, and it was awesome. He picked up the tab for the whole dinner. And now we're attending the Atlanta Symphony Orchestra." She ran out of breath and inhaled before continuing. "I didn't think the guys would want to go, but the music is a tribute to *Star Wars*. Boy, is this trip bussin'. We're working on something special to show our appreciation to Mr. Mackey. You should arrive and be unpacked by the time we get back to the hotel. I've got to go. See you soon, Teach."

I hung up, grinning at the moniker she'd chosen for me and deciding to keep it for as long as she'd let me.

Feet tramped up the stairway, and I almost didn't recognize Dianne in her ratty jeans and bulky sweatshirt. She stopped dead in her tracks when she caught sight of Jane among the passengers, and the words spilled from her lips, "Ms. Mackey, I'm so sorry. I hope you don't mind. Your dad gave us permission to catch a ride to Atlanta." She placed her fingers over the bandage on her forehead.

"It's okay, Dianne. It wasn't your fault, and we all survived."

Dianne lost her footing with a nudge from behind. "What's the hold up?" Noah's head popped in next to her. He glanced around and his boyish smile vanished when he saw me. "Katie. We're glad you're okay. You *are* okay?"

I nodded.

"Where did Wendell think he was taking you?"

"He was headed to a fire tower where he thought he'd get

a line of communication out of the national forest."

"Where is the scoundrel now?" He forced a laugh.

"I have no idea. He could be anywhere or lost forever." I shuddered when I thought I could have been lost forever with him.

Noah stowed his gear and hung his jacket in the front closet. He turned and Jane stood. "I'm glad you still have your great granddad's jacket. It'll be a classic forever. How are you doing, Noah?"

"Good, Jane, thanks," he breathed and opened his arms until he spotted Drew. I'm not sure what he saw there, but his arms danced as if he'd only been stretching, and he straightened up when he met Mitchell's glower. "Hey, boss." He bumped Jane's knuckles and scooted behind us.

Richard entered with more reserve. He caught sight of Mitchell and shook his hand first, then CJ's, Drew's, and Jane's. He bowed toward Pete and me and hustled to join Dianne and Noah.

Renegade and Maverick took up two seats in front. CJ strapped them into the seatbelts wearing special harnesses, and both dogs appeared at ease, much more than I. The engines hummed to life, and Pete grabbed my hand again. His disarming smile eased my nerves enough such that when the aroma of the dinner hit me right after liftoff, my mouth watered. I was ravenous.

Our magnificent dinner included crispy roasted brussels sprouts and a carrot puree. The meal concluded with delicious strawberry macarons. I cleaned my plate to a high shine. Granted, passengers had been expected, and the owner accompanied us, but service on this flight put commercial first-class to shame.

Bougie, indeed.

FIFTEEN

Attending to the completion of a sumptuous meal, I never noticed we'd landed nor that the seat belt light blinked off until both pilots entered the cabin to speak to Mitchell. Noah, Dianne, and Richard bid us farewell and zipped out the door. By the time I collected my belongings, hoisted my bag, and stepped down the stairs, they'd disappeared.

The dogs galumphed onto the tarmac and sat when CJ whistled. Then I panicked, wondering where Renegade and Maverick would go next, but I needn't have worried. Jane sorted the passengers into the two limousines. (It would be difficult not to let it go to my head if our only ground transportation on this trip consisted of Rolls Royces).

"CJ and the pups will be housed at my dad's. I hope that's okay, Katie." Jane looked worried.

"That would be great, but I wouldn't want to put him out."

"He's alone in that huge house and can't wait for company. There's a great yard on the property, even a pool, and the dogs will have free rein. Dad will fly CJ, Renegade, Maverick, and the boys home whenever they're ready, but Drew said they're going to attend at least day one of the competition. And we can visit the dogs, and Dad, day or night."

I rustled Maverick's ears and told him to listen to CJ, as if my words would make the difference. Maverick leaned into me and closed his big brown eyes as I stroked his forehead. "And thank you," I whispered into his floppy ears.

CJ summoned the dogs, and they hopped into one of the cars. Our moment was lost, but the memory would be treasured forever.

I joined Jane, Drew, Pete, and Mitchell in the second limousine. The streets whizzed by, and in no time, we coasted to a stop in front of an exceedingly tall, lavish hotel.

"This is stunning." The doorman in a black overcoat sporting gold braided epaulets and stripes at the cuffs and collar, black pants, and hat with a gold profile opened the door on the sidewalk side, and Jane, Pete, and Drew slid out. "Where're you going? This isn't our hotel."

"It is now." Mitchell grinned. "After such a harrowing experience, I couldn't have my daughter and her best friend staying at the Dapper Inn. You and Jane look a little worse for the wear, but a few days of exquisite service and you'll be right as rain. The Fulton County Superior Court House where the competition will be held is within walking distance, and I'll have a van or bus and driver available for the duration of your stay."

My eyes welled with tears, and I reached over to give him a hug. The hiccup from his throat assured me he felt the same gratitude. "Thank you," I whispered.

"No. Thank *you*." One more clench and he released me into the evening. The limo rolled from the curb and slid into traffic.

I lugged my bag through the revolving doors, where I dropped the handle and stopped to gaze at the imposing entry—the gilded walls, plush ivory carpet, very real greenery, and welcoming maroon leather furniture. A fountain burbled in the center of the atrium. I half expected a troupe of classical violinists to wander among the guests. I heard the snick of a handle and glanced down to find a hand on my bag. "Excuse me, but that's my luggage."

Pete threaded my arm through his. He cast his sparkling eyes and soothing smile just for me and guided me away from the chuckling bellhop to the registration desk. I continued to gawk, open-mouthed.

Jane leaned close and said, chuckling, "You're acting like a small-town kid."

I whispered back, "I am a small-town kid," but closed my mouth and dialed down my awe.

"Hello …" Jane peered at the manager's gold name tag on his jacket breast pocket. "… Augustus. We'd like to check in."

Augustus looked Jane and me up and down. I had to admit, we looked a little worse for the wear. He sniffed and his upper lip curled almost imperceptibly. "Excuse me." He flicked his wrist, and a lovely young woman hurried to the counter to take his place.

"Welcome. I'm Martha. How may I be of assistance?" Martha's fingers hovered over the computer keys, prepared to accommodate the new guests.

Jane handed over her credit card, and Martha typed furiously, recited the on-site amenities, recounted the room details, and ran the card efficiently. "The meeting room on the floor is equipped with multiple charging stations, a printer, and a fridge full of complimentary snacks and beverages. Here are the completed registrations for two additional reservations in the block of rooms under the name Mitchell Mackey."

"Mackey, you say?" Augustus reappeared with an ingratiating smile. "Martha," he said, dripping with condescension, "I'll take it from here."

"Martha and I have concluded our business, Augustus." Jane shook Martha's hand, and Augustus's face fell. "Thank you most sincerely, Martha."

Jane reveled in her delight, visiting her old stomping grounds and spending time with her dad, and Martha mirrored Jane's contagious grin. She handed Jane our keycards. After a quick tour of the lobby level services, Jane stomped to the elevators, clomping her protective boot, and we followed.

"Jane." Gawking at surroundings so unlike the photos of the Dapper Inn, I couldn't even put two words together.

"I know." Her throaty laugh came from deep within. "This time I'll let Dad take care of everything. It's not worth the fight, and we're going to enjoy the rest of the time we'll spend here. We're all on the same floor, men on one end, women on the other." Jane caught Drew's exaggerated eyeroll in the spotless, mirrored walls. She pivoted to shoot her laser sharp eyes first at Pete and then at her fiancé. "I expect you to set a good example for Brock, Galen, and Felipe, not the other way around. You are in the middle of the hall across from the Calders and …" Jane's voice fell, uncharacteristically at a loss for words. She breathed in through her nose and out through her mouth and closed her eyes before adding, "ZaZa."

"Your wish is my command." Drew bowed at the waist.

The elevator stopped and the doors flew open to reveal more sumptuousness.

Jane and I sauntered to our end of the floor. She opened the door and smiled as I strolled into the lavish corporate suite, past a buffed soft leather couch, coffee table, and television, into a large space boasting a stunning view of the city. A beautiful gift box lured Jane to the large table in an alcove surrounded by comfortable leather office chairs. Atop two fluffy bathrobes and matching slippers sat tea bags, hot chocolate packets, coffee pods, chocolates, and shower scents. I rushed into the next room, a grand bedroom, and like a four-year-old, threw myself on the bed nearest the window, claiming, "Mine."

We unpacked our carry-on bags, hanging clothes in a spacious closet and nestling folded clothes in the bureau. I retrieved one of the journals from my new roomy backpack and picked up a promotional fountain pen. The ink flowed over the page, leaving calligraphic loops and decorative strokes so unlike my usual penmanship, and our story unfolded.

As I wrote of our exploits so far, so much had happened, I couldn't believe we'd only been gone a day and a half. Some of the characters we'd encountered took on peculiarities I might not have been aware of before the ordeal. I should have detected Wendell's unusual eagerness to join us. He may have suspected someone was after him all along, even before we discovered the hijacker. Noah and Wendell shared a mutual disrespect of each other. Even the spot of anger I may have seen in Dianne's eyes when we first met felt more ominous. Who was Natalianna Kuznetsov, and what part did she play? The more I wrote, the keener I felt the need to see the kids and make certain they were well. The words in the journal began to sound so bizarre, like speculative fiction, so I put the pen down and turned to Jane.

She lay sprawled out, almost swallowed by the fluffy white comforter, snoring softly, and I hadn't the heart to wake her.

The cryptology book of encoding and solving puzzles called to me. The elementary text gave examples dating back a few thousand years and refreshed the processes with modern-day exercises. The proper tools—the keys to the ciphers—made finding clear-cut solutions to the enigmas my private game, a game won by deciphering a secret message. I covered historical conundrums through the beginning of WWI and messages intercepted about poisonous gases and major attacks—awful stuff.

After unraveling a particularly involved challenge, I leaned into the headrest on the recliner, and my eyelids drifted closed, but too soon they were wrenched open by a knock, and I sprinted to the door.

With my hand hovering near the metal stopper, I whispered, "Who is it?"

"Ms. Wilk. It's us. Open the door." I heard what sounded like a choir of angels sing. "We brought chocolate."

I snuck a peek over my shoulder as I quietly turned the knob, hoping we hadn't awakened Jane, but she stood next to the armoire, returning a brush to the vanity drawer and nodding.

I flipped the stopper, turned the deadbolt, and whisked the door open. Nine apprehensive faces waited for our reaction. I grinned, and my words were drowned out by the collective sigh, followed by the incessant chattering I'd grown to love.

Galen held a decadent chocolate cake covered in hard plastic. Carlee fanned a handful of napkins, and Kindra held plates and forks in her tightly clenched fists.

Marietta Calder clapped her hands and said chatter

ceased. "Let's take it down to the conference room."

The students gave Jane and me a once over, then followed Marietta like a brood of ducklings. Jane slid her tiny, unfettered foot into a plush hotel slipper and flashed her keycard. She gripped my elbow, and we hobbled after them, drinking in every excited word.

"The concert was breathtaking," said Kindra, licking frosting from her upper lip. "The visual backdrop was from the movie. I've never seen anything like it."

"And the food." Galen rubbed his flat wrestler stomach and groaned. "I couldn't eat it all." And I'm absolutely certain he would have tried. After swallowing a mouthful of cake, he used his fork to tap the dessert. "This cake is from the restaurant. Geez, I hope you get to go before we have to return home. If there's time and everything."

The kids emphasized how worried they'd been by our separation and subsequent forced landing in North Carolina. They wished they'd been there to help us, but I'd never have forgiven myself if anything had happened to them.

As Jane entertained them with tales from the wild, Marietta pulled me off to the side. I cracked the cap on a bottle of water and sipped, remembering the words of warning to drink plenty of fluids.

"The kids have been worried sick but were so well behaved. However, we skipped our ticketed events. We didn't visit the Coke Museum today even though ZaZa complained about letting the tickets go to waste. I have to apologize." She looked so contrite I couldn't imagine what she had to regret, and I took another small sip from the bottle. "I told ZaZa to go suck a lemon."

SIXTEEN

It's a good thing I'd only taken a tiny mouthful, or I would've spewed water all over the room.

"I called The World of Coca-Cola and explained our predicament. The local news covered a bit of your ordeal, and they were most accommodating. I planned to reschedule the tickets for another day this week." She smiled. "It's funny how a little communication can go such a long way. They refunded the money and said we could come back anytime— for free. So, I thought, if we have time, we could go Tuesday morning or maybe after the Braves game tomorrow—"

"The Braves game?"

"Didn't Mitchell tell you? He secured a private party suite for the baseball game tomorrow afternoon. My husband was excited for Lorelei to make this excursion. It's so her. But the positive experiences we've had so far on this trip have exceeded Eddie's expectations. Plus, he's a die-hard baseball fanatic, so the game package is a perfect way for him to fully engage his little boy side."

"Marietta, I don't know what we'd have done without you. I can't thank you enough. Jane and I are fine. We could do what we needed because we knew the kids were in good hands."

"Dorene was awesome, but I think ZaZa's a little afraid of her. When ZaZa found out you returned, she relinquished her role to Dorene and made plans to meet some friends."

"Everyone's a little afraid of her, and if they're not, they should be. Dorene is one scary attorney."

"I heard that," a warm alto voice chuckled from behind us.

The kids mobbed Dorene and her handsome guest in the doorway. After reciting our team chant, she sauntered across the room and towered in front of me. She planted her hands on my shoulders. "What do you have to say for yourself, Ms. Wilk?"

"Ah. Hi?"

"C'mere, you." She wrapped me in a hug and rocked me to and fro while whispering, "How do you get in so much trouble?" Holding me at arm's length, she said, "Katie Wilk, meet my criminal co-counsel."

"She means, I assist in trying her criminal cases." The beautiful bass voice resonated in my bones. "Leo George, at your service." He bowed his head.

"Have you known Dorene long?"

They exchanged sly glances. "You could say that."

I cocked my head, hoping to catch a word or two of explanation. His face radiated pride. "She's my big sister."

"Stepsister, but who's paying attention."

"Pleased to meet you, Ms. Wilk. I've heard so much about you. All good and from every corner: Dorene, Marietta, and these great kids. I can't wait to see them in action."

"You'll be amazed, I assure you. They have the nation's absolute best coach." Dorene looked up and puffed out her chest.

"Ms. Wilk, do you have the printout of the schedule for the week? Mom wants to make a copy," said Lorelei.

"It's in my backpack." The thought of it strapped to my back in swirling water caused my shoulders to tremble.

"You don't have to move … yet. If you give me your key, Carlee and I will get it."

I gladly handed over my keycard. "It's a new backpack in the closet on the floor. The schedule is in a plastic folder in the big pocket inside the zippered midsection. I have copies."

They returned in time for me to yawn long and loud.

"Hey, Ms. Wilk, you're beginning to look like something even the cat wouldn't drag in. I think you'd better get some shuteye." Brock nodded as if he'd figured out the next big event of the evening, and I agreed with him.

* * *

Bright shafts of daylight framed the window treatment, and I opened my eyes to dust motes dancing in the narrow beams shooting into the room. I quietly stretched and painfully remembered the last forty-eight hours. When I snuck a peak at the empty bed next to me, I let out a groan and sat bolt upright. The clock read dark-thirty.

"Jane?"

The bathroom door opened, and Jane emerged with her hair cascading in gentle curls about a perfectly made-up face. Her intense brown eyes glinted as she stomped to the window and whipped open the curtains. "Morning, sleeping beauty. Breakfast in forty. Chop, chop."

Then she ripped off my comforter. No longer swaddled in its downy softness, I had nothing better to do than get up. Thirty minutes later, with damp hair and a fresh clean face, I pulled the door closed, and we headed to the busy dining room.

It seemed many of the hotel patrons began their day early, and it took a moment to locate our students, sitting at a table near the window, laughing at Galen completing yet another run at the prime rib station. After attacking the savory breakfast options, Jane and I took the last two seats at the adult table next to the kids as ZaZa downed what remained of a pink drink in her cocktail glass. She stood, and announced with such passion, "*Mon Dieu!* They are all yours. I assume you can handle them."

"Thanks, ZaZa," I said as she walked away. I sincerely meant it.

I downed grilled shrimp and cheesy grits but couldn't pass up the colorful produce buffet and dug into the heaps of fresh fruit and green leaf accompaniments as well. After attacking the dessert bar and nabbing a decadent caramel covered chocolate truffle, I leaned back, patted a full stomach, and sipped ambrosial espresso from a dainty white porcelain cup.

"We'll keep the kids occupied and well supervised. I don't think they'll find time to be nervous. We've already had plenty of that," Marietta said quietly, with a mischievous grin. "Mitchell has graciously provided access to some grand activities."

Drew asked, "Can you text me a copy of the itinerary?

I'd like to do some reconnaissance beforehand. But Pete and I will join you for the ballgame." His phone pinged. He read the text, looked up, and said, "Thanks, Marietta."

She stood and tapped her glass. Her lyrical voice nearly put me back to sleep as she detailed the proposed agenda for the day. "Our first order of business is to visit Margaret Mitchell's house. Mr. Mackey has assigned a bus to pick us up out front in …" She glanced at her wrist. "Fifteen minutes. Meet in the lobby. Mr. Mackey is on the board of the Mitchell House and has arranged a brief private tour for us. Sometimes it pays to know the right people. And remember, when we pick up Dr. Erickson and Mr. Kidd, we won't have much time to return to our rooms until after the baseball game, so slather on the sunscreen, wear layers, and bring your water bottles." She voiced total mom concerns I hadn't thought to share.

When we unloaded at the address, Marietta took the lead. "The museum includes the architectural history of a house built in 1899 as well as biographical information of the famous author who published *Gone with the Wind* in 1936. The newly renovated structure displays the original suitcase, which carried the beloved manuscript in a number of manilla envelopes from Atlanta to New York, as well as period furniture and the original Remington typewriter Margaret Mitchell used to compose the Pulitzer Prize-winning story."

The kids spoke in hushed tones and read the placards detailing the sale of thirty million copies of the decades-old masterpiece having been translated into twenty-seven languages, as well as reverently perusing articles and editorials exposing the controversy surrounding the familiar work.

When we completed our tour, we sauntered into the bright sunshine and onto the bus waiting to transport us back to the hotel to pick up Pete and Drew. Trying to read the faces of the kids, I wondered if they, too, respectfully contemplated the stunning life and, sadly, the tragic end of a true wordsmith. Margaret Mitchell died as the consequence of being struck by a drunk driver on a street outside her home.

The bus pulled in front of the hotel and the door clacked open. We waited. I texted Pete, but didn't get a response. Jane texted and winced.

"What's wrong?"

"I forgot to take my pain pill this morning, and Drew doesn't have a key to get into our room." She painfully climbed to standing.

I jumped up and flashed my keycard. "I'll get it. Just don't leave without me."

I hopped off the bus and dashed past the doorman, in through the revolving door, waved at Martha, and skidded to a stop in front of the elevator doors. The up button was lit, but I pressed it again—twice. My shoulders jerked up and down while I watched the numbers flick on and off, hoping to speed the descent. A ding preceded a mass exit, and ZaZa emerged from the packed car, pointedly ignoring me.

I shrugged, hopped on, and pressed our floor button. Heels clattered across the floor, and I heard, "Hold the elevator."

SEVENTEEN

Felicity stepped in and turned her back to me. Her finger hovered in front of the floor button I'd already pressed. She shrugged and withdrew her hand. We rode up to the sound of her tapping keys on her phone. When the elevator stopped, she looked up, saw me in the mirrored reflection, and froze. Her face pinched in recognition.

She didn't make a move, so I said sweetly, "Excuse me, please," and glided past her.

With everyone waiting on the bus, I hurried down the hall. A cleaning cart blocked the path to our room, so I knocked.

"I told you I could not let you in without a key," a heavily British-accented voice called out. "It is company policy."

"I have a key. This is my room. I have to get something."

A tall, beautiful, dark-skinned woman came into view.

She smiled broadly. "Prove it," she said and slammed the door in my face.

I hadn't used my keycard yet, so I thanked my lucky stars when the tiny light turned green. As I opened the door, she picked an imaginary piece of lint off her gray and black uniform and greeted me teasingly. "Next time, tell your husband he needs to carry his own key. We do not let anyone without a key in while we are cleaning. Security is one of the key tenets of our hotel's success."

Drew? My husband? "I'll tell him." *Just not the husband part.*

My immediate task was thwarted for a heartbeat when I spotted the origami towel art placed on our beds. "That swan is so cute, and I've never seen a bear before. Thank you. You don't have to do that every day, but I'm sure my students will love it."

"I aim to please." She flipped long black braids over her shoulder, and I read her name tag, Samara.

I could have listened to her deep honeyed voice all day, but I opened Jane's kit and grabbed the little plastic medicine bottle. "Thanks for taking such good care of us." Rushing through the living area, I noticed the spray of daisies on the conference table and hesitated. To reconcile my sense of order, I slid the vase to the center of the table. "And the flowers are gorgeous. What a nice touch, but I've got a Braves game to go to," I said, waving and squeezing between the cart and the door frame.

"Make sure to tell that man of yours," she called after me, shaking her hand. "Keycard."

My trip down took half the time. Augustus materialized behind a smiling Martha, scowling. I waved at both of them and rushed out the door. The doorman hastily cleared my path to our chariot. I clambered up the stairs and handed the rattling bottle to Jane.

My seat was occupied, so I dropped next to the handsome hunk with the dark eyes wearing a Minnesota Twins' jersey. He stretched and nonchalantly reached his arm around my shoulder. My heart tumbled.

The driver checked the mirror, smiled teasingly, and adjusted his cap. He threw the idling bus into gear, and we were off on another adventure.

"Drew, the lovely housekeeper wanted me to remind you to bring your keycard with you." I giggled. "But yours wouldn't have opened our room anyway."

A curtain of confusion closed over Drew's face.

Before I could elaborate, Carlee tapped on my shoulder. "Ms. Wilk, did they ever find that guy? It turned out he was way creepier than I thought when we first met him."

"I don't know. Drew?" If anyone had news, it would start with him, but he shook his head.

"Sorry, Carlee. He hasn't turned up, that I know of."

"You don't think he's around here, do you?"

"I would think Atlanta would be the last place he'd go. He must know, by now, he's being sought in connection with the kidnapping of Ms. Wilk."

Not to mention, I thought, the theft of whatever super-secret plans he'd stolen.

She nodded and weaved her way through the seats to the back of the bus. The serious timbre among the students had brightened, and I welcomed the laughter, imagining our next escapade. I glanced at my kids and noticed them all similarly dressed. My forehead scrunched, and I turned my eyes to Pete. "Who are the Braves playing today?"

Pete reached into a bag at his feet and retrieved a navy-blue jersey covered with scripted letters. He tore off the tag and winked.

"For little ole me?" I tried to mimic Jane's smooth

southern drawl but failed miserably. "They're playing the Twins? How did we luck out? Mr. Mackey … I mean, Mitchell couldn't have arranged a schedule change." I pulled on the jersey, and as my head popped out, my eyes widened. "Could he?"

"The game was on the schedule, but because it's an afternoon game against the Twins, Mitchell was able to get the party suite. I think the kids are going to have a great time. Brock is nearly beside himself."

Brock had overcome a painful shoulder injury to finish his high school pitching career on a win, and he would play for the local community college next year. The Twins game would be an extra graduation treat for him.

By the time we reached Truist Park, we'd sung "We're Gonna Win, Twins," and "Take Me Out to the Ball Game" too many times to count.

Eddie had researched the stadium. He marched ahead, swiped the tickets through the scanner, barreled through the turnstile, and shepherded us to Party Suite V reserved by Mitchell Mackey.

"Can you smell that?" Galen said as we approached the door, inhaling with the appreciation of a connoisseur.

Eddie entered our code and bustled inside. He hurried past the sideboard covered with heated servers mounded with chicken wings, hamburger sliders, and mini tacos, and through the obstacle course set by the couches and chairs. He slid the glass doors aside and strode onto the balcony to park himself on a stool at a bar height table nearest the turf. Brock joined him.

Marietta grinned, leisurely filled two plates, and placed them within reach of Eddie and Brock. Absentmindedly pecking at the food that magically appeared before them, their eyes remained glued to the action unfolding on the field.

I hadn't fully recovered from breakfast yet, but the sweets table caught my attention, so I grabbed a bottle of water and a piece of chocolate cheesecake before settling into a seat next to Pete with a good view of the kids and the ballgame. I savored the first delicious bite of protein and calcium, thinly disguised as dessert.

The inspired Twins scored in every inning and twice in the top of the seventh, increasing their lead to four. During the seventh inning stretch, Eddie, Drew, and Jane escorted half the kids to the restrooms, while Marietta, Pete, and I kept tabs on the other four. The caterer delivered more tasty tidbits, and the kids with the bottomless stomachs circled like vultures, knowing when Galen returned, the repast would disappear.

We had a great right-field view of the stadium. My eyes wandered over the host of plebians—smirking at the peasants from our catered private post. Pete was a Duke fan, at least when their opponent wasn't a Minnesota, Iowa, Wisconsin, or Michigan team, so I kept my eyes on the stout man in the white sweatshirt with the royal blue D emblazoned across the front. He climbed in front of everyone in the last row, making them all stand to accommodate his girth.

"Look at that guy crawling over the whole row. Why wouldn't he go around? It's so impolite. He's making everyone stand up."

"Which guy?" Marietta said, panning the crowd.

"The blond wearing a man-bun and messy beard." I pointed. "There. He's still creeping over the whole row. He isn't even pretending he's in the right place."

As if he heard me, the man raised his face to view our suite, and I choked back my alarm. I grabbed Pete's arm and pointed. "There."

EIGHTEEN

K atie, you look like you've seen a ghost."

"Pete, tell me you saw him?" I searched the stands, but the blond had melted into the crowd. I grabbed my phone. Jane was near the top on my list of favorites, and I called her.

Pete scanned the faces of the fans. "Who?"

"Please call Drew." I paced, waiting for Jane to pick up. "I'm sure I saw Gromm."

Jane and Drew returned to the suite, dragging their petulant charges behind them. "We're back." Though the lilt in her words was positive, I could read the enquiry in Jane's face.

"Where's Gromm?" Drew asked in a stage whisper, scanning the scene from the balcony.

I rubbed my arms, trying to get rid of my goosebumps.

"He took off as soon as our eyes met. But his sneer freaked me out."

"Pete, did you see him?" Drew asked. I think he wanted to believe me.

"I'm sorry, no, and to be honest, even if he'd stood right in front of me, I don't know that I'd recognize him."

"Carlee's the only team member who saw him, and if she'd been here, I'm sure she'd have recognized him, but I wouldn't," said Marietta.

Eddie laid his large hands on his wife's shoulders. "What could he possibly want? What's he doing here? Is he following you?"

"Do you think he recognized you, Katie?"

"Oh, yes. But he tried to disguise himself wearing a beard and long blond hair." Then I second guessed myself. "I think."

"How would he get to Atlanta? Why would he be here? While you wandered the forest, did he tell you anything? Can you think of anything he let slip?" I shook my head, and Drew started itemizing our next steps. "We're not taking any chances. No one goes anywhere alone. I'll take care of the announcement on the bus, meanwhile I'm reporting this sighting to the proper authorities, and we'll get some extra protection." He lifted his phone to his ear and walked to the far side of the room.

Marietta reached out and squeezed my shoulder. "We're not going to let one evil little man take the fun out of our trip. Everything will work out."

Jane meandered close and whispered, "He had to have help. I'm just not certain who would help him." She blew a tendril from her face. "Unless that's why Felicity was in Franklin."

I cornered Drew. "Well? What's the plan."

"My contact can't believe Gromm would return to Atlanta, but he's sending a protective detail. They should arrive tomorrow sometime. Gromm would have to be pretty crazy to try something with all of us here. Don't worry."

But worry was my middle name.

The kids devoured the chicken, burgers, and barbacoa. The baseball game ended, and I couldn't have repeated the score under any circumstances, but I could tell by reading their cheerful faces, the Twins won.

Jane fretted for a moment when our driver didn't pick up his phone, so she sent a text. She read aloud the reply from an alternate number.

Be right there—one block away. Your driver ate something that disagreed with him, and he passed along your info. I'm Lester.

The bus pulled up next to us. The new driver handed an envelope to Jane. "It's from Dad." As she ripped it open, she said, "Don't forget, mock trial registration begins at five, so we won't have enough time to visit the Coca-Cola Museum tonight." She scanned the contents of the enclosed note. "Lester, you need to drop off Katie on our way back to the hotel."

He scowled intensely and balked at Jane's request to take a detour saying it wasn't on the itinerary, but she wielded her super-Georgian look, and with a shrug, he altered the address on the GPS, made the proper turns, and pulled in front of the Fulton County Courthouse.

Pete wove his fingers through mine and winked. My heart pitter-pattered when he hopped off the bus with me.

"If you two don't want to walk back, just give me a jingle, and I'll send a car," Jane yelled out the open door. Flicking the envelope, she added, "When you return, I'll share another awesome surprise Dad has arranged for tonight. We'll keep the kids too busy to worry about tomorrow."

Fifteen minutes early, we ended up second in line to register. I'd completed most of the paperwork online. So, after affixing my signature to the bottom line, I collected seven heavy welcome bags for the students and four more for the coaches, gladly sharing the responsibility of carting the goodies with my attractive accomplice.

We walked the half mile, and our conversation circled around Wendell. "If it really was Gromm, what do you think he wanted?"

"I can't imagine." I worried, though. I'd survived our first encounter, and I didn't relish another.

The ever-present doorman bowed, and a bellboy rushed to my rescue, lightening my load, ushering us past the busy registration desk, and following us to the elevator.

It opened three floors shy of our destination to Samara's dulcet words. "I will take the next car." Her dancing eyes looked from Pete to me, and her hands flew to her cheeks. "This is not your husband."

Her laughter burbled like a brook, but before the sound was cut off by the closing door, Pete's hand shot out to reverse its course. He tilted his head and watched my reaction as he repeated, "Husband?"

I shuffled to the back, and Samara joined us, filling the car with a warm hoot. I leaned forward and caught the twinkle in Pete's eye. "Tell me about her *husband?*" he said with a smile designed to melt solid iron.

"She means Drew. She wouldn't let him in to our room to get Jane's meds."

"No, I would not." Samara crossed her arms in front of

her. "I told him it was company policy. You must have a key, whether or not you bring flowers." Her head nodded, and there was a finality in her voice I trusted. She waggled her eyebrows at Pete. "You are much more handsome."

The light dimmed in Pete's eyes. "Can you describe him?"

"Blond. Loud. Robust."

I wouldn't use those particular words to describe Drew.

"Did he say what he wanted?"

"It did not matter what he wanted. I told him to go get a key."

I said softly. "Did he have glasses and a buzz cut?"

"Glasses. Yes. Buzz cut?"

"Military cut."

"Short hair. No. He tied it back." She reached up and pinched Pete's cheek. "And I like my man clean-shaven."

Blood pounded in my ears. The man who'd attempted to get into our room hadn't been Drew, but it could've been Wendell.

The doors opened, and Samara exited. "Have a good night."

Before the doors fully closed, Pete had punched a number into his phone. "Bring everyone down to meet in the conference room. We need to talk."

The bellboy welcomed the kids into the large room and delivered their hospitality bags. Before he excused himself, Pete tipped him well. He bowed and said, "Anytime, sir."

My students had known Dr. Pete Erickson, or of him, for a very long time. He grew up in Columbia, was homecoming king, a star athlete and brilliant academic, and had returned to help staff the emergency room. His father had been the chief of police for almost their entire lives. They knew when Dr. Erickson spoke, they needed to listen.

Pete took a deep breath. "We have some rules that absolutely must be adhered to. It's possible the man who kidnapped Ms. Wilk might have followed her to Atlanta. I'm going to repeat what Mr. Kidd said on the bus."

A few of the youthful voices murmured, "We'll take care of you, Ms. Wilk."

"That's a wonderful sentiment, but it's not your place to take care of Ms. Wilk. You are here to do your best at the Mock Trial America competition. There are nine adults you can trust."

Someone murmured, "Eight."

"You might not like all nine of us, but we're here for you, and we'll watch out for Ms. Wilk, but you can't go anywhere alone. It's imperative you always tell one of the coaches where you'll be if you need to leave the group, and again, never by yourself."

"Everywhere, really?" Galen flexed his biceps. He'd take on the world for any one of his teammates, and with his strength he'd make a dent.

"Everywhere, Galen," I said. "It's your job to watch out, stay alert, and have fun. Mr. Kidd is our go to. You've programmed his number into your list of contacts. Hopefully, we've been mistaken, and you won't need to use it, but if you see anyone you don't know on our floor, call Mr. Kidd. If you have a funny feeling, call Mr. Kidd. If you get separated from the group—"

They announced together, "Call Mr. Kidd."

Drew smiled. "I just got off the phone with Coach Dvorak. She and Mr. George will be moving into the two empty rooms at the end of our floor. You should recognize every face, and assure your parents, we are taking every precaution to make this event successful and safe."

Eddie raised his hand.

"Yes, Mr. Calder."

"Thank you, Mr. Kidd." He gave the *dad* look. "We'll do exactly as we've been told. Right kids?"

"Right, Mr. Calder."

I saw a look pass between Galen and Brock. *Yeah, right.* Famous last words.

Jane raised her hand too, and Pete called on her as if in a classroom. "Yes, Ms. Mackey."

"I'd like us to take a moment and reflect on those who have died defending our nation and our values, be aware of the sacrifices made, and honor those individuals on this Memorial Day." She bowed her head, and before I closed my eyes, I caught several others following her lead. When a minute passed, she said, "Now…" She drew our attention to the big round analog clock on the wall. "It's time to call it a night."

The students frowned and groaned indistinguishable unhappy kid words concerning the early hour. I read the clock hands at six and twelve twice myself. What could she be thinking?

Her eyes took on an impish gleam. "Then how about a game instead?"

The surprise silenced the grumbling.

Jane clapped her hands. "Tonight …" She sought confirmation from Drew who nodded. "Tonight, my dad reserved an escape room." No one moved, and when no one said anything, she frowned and added, slowly, "Unless you don't want to go."

The room erupted with applause and cheers. Brock and Felipe jumped and chest bumped. Lorelei and Kindra high-fived, and Kindra used her ever-improving ASL to relay the responses she might have missed to her sister, Patricia, who was trying to read their ever-moving, excited lips.

"By unanimous decision, we're going to solve some puzzles and immerse ourselves in a mystery. Get ready. Our transportation will be here in twenty minutes." The kids caught Jane's infectious excitement and raced from the conference room, only to rendezvous in the lobby with ten minutes to spare, ready and raring to go.

Our replacement driver, Lester, dropped us on the street in front of a shop with a marquis touting the word "Open" in flashing neon teal.

As she hopped down the stairs, Jane said, "Thanks for the ride. We'll be finished in ninety minutes. We'll see you then."

Jane opened the door and marched to the desk with a smile so wide and proud it made *my* cheeks ache. She presented our passes, and the ticket taker said, "With the purchase of ten admissions, you get one free. Which one of you is Mitchell Mackey?"

Jane said bashfully. "He's my dad, but he's not here."

"I can only give the free admission to the purchaser," he said and sounded as if he expected an argument.

"No worries." Jane turned her bright eyes to the kids. "Are you ready?"

The ticket taker snapped his gum and took the wind out of Jane's sails with his next statement. "Only eight at a time per any single escape room experience."

Befuddled, Jane stammered. "But there are thirteen of us."

NINETEEN

C an't do more than eight in one room at a time. Fire code. No exceptions," he said unsympathetically. He brushed the back of his hand across the sparse hairs on his chin.

Jane's shoulders slumped. I thought she was about to cry until Drew said, "I'll join the kids. They won't be unsupervised. You *adults* ..." He said the word as though it signified a repugnant stage of life. "You can try one of the other games, and we'll see which team comes out victorious—"

Jane broke in, "—in the shortest amount of time." Her cheeks glowed as her excitement grew at the prospect of competition. "There are multiple games with similar difficulty ratings so complexity shouldn't be an issue."

"As long as both teams compete at the same level of difficulty," Brock said, "you're on."

The bored worker held a lock box labeled 'phone.' After grudgingly surrendering our devices, the young man stepped behind the counter and completed the instructions in a monotone. "Using teamwork, clear communication, and strategic thinking, each team must find clues and complete tasks to escape within sixty minutes. If something doesn't move easily, don't move it. If I can't reach it ..." He raised his arm perfunctorily and let it drop. "... it isn't part of the puzzle solution. The rooms are monitored, and three hints are available. All participants must agree to use a hint. Just say, 'Hint, please.' There is a penalty. Using a hint subtracts ten seconds from the team's remaining time. Any questions?"

Before I could fully process his instructions and formulate a query, he continued on a long exhale, "And no, you're not really locked in, but an alarm will sound should you leave before accomplishing the escape or failing to do so. Prior to entering, participants need to read and sign a waiver."

We completed the digital agreements, and Jane held out her phone to scan. He checked us in one-by-one and confiscated her phone as his last official act.

The attendant sighed. "Take your pick."

Galen perused the descriptions in front of each game's door and stopped to read one aloud. "How about Moon Madness with a difficulty rating of eight out of ten? 'For a phenomenal dual-room experience, immerse yourself in an alternate time and place. Test your reasoning skills and powers of observation to determine if your team can escape. The year is 2200, and all humanity is depending on you.'"

The kids crowded around the poster, approving and confirming their choice.

Eddie read the summary of the second room with a rating of eight. "Bewildering Broadcast. 'For a phenomenal dual-room experience, immerse yourself in an alternate time and place.'" His eyes raced ahead. "'Test your reasoning skills and powers of observation to determine if your team can escape. The year is 1932, and all New York City is depending on you.' Not very original, but it works."

Brock rubbed his hands together. "This is gonna be great. We'll be patiently waiting in the lobby for you to finish your puzzle."

The worker said, dripping with ennui, "Ready?" A buzzer sounded and the doors opened. "Timer begins when you cross the threshold."

The kids disappeared, lugging Drew with them. Eddie dragged a giggling Marietta through our door first. Jane and I followed, and Pete brought up the rear. The door snapped closed, throwing us into the shadows. An old-time radio voice recited the creepy words from a crackly nineteen thirties broadcast, "The weed of crime bears bitter fruit. Crime does not pay. The Shadow knows," and a light slowly blossomed over a work of art signed by Edward Hopper. As the light brightened, aspects of the painting became evident in the room—a three-dimensional partial reproduction which included the piano, coffee table, art on the walls, newspaper, and multi-paned glass door—bringing the painting to life.

Marietta stood in front of the print and regarded the room. "They're almost identical."

"Have any of you done an escape experience before?" asked Eddie.

"I have." I straightened the painting, an annoying habit of mine, and a playing card floated to the floor. Eddie retrieved an Ace of Spades. I examined each of the walls in turn. "This is a multi-room puzzle, so there is an exit to an additional area somewhere in here. We have to unlock a door by solving puzzles, so read everything, try whatever comes to mind, and scrutinize the smallest details. Share your findings. If something looks like a clue, it probably is."

I peeked behind a large black-and-white movie poster of the striking woman from the Golden Age of Hollywood, Hedy Lamarr. As I circled the room, lifting items from hooks on the wall and restaging the décor, I said, "Did you know that Hedy Lamarr was not only an actress, but also an inventor? She theorized varying radio frequencies at irregular intervals to prevent interception or jamming of transmissions—a cryptanalyst's boon or bane, depending on whose side you're on. She shared her concept for using frequency hopping with the U.S. Navy and co-authored a patent in 1941, which helped make possible today's wireless communications technologies, including Wi-Fi, GPS, and Bluetooth."

The red coffee cup Jane turned over in her hands stopped rotating. She rolled her eyes. "Why do you know these things?"

I marched to the far side of the room and tipped random books forward on a shelf until a panel slid away, revealing a padlocked door. The unforgiving knob rattled in my hand.

"How did you know that was there?" asked Eddie, standing in front of an oval mirror.

"I didn't. That's the key. Take a stab at a solution. It might seem crazy, but just try out your wild ideas."

Everyone moved at once.

Pete sat at a keyboard and tickled the ivories, playing the jazzy riff from the sheet music on the stand. When he struck one particular key, a card popped from the lid—the Queen of Diamonds. "How is *I've Got Rhythm* a clue?" He scanned the room, and a flicker of amusement flew across his face. He removed a tome from the top shelf of the bookcase and paged through the book entitled *Annals of the 1930s*.

Marietta observed the jigsaw pieces trapped between two panes of glass on the coffee table. She tentatively lifted a magnet from the wall and slid it across the top, dragging the metal puzzle elements around, fitting them together. "There's a message here. It reads, 'Asta only.'" With a nervous smile, she shimmied beneath the table. "And the pieces fit together to make the King of Hearts on the back."

Jane flitted from one corner of the room to another, moving cushions on an Art Deco couch, fanning pages of a vintage telephone directory, shuffling thirteen oversized playing cards, and ended up at a makeshift bar, scanning the cocktail recipe for an Aviation. She gave me a curious look, and I joined her. The inscriptions etched into the sides of wooden dowels standing in a bottle matched the ingredients for the cocktail recipe. We tossed the required sticks into an aluminum cocktail shaker, but nothing happened.

Eddie opened the cupboard above the faux bar and about a hundred ping pong balls tap-danced onto the floor, around the chairs, and under the furniture.

"Make sure there isn't a clue on any of the balls," Jane laughed. She stood on her tiptoes and stretched. "There's something in this cupboard. A little help here."

Eddie reached over her head and removed a scale. He calibrated the digital gauge. "What do we have to weigh?" He plucked the cocktail shaker from my fingers and set it on the scale. Still nothing happened.

He opened another cupboard and identified sets of glasses. "Martini, margarita, highball, champagne flute, snifter, wine, and coupe." Eddie removed a glass and held it up. "Anyone know what you call this one?"

"It's called a Nick and Nora cocktail glass," Pete said. "And their pet's name is Asta. May I?"

He tugged the glass from Eddie's fingers, used it to replace the shaker on the scale, then precisely poured the shaker contents into it. We watched as an alphabetic key appeared on the wall beneath the cupboard. My head tilted, and I examined it more closely. Each letter paired with a circular symbol.

I'd seen the images before, but I couldn't place them and searched for a similar encryption around the room. "Anyone find these markings?"

Jane handed me a comic book. A host of similar circular symbols covered the back page.

Ignoring the bustling behind me, I focused on the round figures, memorizing the quasi-predictable progression in the symbols and matching them to the appropriate letters. When I finally tore my eyes away from the code and its attribution to Walter Gibson, best known for his stories written about the pulp fiction character, the Shadow, I mapped each symbol to a letter. Before I could share my possible solution, Jane squealed in delight. She and Eddie had gotten into the swing of the puzzle solving.

"Jane, hand me those playing cards," said Eddie. He fit arbitrary cards into a depression within each of four white rectangles of the exact same size he'd discovered under a runner on an end table. Then he switched the order and switched again, trying to get something to happen.

Usually, my personal filter kept math solutions in my mind, but still overly tired from our latest ordeal, the number just issued from my lips. "There are seventeen thousand one hundred sixty different ways to order those cards." I stammered in an effort take back the words.

Eddie ignored my embarrassment. "How do we know which one is correct?" He fanned out the cards in his hand

and looked downright frustrated.

Marietta bent to collect the last of the little white round wonders. "There are phrases glued to the sides of a few of these balls. This one says, 'One is the loneliest number.'" She selected others. "'Three's a crowd.' 'Two is company.'" She continued to pick up the balls, tossing them into a basket on the floor. "Here's a new one. 'Four, five, and six is what?'"

"Fifteen." The sum slipped out again without preamble. My fingers flew to cover my lips, hoping to staunch any more numbers from pouring out.

Pete chuckled. "Let's store that one for future reference." He opened the annals and found references to the items we'd already uncovered. "How about placing the cards in the rectangles ordered by date: Gershwin's *I've Got Rhythm*, 1930, Queen of Diamonds; Hopper's *A Room in New York*, 1932, Ace of Spades; and *The Thin Man*, referencing the Nick and Nora glass, 1934, King of Hearts. Look for other playing cards."

Jane inspected the cocktail recipe and flushed with excitement when she turned it over. "Jack of Clubs." Her shoulders rose, and she silently shook her fists in triumph.

Pete ran his finger down the index of the annals, flipped the book open to a page, and read, "Although first concocted in 1916, Craddock's *The Savoy Cocktail Book* from 1930 featured the specialty cocktail, Aviation, in its new form. Try the Jack of Clubs before Gershwin's hit song."

Eddie meticulously laid the cards inside the white outlines again, and as the fourth card snapped into place, the landline trilled. Eddie held the receiver to his ear. His face went blank. "We have thirty-five minutes to save New York City. And the last number is seven?

"I might have deciphered the encryption on the wall. I

believe the message spells out thirty-nine and forty-eight. We have four numbers to use for a combination, and because we know the last digit is seven, there are only six permutations."

Jane clapped her hands. "Let's do this."

Pete crossed the room and hefted the lock. He spun the dial and stopped. "Fifteen." He carefully turned the dial again. "And?"

"Try thirty-nine, forty-eight, and seven."

The shackle released on the first try. Pete pulled up, smiled, and removed the lock. The knob turned and the door opened. He took a step back. A soft light went on inside phase two.

"After you," he said to Jane.

We entered a smaller room and, building on our prior successes, explored with more daring, spinning dials, opening doors, moving items, reading messages, using all our senses, throwing ideas at each other, and laughing.

We scoured the room one final time, and Marietta glanced at the countdown on the wall. "Three minutes."

Pete read the directions for possibly our final puzzle. His eyes lit up. He confidently strode to the door and performed his intrepid magic using the clues we'd amassed. The mechanism made a loud clank. This time he turned to me. He smiled, and my knees gave way, eyeing his deliciously tantalizing dimple. "Ladies first."

I grasped the doorknob and inhaled.

"Two minutes," said Marietta, her hand revolving in a gesture encouraging me to speed up the process.

I smiled and tugged on the door. It wouldn't open. "Maybe we're wrong." My forehead wrinkled. "But we all heard the sound of a lock releasing, right?" With more determination, I pulled again. The door creaked, swinging slowly. A figure in a long trench coat and brown Trilby hat filled the entry.

"Not another puzzle," Marietta groaned.

The form reached its arms toward me. I gulped, and as it tumbled forward, I collapsed under its weight, trapped, breathing faint onion-like fumes.

Pete rescued me, rolling the bulky shape to the side. I skittered back and a voice boomed from overhead, "Fifty-eight minutes, twenty-two seconds. You have succeeded in … Hey, what's going on in there?"

TWENTY

I looked onto the floor into a slack, pasty face, split by a dark gash of a mouth. Red rimmed, puffy, unblinking eyes stared at the ceiling, but that didn't stop the doctor from getting on his knees and pounding the man's chest, yelling orders to the omnipresent voice overhead. "Get help."

"What do you think you're doing?" The voice bordered on hysteria. "I'm calling security."

I rushed out the door into the lobby, clearheaded, with a purpose, and calmly said to the frazzled young man, "There's been an accident."

Drew rushed past me to join Pete, or maybe to check on Jane.

The young man's face paled. He latched onto the edge of the counter as my students hopped off their perches and stood at attention, their winning grins fading. Their faces wore knowing looks, and sadly, with all we'd encountered throughout the year, they were taking the occurrence in stride.

With wisdom and self-possession well beyond her years, Lorelei stepped behind the reception desk, cleared the waxed paper food wrapper to one side of the workspace, picked up the receiver, and punched in some numbers.

"We have an emergency at—" She rattled off the address painted on the window and answered a smattering of questions.

I commandeered the collection box and extended it, lock forward, toward the shaken man. "We need our phones." I jostled the box and rattled the game room guardian free from his stupor. He fumbled for the key on his ring, trying four times before he found the right one and jabbing it murderously into the lock.

The lid on the box popped, and I distributed the devices. The kids sat back down, stoically waiting for whatever would come next. Brock and Eddie flanked Lorelei. Marietta spoke softly to the young man. And when Jane stepped into the foyer and sat between Kindra and Patricia, Patricia's head dropped onto her shoulder. I only recognized two of the signed words she and Jane exchanged, escape and sad, but agreed with both.

I inhaled and stood taller, but before I could think of any words to say, a roly-poly uniformed man barreled through the front door, taser drawn.

"Mitts where I can see them." He made a point of jangling handcuffs suspended from the belt snugged in below his gut. We raised our hands. "Why'd you set off the silent alarm?"

A two-way radio crackled at the man's shoulder and a voice said, "We shut down the siren on our end. What'ya got, Zeb? Need help?"

Zeb depressed a button. "Full house at the Escape Room."

"What's going on? Where's Junior?"

The young man stepped forward to be recognized despite his ashen face and twitchy movements. "Here." He slowly lowered his hands.

"What happened?" Zeb asked. Junior stared at Zeb's chest. Zeb looked down and swiped his hand across a dripping splotch in front, smearing fresh red sauce down his blue shirt. He brushed his fingers on his pants leg, and when satisfied they were clean enough, encouraged Junior to explain.

"They messed with the solution to the 30s game." Junior's voice had grown stronger. "There's something wrong in the room."

Zeb hitched his pants. As he edged forward, a palm slammed into the glass entry followed by two more uniformed officers. "Who called the APD?" The older, taller officer surveyed the average age of our troupe. "Which one of you is Agent *Kidd*?" The word kid brought the slightest sneer to the officer's face. "This better not be a crank call."

Lorelei bravely drew her hands to her sides and in a stentorian voice said, "I requested the presence of the Atlanta Police Department in Agent Kidd's name. Dr. Erickson called out and I responded." She used the index finger of her right hand and pointed through the doorway, suggesting the uniforms take a look for themselves. "You'll find *Agent* Kidd through there."

"Stay where you are. Don't anyone move. Zeb, watch them," the younger, curly-haired blond officer ordered as she marched through the door followed by her partner.

Seconds passed, and one by one we all lowered our hands.

Troubled voices from inside the room clearly said, "Back

away," followed by an "Oh, no," and "Who are you?"

The officers paraded Pete and Drew out of the back room. Pete's head moved from side to side; the victim had not survived. After presenting credentials and identification, which were thoroughly checked, and exchanging professional courtesies, the officers introduced themselves.

Day and Knight?

"But I wouldn't go there if I were you," said the female officer, Knight.

"Wouldn't dream of it." Drew sorted most of the answers to questions the officers posed. Junior corroborated our arrival time, and the clocks on his desk indicated the minutes we'd been figuratively locked behind doors.

Officer Day glared at Drew. "You don't have jurisdiction here."

Drew raised both hands in surrender. "True, but if there's anything I can do to help …"

Officer Knight pulled out a notebook. "Whose idea was it to try the escape room?"

"My dad bought the tickets," Jane said, balanced on the edge of one of the uncomfortable plastic chairs. "The victim—"

"Her dad booked the entire experience," Junior said quickly, excited to provide accurate additional information.

Jane almost smiled appreciatively and emphasized the next words, maybe hoping to shake us loose from the interview. "High School Mock Trial America competition begins tomorrow. Dad wanted to give our students something to take their minds off their upcoming contest."

"Huh. Well, he certainly did that. And who is your dad?" asked Officer Day.

Jane sat up straighter. "Mitchell Mackey."

After Officer Knight pursed her lips and blinked a few times, she turned to Junior. "And no one else came in while they were locked in the room?"

Junior chewed on his cheek. "I don't think so."

"What do you mean you don't think so?" asked Drew gently.

"No one's ever completed one of our escape rooms in less than forty-five minutes."

"And?" Drew prompted.

Junior's head bent. "I picked up supper." His head jerked toward the flashing sign on an establishment across the street. "I was starving." He gazed longingly at the remains of a large burrito cooling on the desk. He glanced up, and his eyes found Drew's. "I was only gone for like five minutes, tops."

Brock stood tall to emphasize his point. "What if we'd have asked for a clue?"

"Would you have asked for a clue in the first twenty minutes?" Brock's shoulder sagged in response. "No one ever wants to be the one who can't get out of an escape room game."

The officers exchanged looks. "So, the vic enters and any one of these thirteen escapees could've done him in," said Day, nodding to himself as if he'd just solved the case.

"Excuse me—" Jane began again.

Day shook his head to quiet Jane.

"Nope. Not possible." Junior stood straighter and said with assurance. "The clocks stop when the doors open. They …" He read numbers on the monitor and pointed to Jane and me. "… came out at fifty-eight minutes twenty-two seconds and the kids came out in fifty-eight minutes—"

Knight put up her hand and cut him off before Junior could declare a winner. "Not important now."

I felt twelve heads perk up and twelve pairs of eyes shift expectantly. It was a little important to us. But we all knew our tiny challenge occupied the least important rung at the bottom of this ladder.

"But, officers—" Jane tried again.

Day said, "Quiet, please."

"That means when the vic wandered in, he could have been followed by anyone." Knight closed the notebook and slid it into her back pocket. "Day, call the medical examiner to pick up the body."

We heard a gasp at the door.

"Body?" Lester's shaky voice repeated. "This is the last time I sub in. I'm outta here." He turned to leave.

"Hold up. Who are you?" Officer Knight retrieved her notebook.

Lester bowed his head of blond curls. "I drive the tour bus. I was told to return in ninety minutes, and here I am, but I want no part of this."

"Where have you been for the last ninety minutes?"

Jane glanced at her watch and growled, "One hundred minutes."

"I had dinner at a dive in Midtown. You can check the tracker on my GPS."

Officer Day accompanied Lester outside to confirm his alibi and returned without the irascible driver. "I have his contact info. He's new to Atlanta." The officer spoke over Jane's head, never a good idea, directly to Drew. "He'll wait for you on the bus in the parking lot."

"Excuse me." Jane huffed to get their attention and said in a stern teacher's voice, no longer to be misunderstood or ignored, "Officer Day. The victim has a name. It's Wendell Gromm."

TWENTY-ONE

Knight panned the room, searching our faces, and her eyes landed on Jane. "How do you know the victim?"

"He kidnapped my friend, Katie." Jane's face had lost all color as she looked at me. Knight scribbled on a page in her notebook. "He's a wanted man. I've known—"

Day consulted his phone and cut Jane off—again. "Gromm's wanted by the FBI and Buncombe County Sheriff's Department for theft, kidnapping, and a host of other crimes. Last seen in Nantahala National Forest." He read a few more words, then pocketed his device and looked at me. "How did he get here? You're Katie? Was he wanted by you as well?" He seemed to hold back, chuckling at his own poor play on words.

Marietta could calm a hurricane. "Officer Knight, we

need to get our students to their hotel. You know where we were during the time in question, and you have our contact information as well."

"I don't think the kids need to see Mr. Gromm." I lowered my voice and tipped my head at our kids. "Or hear any more, for that matter." I looked to Drew for confirmation.

He held out a card to each officer. "If you need anything further, give me a call. I'll make the arrangements you might need."

Knight took it and shook his hand. "Thank you all for your cooperation. Please notify our office if you plan to leave Atlanta."

Marietta and Eddie led the group out of the building. Pete and Jane guarded the middle, and I herded the straggler, Patricia, to the door when Drew sucked air through his teeth. "One thing, though." As I urged Patricia through the door into the cool evening, I slowed to listen. "According to the victim, he had a professional hit woman after him. Maybe he was right."

Knight glared at Drew. Officer Day took out his phone again and tapped a few more keys. He read his screen, swiped up, and shared it with his partner. "This Kuznetsov? She's got quite a sheet, but no convictions."

Knight took the device and scrutinized the contents. She caught Drew's eyes and said, "You're free to go ... for the time being."

We tromped up the bus stairs. A sullen Lester gripped the steering wheel, focused on the windshield, and wouldn't acknowledge his passengers. Drew brought up the rear and when we were seated, Lester cranked the door closed and tapped the GPS unit. A crew of four, wearing navy-blue windbreakers with DOFS plastered across the back, met Knight and Day at the entry. After a brief exchange, Knight and Day jogged to their patrol car.

Drew ducked his head to gaze out the window and said, "They brought in the A-team. Their Division of Forensic Sciences has a great reputation. I should be able to check in with them tomorrow and get the official determination of death."

"Drew, did you see the strange look Knight had when she read about Kuznetsov?"

"I think I'll do some checking on my own." Drew made a quick inquiry on his phone and pocketed it with a deeply furrowed brow.

"What's the matter?" I asked.

He leaned forward. "We've been kept out of the loop. Safety reasons," he said derisively, "but my contact just found out they had to release Kuznetsov Sunday evening. Without the weapon in hand, and no solid evidence, they didn't have enough to hold her. It seems they never do. She's in the wind. I don't want to add more to worry about, but just in case …"

Multiple phones pinged.

Drew's disclosure added Kuznetsov to my growing list of concerns. He turned in his seat and said to everyone, "I've sent you the most recent photo of a woman with ties to the man who died at the escape room. If you see her—"

"Call Drew," Jane and I finished in a whisper, unified with the voices of our students.

The bus pulled away from the curb.

"Meanwhile," Jane yawned and stretched, "I can't wait to hit the hay."

But sleep would still be hours away.

Cars lined both sides of our street, so Lester delivered us a block past our hotel. I thought the walk would do us all some good until the gruff unfamiliar doorman, replacing our affable friend, asked for identification.

As Pete and I approached the registration desk, a red-eyed Martha stepped forward, struggling to affix a smile onto her youthful face, and sniffled. "How can I help you?"

"Where is everyone?" Pete took out his ID. "I'm a doctor. Is someone in need of help?"

Tears filled her eyes. She wiped them away, and I thought I heard her say to herself, "You can do it, Martha."

"Someone tried to break into one of the rooms and attacked our head housekeeper. The police are talking to her now. She assured us she's fine, but the assault put everyone on edge." She inhaled and said nervously, "We've increased security. Everyone is safe here. We're just a pretty close-knit group, and when you hurt one of us, you hurt all of us."

"Sorry to hear that," said Pete.

Like the escape room, the elevator had a capacity cap by order of the fire marshal, so we split up again. Pete, Eddie, and I rode up with Kindra, Patricia, Carlee and Galen. When the doors opened to a hall filled with faces we didn't know, Galen joked, "Think we need to call Mr. Kidd?"

Samara sat in a lounge chair between Dorene and Leo outside their rooms at the less crowded end of the hall. When they recognized us, Leo stood and gestured for us to join them. As we neared, I could see the cold pack Samara held against her cheek.

"Samara, what happened?"

Leo said, "Someone tried to break into your room, Katie. Samara happened upon them using a crowbar. She called them on it and received a fist to her face in answer." His tone indicated it could've been so much worse.

"What do you have in your room, girl?" Samara's laugh ended in a groan.

"Nothing of importance. Was it the same man as earlier?"

Dorene's eyebrows shot up, and Leo let loose a tiny whistle.

"I do not know. I could not see his face. This one wore a

scary rubber mask."

The elevator opened and expelled the remainder of our group.

"Why weren't we invited?" said Jane with a hearty laugh. "What's going on?"

Pete and Dorene looked at me, and I said, "Someone broke into our room, and Samara stopped them, but she took a punch before they took off."

The smile dropped off Jane's face. "What do we have worth taking?"

Dorene introduced us to a tall woman in a black suit. She smoothed the front of her crisp uniform and said, "I'm head of hotel security. We're so sorry. This has never happened at our hotel. Please accept our sincerest apologies. I think Samara caught the perpetrator before he or she had time to enter, but could you please check your room to make sure nothing's been taken?"

The kids followed Marietta and Eddie with the admonition to stay together and call Mr. Kidd if they had qualms about anything. As we followed the head of security down the hall past the elevator, the doors opened. ZaZa took one look at me, gaped down the hall, and rolled her eyes. "It is always something with you, drama queen." She backed into the elevator, and the doors closed on her smirking face.

Just as Samara had done earlier, the head of security closed the door, and insisted Jane open it again with her keycard. "As a precaution," she said, unapologetically.

The key opened the door, and Jane and I tiptoed inside, not wanting to trouble law enforcement already hard at work, when a low rumbling voice said, "What are you doing here?"

TWENTY-TWO

Officer Day, you got here quickly," I said, trying to keep the unhappy surprise from leaking into my words. "This room belongs to Jane Mackey and me."

He gazed at the deluxe space and back at me, his mouth opening and closing like a curious walleye. Although he looked taken aback, he finally said, "Why am I not surprised?"

Officer Knight flipped the light switch on the bathroom fixture, and her head swiveled, scanning the room, but stopped abruptly when she saw me. She covered her surprise well and had complete control when she asked, "Ms. Wilk, we were told a staff member caught someone trying to break in. She was adamant she thwarted the plan. But, just in case, do you see anything missing?"

Jane and I slid hangers from side to side, burrowed

through our drawers, and dug into our packs. My head fell back in relief when I carefully brought out Brock's diploma. "I can't see anything of importance. What do you think someone would want to take?"

"The attack happened minutes after we were called to the escape room," Knight offered at the same time Day smirked. "It's one thing after another."

My mind reeled. Even if it had been Wendell trying to get into our room the first time, it certainly hadn't been Wendell this time.

"And you have no idea what anyone could want." Day didn't sound like he believed me.

"No, Officer, but if I figure it out, I'll be sure to give you a call." I tried to keep the brewing testiness at a simmer.

"There will be two plainclothesmen on guard in the hall tonight. We do take your safety seriously, but please do not impede our investigation." Knight could have pinned me to the wall with her look. She handed me her card. "Goodnight, Ms. Wilk, Ms. Mackey."

The door closed, and I said, "I miss my dog." I wandered from the gathering space, followed by Jane.

"What? I'm not good enough." Jane dropped onto her bed. "CJ's bringing them by tomorrow." She scooted to the edge. "Who do you think did it?"

My eyes widened. "Officer Knight told us to stay out of the investigation."

"We won't, though, will we?"

"Jane, we have seven students depending on us."

"All the more reason to solve this horrible mess and put it behind us. So, what do you think?"

"I think if we make any discoveries, we will turn them over to Knight and Day."

"Deal. I can't help wondering what trouble Wendell got into. What could he have stolen?"

"Would Drew know?"

"Maybe, but I'll have to employ every ounce of my feminine wiles to get him to disclose that information. Let's brainstorm the entire list of questions we'd like answers for."

"Can you ask him if he knows the company Wendell stole from, the value of whatever he stole, and what ties Natalianna Kuznetsov has to the company?"

Jane snatched a notepad from the nightstand and one of the fountain pens and scribbled as I spoke.

"We might ask if Felicity could have picked him up in North Carolina and returned him to Atlanta. Or is there a reason for her to want Wendell gone? Felicity said she had proof you were seeing Wendell." Jane's lips puckered, and she started to protest, but I quickly added, "I know it wasn't you, but the proof might point to someone else and, whether or not it was true, does Felicity have an alibi?" Jane nibbled on her lip and her eyes grew round. I continued. "What other enemies does Wendell have we don't know about? I think we might find a clue if we knew what was used to knock out Noah and Richard. And also, I wonder how Wendell died. I assumed he was killed, but he may have died of natural causes."

Jane stopped writing and observed me as if examining an unknown species. "Did he look like he died of natural causes?"

"You never know." I shrugged and sighed. "I can't wait to see Maverick."

"I could use a sloppy kiss too." Jane made a production of fitting the cover on the pen and said, "Give me a few minutes." She grabbed her notes and hobbled to the door, opened it, and disappeared down the hall.

I ripped the cellophane off the box of chocolates included in the welcome basket and bit into a dark chocolate raspberry cream. Three truffles and one sea salt caramel later, Jane returned with Drew in tow. Stars filled his eyes. Pete wasn't far behind, hiding a smirk. I held out the candy and three more pieces disappeared.

Jane flopped onto the couch and ordered, "Spill."

Drew read the list. "I'll tell you what you could dig up for yourselves. A.B.SEE is a mechanical design company best known for the research and development of remote guidance systems like the one found in the cargo hold, but that's just one area of their expertise. They have a video of Gromm downloading and saving a copy of some new plans from an interoffice computer to a portable storage device—a flash drive. Gromm allegedly pocketed the drive and left the Twin Cities hours later on your flight to Detroit. It seems his reputation for being a little light-fingered preceded him. Although the CEO reported the security breach and the value has yet to be disclosed, he assured law enforcement they could take care of the problem internally. It had happened before."

"Is that where Kuznetsov came in?"

"The FBI confirmed Kuznetsov is being investigated as a person of interest in a number of high-profile crimes, but so far, she's been able to avoid prosecution. Not finding a connection between Kuznetsov and A.B.SEE doesn't mean there isn't one. She may have just happened to be at the wrong place and her appearance coincidental—"

"You can't believe that. We discovered her with all that gear."

"The cargo listed on the manifest looked legitimate. Kuznetsov claimed she wasn't part of any hijacking operation, but rather was in charge of a trial run of the hardware for a potential buyer, not part of a conspiracy. She didn't know the pilots had been incapacitated. Gromm used the situation to further his own agenda. Why else would he tie her up and kidnap Katie?" Drew ignored my comment and cleared his throat. "Felicity Williams had a rocky relationship with Wendell for ten years—"

"Twelve, but who's counting?" Jane flopped back onto the downy pillows.

"If he found a spot for his phone to connect and was able to contact her, she could've picked him up and driven back to Atlanta in plenty of time for him to make an appearance at the Braves game. Although how he knew you were there is a conundrum." Drew inhaled deeply. "We do know Williams returned. Naming other suspects would be purely conjecture at this point and would negatively impact the investigation. That being said, I found out what caused the pilots' unconsciousness."

I didn't breathe for fear I'd miss his next words.

"Fentanyl. It was ground very fine. Richard accidentally opened a can booby-trapped to disperse the drug into the cockpit. Fortunately, you and Jane covered your mouths and noses, or you could have seen some effects from the drug as well. The autopsy on Gromm hasn't been completed, that I know of. I'm being held at arm's length when it comes to sharing information."

Pete shifted uncomfortably. "I'm fairly sure he died as a result of a toxic inhalant."

TWENTY-THREE

The plainclothes officers had seen no activity overnight and left before we breakfasted Tuesday morning. Our bus, minus Lester, picked us up and delivered us for an early tour of the World of Coca-Cola. Everyone had an interest in the museum showcasing the non-alcoholic version of Pemberton's French Wine Coca. Invented in 1886, John Smith Pemberton's temperance drink sold for five cents a glass and has grown to be a dominant contributor to the global soft-drink market.

We raided the learning modules, experiencing the powerful connection between smell and taste, sampling the varied flavors of Coca-Cola, crackling across the tacky floor sticky from spilled soda, creating new combinations—some successful, some not so much—and experimenting with the science behind the soda. Carlee, Galen, and Felipe proudly displayed the custom cans they designed, but the photo op in front of the vault containing the secret formula for the beverage of the century highlighted the tour.

Eddie read from a placard on the wall, "It says here, the drink gets its name from the coca leaves and kola nuts used in its creation." His twinkling eyes drew me to his narrative. "I've heard Coca-Cola at one time contained something more stimulating."

Of course, the statement sent fingers flying over phone keys to verify said ingredient.

Felipe's jaw dropped. "Evidence suggests Coca-Cola contained cocaine until 1903 when they removed fresh coca leaves from the secret formula." As he pondered the soda's past, he fixed his gaze on a group of chatty girls wearing black leggings, pink high tops, and matching bubble gum pink satin jackets with polka dot scarves tied at their necks. One of the girls waved. He saluted with two fingers, and she split from her crew.

"Felipe," she squealed. "What are you doing here?"

"My team is competing in the Mock Trial America competition. What are *you* doing here?"

"Dancing. Our troupe is here for a regional dance competition." She tossed her wavy blond ponytail over her shoulder and batted her ultra long false eyelashes, flirting with her sky-blue eyes. "I dropped out of speech, so I won't see you at the meets anymore, but I wasn't very good anyway." Felipe tried to dissuade her, but she shook her head and said, "It's alright, really. And I simply love dance. But we should get together while we're here."

Kindra cleared her throat, reminding Felipe of our presence. He stood at the edge of our group and wore a lopsided grin. "Hey guys, this is my friend, Rocky. She's from Duluth, and her team is here for a high school dance competition."

"Can I hang with you for a bit? My aunt lives here, and I've been to this museum like a gazillion times." She rolled her eyes. "My friends want to try every single experiment." She noticed Felipe's personalized can. "Ooh. I like that. I did one last year."

"We're having lunch on the premises. Join us?" I said.

"If you're sure it's okay."

The girls welcomed her with open arms and dragged her with them to try the tasty tidbits.

"This Bottle Cap Café is my jam," said Brock, taking a humongous bite of a burger dripping with cheese, loaded with onions, tomatoes, and lettuce, and drenched in ketchup and mustard. He swallowed hard and wiped his mouth, taking a long sip of his beverage. "Look at the size of my sandwich, and I even have enough fries to feed Galen." He received a gentle shove from his friend, who reached over and grabbed a handful. "And it goes perfectly with my regular Coke."

After finishing lunch, ever the gentleman, Felipe made certain Rocky hooked up with her friends before he let us leave. The bus dropped us off at our hotel, and thirty minutes later, we walked to the Fulton County Courthouse. The healthy activity helped the kids decompress, as much as seven kids surrounded by eight eagle-eyed adults could. (ZaZa declined the promenade, but promised she'd attend when the real competition began).

I kept my eyes peeled as we made our way through the streets of Atlanta, but I had no idea who I was looking for. Wendell was gone for good. Although Natalianna had disappeared from the FBI's radar, Drew didn't expect to see her near us. Felicity lived here, but I thought she'd keep herself well away from us now that she knew where we were staying.

Drew stood on the bottom step in front of the multi-story county building and began a little pep talk. "While you're hard at work—"

Always one to lighten the mood, Brock snickered and received a soft elbow to his ribs from Lorelei. "Sorry, I thought you were kidding."

Drew laughed. "Dr. Erickson and I are off to take a localized tour of the city as we wait to hear about possible extra protection. If you need anything …"

The kids echoed, "Call Mr. Kidd."

He nodded. "Have fun."

Pete squeezed my fingers. "Let us know when you're ready to return. We'll walk back with you." Before I could protest, even if I wanted to, he added, "Better safe than sorry."

Once onsite, the greeter handed us an updated schedule. The host of sponsored activities included voluntary scrimmages, team meetings, coaches' orientation, student orientation, a welcome reception, and the official opening of the tournament.

Dorene and Leo led the kids to our assigned room. They blocked out their final moves, practiced opening and closing statements, and took a discovery tour to familiarize themselves with the courthouse. Knowing the students felt more at ease, Dorene and Leo retreated to the attorney coaches' meeting, and we entered the meeting hall.

Usually quite self-assured, after attempting to greet the other teams and being nearly shunned, my students hugged the perimeter of the humongous room and warily eyed their confident opponents circling the beautifully decorated banquet tables. Even Galen, who'd never let food go untasted under my watch, hung back, observing the piles of hors d'œuvres shrink rapidly. If they hadn't been nervous before, as the target of surreptitious finger pointing and susurration, the cause of their palpable anxiety angered me. Whatever the reason they'd been singled out, they'd earned their chance to participate, to compete with the best in the nation.

I had many years of experience dealing with those who felt the need to belittle and disparage anyone unlike themselves and easily pinpointed two pompous young people parked at a table near the stage who appeared to orchestrate the campaign to avoid my kids. Seemingly at the top of the pecking order, they ran the show, greeted other teams as old friends, and glanced our way, gesturing and sniggering. When one happy-go-lucky young lady deigned to break the rules and head our way, she received a whistle, a shake of a head, and an obvious nonverbal admonition. She almost bucked the system but lowered her head and drifted to the opposite side of the room.

Jane clomped next to me. "Do you see that guy? Who does he think he is? And she's no better. What are they doing? I'm going to go over there and give them a piece of my mind."

"Be careful, girlfriend. You don't have much to spare."

She blinked and when she understood my really bad joke, she rolled her eyes. "They're nasty."

"True."

"What should we do?"

"If you or I take them on, we'll lose the image of Minnesota nice. If we leave, they win. If we herd our students over there, our kids will be embarrassed. If we call out the bullies, our kids will lose their edge. Instead ..." I raised my eyebrow and pursed my lips mischievously.

Jane shook her head. "You wouldn't, would you?"

I whipped out two decks of cards, tossing one to Lorelei and one to Carlee. I watched lights go on in both pairs of eyes. *If you can't beat 'em, change the game.*

The girls sat on opposite sides of a table surrounded by our Columbia companions. Lorelei shuffled and asked for someone to cut the cards. She counted out what she needed. Her guinea pig chose one card, and through mathematical genius, her final spelling always produced the chosen card. Carlee's trick required sleight of hand, and dexterity was one of her many talents. Soon we were all laughing and a few of the braver souls from around the room meandered over to find out what the giggles were about. Neither girl faltered, and the mystified crowd grew.

Lorelei repeated the routine a half dozen times. She shuffled the deck and asked, "Anyone want to test this card trick?"

The happy-go-lucky young lady shot a defiant look over her shoulder and said, "I'm in."

Channeling her game show hostess genes, Lorelei said, "I'm Lorelei Calder from Columbia, Minnesota. Who are you, and where are you from?"

She'd broken the ice and hopefully the ties that bound as well. In the ever-expanding circle, our kids intermingled with other teams, munched on the appetizers, and made new acquaintances. More and more of the students introduced themselves, and our kids exchanged the swag they'd brought— lapel pins in the shape of the Minnesota state bird, the loon.

"What a sick trick," said one teen Carlee outfoxed. Before I could figure out what the comment meant, another said, "Totally boggers." The magnetic laughter drew the two negative bodies from the front.

"What's going on?" sneered the young man, running his

fingers through a thick lock of brown hair.

"Math magic. Care to try?" said Lorelei.

I witnessed a short non-verbal debate. The young man snorted and walked away. The young lady reluctantly followed behind, although she cast quizzical glances over her shoulder.

"Don't mind them," said one of our new friends. "They've won the mock trial competition for three years running, and fully expect to be treated like royalty. They've earned it, I suppose, but not at the expense of others. They kinda told everyone trouble follows you. It made me a little leery. Sorry to have been such a dork."

I wondered how they knew. Jane and I shared an understanding look. For good or ill, things happened. She straightened her shoulders before trying to enlighten our new friend, but her eyes widened at what she noticed over my shoulder and caused me to turn.

Drew and Felipe were in deep conversation. Knight and Day and two more uniformed officers fanned out and strode purposefully through the assembly.

Our new friend whispered, "It's true." Rather than turn away, she grabbed Kindra's arm and said, "I'm so amped."

Felipe pointed at a woman dressed in the crisp black and white uniform of the caterers. The woman caught my eye, smiled coolly, and fled between the sectional screens and out the door. They were too late.

TWENTY-FOUR

Natalianna Kuznetsov vanished at the same time the lights dimmed and a tall, white-haired gentleman with piercing blue eyes, a patrician nose, and shining white teeth mounted the stairs to the stage for his grand opening. He wore a black suit and starched pinstriped shirt. Straightening a subdued blue tie, he stepped into the spotlight. After accepting a lengthy round of deafening applause, he batted the air to silence his audience.

"Welcome to Fulton County Courthouse and the latest edition of High School Mock Trial America. You are representing your home states in a grueling legal contest. I am—"

"Katie Wilk." A very loud electrically modulated voice reverberated from every quarter. "Give it up, and you'll be left alone. Otherwise …"

The program director eyed the ceiling, waiting. With no more words forthcoming, he forced a chuckle and waggled his eyebrows. "I am NOT Katie Wilk."

I missed the rest of his speech. Day tugged on Felipe's arm. Felipe and Drew exited the hall, and I trailed after them.

"Good job, Felipe," said Drew as the doors closed, muffling the speech.

"Thanks, Mr. Kidd." Felipe pulled up the photo. "I saw her." A huge grin lit his face. "And called you."

I peeked at the screen. The photo matched the face of the woman in the catering duds with one minor difference. The eyes of the woman in the hall were fierce.

"Whose voice came over the speaker?" asked Knight. "Was it her?"

"I've never heard her speak." I shrugged. "And I couldn't tell if that voice was male or female. Could you?"

"What do they want from you?" asked Day.

"I have no idea."

"I think we need to have a more detailed conversation and check your belongings immediately," said Knight, heading toward the exit. "This character thinks you have something important."

"I can't leave my students."

She stopped and stared. "And just what do you think was meant by 'otherwise'?"

I stared back. "I won't leave them."

We waited. Minutes passed, and the doors opened. An echo of the director's final words, "Let the games begin," resolved our standoff. Students poured out and most gave us wide berth as if repelled by some catchy uniformed disease. My students were, of course, last to quit the hall.

"Ms. Wilk, may we trouble you for a moment of your precious time and meet you at your hotel?" Day said with just a hint of sarcasm.

I paused, as if deliberating. "I suppose. I realize you are investigating a murder, but you know none of us could have possibly killed Gromm. I'll meet you, but I don't know what you hope to find."

After dragging her massive boot around all day, Jane started slowing down, so Drew called for the van to pick us up. My students quietly climbed inside the vehicle driven by a new driver, still not Lester. The kids opened phones or looked out the windows. Aside from the music wafting overhead, the silent ride gave me time to think.

Maybe we should return to Columbia.

We parked in front of the hotel, and before we disembarked, Drew turned to address his captive audience. "I'm ordering pizzas from Jeeno's, a five-star venue with three thousand reviews. The menu should be on your phones. Text me what you'd like, and I'll let you know when it's time to eat."

We'd come to expect the hotel staff to man their stations, except under duress, and it was comforting when the doorman and the bellboy greeted us by name. Augustus's eyebrows rose, but Martha smiled a welcome. All seemed right with our accommodations.

Drew's phone dinged multiple times before we made it to the elevator. He nodded in approval of the choices and placed the order as the elevator carried us to our floor.

"Pizza will be here in thirty minutes, or we get it for free," Drew called. "We'll meet in the lounge at the end of the hall."

The kids glanced at each other, opened their doors, and slipped quietly into their rooms.

I used the keycard, and Drew helped Jane get settled on the couch next to an origami towel monkey. Dorene took one chair, Leo another. Pete leaned against the wall and crossed his arms, his eyes focused on his walking shoes.

I could sense their minds whirring, bouncing thoughts off the walls. When Drew and I began to talk at the same time, he said, "Go ahead, Katie."

I blurted, "Maybe we need to go home." Having voiced my concern, I gazed around the room. I hoped I'd feel relief, but instead I sagged with intense failure. My head dropped into my hand, and I kneaded my forehead, massaging the tiniest kernel of a headache. Heavy pounding on the door intensified the pain.

I stiffened, thinking Knight and Day had arrived, and I had no better idea what I might have that someone else would want. Pete raised his hand in a gesture for us to remain seated, and he walked to the door. He leaned toward the peephole and pulled the knob. Marietta stood, arms akimbo, head shaking. She stepped to one side, revealing our seven wards in addition to her husband.

Lorelei raised her chin. "We need to talk."

Pete pulled the door wider and nodded.

Dorene and Leo pulled their chairs together, making space for the last person to cram into the room.

Eddie puckered his lips and clicked his tongue before saying, "I think you should listen to them. They provide a valid argument." With a nod to Dorene, he said, "They learned from the best." He stepped next to Marietta.

Felipe cleared his throat. "We've been talking to our parents about what's happened. They have a message for you."

He held up his phone and his mother's bubbly face filled

the screen, "Hello Ms. Wilk, Ms. Mackey." Her phone zoomed around a kitchen, catching visual snippets of all the other parents, waving or tipping their heads in greeting. "We just want you to know we've been in contact with our children and are aware of what's happened. Are you okay?"

Tears pooled in my eyes. "Yes. Thank you."

Jane, too, was overcome and garbled, "I'm fine."

"We know Mock Trial America is a once in a lifetime opportunity, and we are so incredibly proud of our kids."

This is it, I thought. *We'll return to Columbia tomorrow.*

I tuned out the phone call as I calculated times and mentally compiled a list of what needed to get done to provide new transportation and get us home efficiently. Mitchell Mackey's expertise would be a great resource. In addition, changing travel plans midweek should be much easier than trying to do so on the weekend.

As I prepared my exit strategy speech to gracefully accept the inescapable, I quickly lost track of the conversation until the quiet, hopeful looks on my kids' faces brought me back to the present exchange.

"What do you think?" said Felipe's mom.

I didn't want to appear too eager. I took a huge breath, carefully formulating my first words accepting the inevitable.

Felipe's mom added, "We trust you both and sincerely hope you'll consider staying."

I rewound and wrapped my head around what she'd said. They didn't want us to go home. They'd chosen to have their children compete in Atlanta. I adjusted my plan, but before I could utter any words, Pete answered another knock at the door.

Officer Knight surveyed the occupants and said uneasily, "We'd like a word. When y'all finish, we'll be just outside."

She pulled the door closed.

I concentrated on the lovely face on the screen. "Are you sure?" I asked.

Felipe's mother muted her side of the call, and we watched a brief discussion tumble behind her. She came back on and said, "The consensus is to allow our children a shot, Ms. Wilk. Mr. Kidd has consented to remain onsite with our kids for the duration."

Drew nodded and Jane relaxed.

"We feel confident they will be as safe with you as anywhere else."

"Please," came the plea from every corner of our room.

Drew said, "It's up to you two."

The kids waited. Everyone waited. Jane and I often communicated with a look, and this time she reinforced her affirmation with a resolute, "Let's do it."

I puffed out a lungful of air and said, "Okay."

I quieted the rowdy cheer with a screeching whistle and said to the parent portal, "We will keep in touch, and we can change our plans any time someone feels the need."

Drew's phone dinged. He read the screen, grinned, and said, "Pizza."

TWENTY-FIVE

With a promise to save six slices of the deluxe meat lovers, Dorene hurried everyone out of the room, closed and turned the lock on the door. Someone knocked.

"Knight and Day are law enforcement," Dorene said in a rush. "I'll be here with you. Before you answer a question, look my way. If I shake my head, please refuse to answer. Is there anything in here you wouldn't want Knight and Day to find? They don't have a warrant and most probably couldn't get one, but …"

Jane laughed. The knock sounded again. I tried to look incredulous.

"I won't leave you alone. If you need representation, I know skilled attorneys who practice in Georgia, and I believe I can get an admission on motion without examination."

Sounds impressive, I thought.

We agreed to abide by her recommendations. She sat down and I opened the door.

Knight asked the same questions she asked after the almost-break-in, "Are you certain Gromm didn't give you something or leave a hint?"

Day snorted and gave me a withering look. "Or did you take something?"

I ignored him and gave Knight the same answers I'd given the first time she asked. "Unless there was a chance for me to escape, which I would've taken in a heartbeat, I stayed away from him. I didn't want to have anything to do with him. What are you looking for?"

"He could have been carrying the plans he stole." Day searched my face.

"What did he steal?" Day didn't acknowledge my question. "I never saw what was in his backpack, and it was heavy. His only contact with my pack was to remove food, but everything was ruined when I fell in the river." I slid open the door on the closet, whipped out my replacement bag, and slammed it onto my bed. "This is my new bag, compliments of Mitchell Mackey."

Knight stayed Day's itchy hands, ready to open the pack. "May I?" she asked.

Dorene gave the go-ahead. Knight removed the two journals covered in navy and white gingham and a book on cryptology. She paged through the thick three-ring binder containing material from the mock trial competition, withdrew three pens, a notebook, Brock's diploma, and paper receipts, before patting the sides, looking for a hidden pocket.

Jane said, "Wendell never touched our luggage, but feel free to search."

The mundane contents of my drawers ended up strewn all over my bed. I almost laughed as the frustrated Day continued his search through the closet, sliding hangers across the clothes bar and lifting shoes and examining the soles. Knight was more considerate, carefully replacing the items she removed from Jane's drawer.

I tried again. "Who did the plans belong to? The plans Wendell stole … what were they for?"

Neither officer volunteered an answer. Maybe they didn't know.

I tried again. "Do you know how he died?"

Knight raised her chin. "He died as a result of exposure to an extremely high concentration of commercial grade dimethyl sulfate. You wouldn't know anything about that would you?"

I felt like a marionette, my mouth opening and closing, waiting for a puppeteer's voice to fill the gaping hole. I'd never heard of dimethyl sulfate before this trip, but Knight's pronouncement made me queasy. Two times in one week was two times too many.

Dorene knew me well enough to read distress. "Officers, this is clearly a fishing expedition, and you've come up empty." She stood and moved toward the door.

Day narrowed his eyes. I almost laughed. The scare tactic of pretending to use x-ray vision wouldn't be effective on our legal superwoman.

"Let me introduce our winning mock trial attorney coach, Dorene Dvorak."

Day's eyes closed tightly as if warding off a splitting headache which Dorene could easily dispense.

Dorene threw her shoulders back and raised her chin. "Ms. Mackey and Ms. Wilk are the victims. If you have more questions, please let us know. Until that time, you need to let these lovely ladies return to their charges."

The impasse lasted five seconds, at the most, but felt like an eternity. After they'd gone, I breathed. "Thank you, Dorene."

"Don't thank me yet. I couldn't get a read on what they were looking for." She stopped and stared. "What's going on with you? You look … guilty. Again."

I dug out my cryptology book and flipped to the offending page. "The encrypted message was intercepted by the French resistance during the great war." She nodded, rapidly losing interest. I read my hastily penciled interpretation. "'Four parts dimethyl sulfate to one part chlorosulfonic acid.'"

I stumbled over the chemical names, but Jane didn't. "Rationite."

"I never heard of it before."

Jane continued to talk while she stood in front of the decorative mirror and touched up her mascara, as if making everyday conversation. "One weapon of World War I chemical warfare. Awful, suffocating stuff. Smelled like onions. Sometimes the effects were delayed, and the victims died a painful death." Her bright pink lipstick stopped halfway to her mouth as her gaze shifted to the reflection of our astounded faces. "What? I'm a history buff. What else do you want to know about World War I?"

Dorene's piercing eyes drilled into Jane and me. "Pure coincidence. You don't know anything. Remember." Her eyes intensified. "And not a word until we know where this is going."

I pressed my lips together and placed a marker on the page before tucking the book back into my bag. Jane mimed zipping her lips and tossing the proverbial key.

We joined the super excited kids. It seemed nothing could curb their enthusiasm for the upcoming competition, except maybe food.

"That's the dankest pizza ever, Ms. Wilk."

"Is that good or bad?"

"If you can't finish yours …"

I didn't want to let Brock down, but famished, I nearly swallowed my two delicious pieces whole.

Lorelei gave last-minute orders disguised as suggestions. "If no one has anything else," she said, catching the eyes of each of her teammates. "We want to be fresh tomorrow. Let's call it a night." No one resisted.

"What time tomorrow, Ms. Wilk?" asked Carlee.

"Let's do breakfast at eight. That'll give you plenty of time to get ready, and we'll head over to the courthouse at nine fifteen."

"My friend, Rocky, asked if she could come watch," said Felipe.

"Absolutely," said Dorene, herding them like stray cats. "But they unequivocally prohibit late admittance, so make sure everyone understands what time they should arrive." The teen voices receded down the hall.

Drew ushered Jane back to our room. It took Pete and me less than a minute to toss the garbage and clean up. As we turned to leave, he entwined his fingers with mine. I barely had time to blush before Maverick and Renegade filled the doorway and sat patiently, panting. CJ stood behind them, watching silently. Pete released my hand, and I dropped to my knees, and even CJ couldn't contain my dog's exuberant dash across the room, wicked tongue-lashing, and tickling nuzzle.

"I missed you," I giggled as we snuggled on the floor.

A door slammed, and Carlee's voice carried well.

"Renegade." All the doors flew open, and she was joined by her friends.

Renegade yipped, broke her hold, and galloped down the hall. For the first time in what seemed like forever, CJ's clicking cue went unheeded. I couldn't have cared less. The presence of the dogs raised the level of endorphins and relaxed everyone.

When CJ finally restored order, I asked, "However did they let you bring the dogs in?"

"I had a short discussion with Augustus." His eyes twinkled. "It pays to know the right people."

"I know the right people." Carlee gave her dad a hug and reminded him of the round one start time. She had her mother's beautiful silver eyes and gentle smile, but her dad's straight black hair and his temperament. "Don't be late," she said, strolling back to her room and waving. "They won't let you in."

"We will be on time."

I tilted my head, watching CJ admiringly as he interacted with Carlee. Once he found out he was her dad, he'd been all in.

He turned to me. "The dogs have behaved well—until now." CJ's voice held a tiny reproach. "Maverick has been a bit stressed by the flight and his unfamiliar arrangements, but he is happy to see you."

"And I'm happy to see him." Maverick's eyes closed, and he leaned into my fingers, smoothing the soft fur on his head.

"If it works for you, with Mitchell's permission, I plan to remain with the dogs until Drew returns to Minnesota." CJ's cue worked perfectly the second time. The dogs jumped to attention at his side, a perfect double heel as they headed to the bank of elevators. "Drew has called in a few favors and there should be extra security beginning tomorrow. I would, however, like to see for myself."

Pete said, "It's taking a bit more time. Drew's been coordinating with his contacts since Gromm's murder, and you know how some agencies work."

"Fingers crossed." A rare smile formed on CJ's lips. "Tomorrow," he said, as they disappeared behind the elevator doors.

Pete accompanied me to our room, and the serious conversation we interrupted ceased upon our arrival. Drew put a hand on Jane's arm. She ignored him. Through tight lips, she said, "Drew said wherever we get together, there's trouble. I assured him that wasn't the case and promised we would let Knight and Day do their job."

"No sleuthing." Drew reached for Jane's hand. "I love you. Get some rest." He kissed the top of her head.

Dorene headed for the door, saying, "We're out of here, bro." She and Leo disappeared.

"We'll try to meet you for breakfast, but if something comes up, we'll be at the courthouse rooting for you. Good luck tomorrow." Pete leaned over and whispered, "Sleep tight," before I received a chaste kiss on the cheek.

As soon as the door snicked, Jane bounced forward. "Who do you think killed Wendell?"

"Jane? You just promised Drew—"

"I know. I know. I promised to let Knight and Day do their job, and I am perfectly willing to do that. I know you're curious." She hobbled to the closet and retrieved one of the journals, opening it to the last page where I'd begun a list of my own. "I jotted down a few more thoughts is all."

She'd written 'suspect' at the top of the next page, and under the heading, she had written Felicity, Natalianna,

Unknown Girlfriend, Mr. X, Driver 1, Lester, and Junior. In the second column, she also included Samara, Richard, Dianne, Noah, Jane, and Katie, and I cast a wary look her way.

"Jane? You can't be serious."

She drew a heavy line through my name, and my shoulders relaxed a tiny bit. I pointed to her name. She huffed and drew another line through her name, reducing the long suspect list by two.

"Tell me why you chose these names." I hadn't meant to become embroiled in another investigation, but I had to admit, my curiosity had been roused.

"I would put Natalianna at the top of the list. According to Drew's sources, she had the wherewithal to do away with Wendell. But if it wasn't Natalianna, it still could have been someone from the A.B.SEE after those plans, and that is my Mr. X."

"Felicity's on the list because significant others are always considered a suspect, and she believed Wendell had a girlfriend."

"Correct. And our first driver suspiciously ate something that didn't agree with him, or not. Then, Lester conveniently took over the job and was onsite when we found Wendell. They were on location."

"Which is why you've included Junior too. But that's pretty lame." My lips shifted to one side of my mouth, considering. "I like Samara, though I suppose she does have access to our room, but she wouldn't have hurt herself, would she?"

"Ever heard of an accomplice?"

"Richard, Noah, and Dianne were on the plane when it went down, so they also had what? Opportunity? Means?" My hands flew in a gesture of surrender. "That's pretty much all we have for any of the suspects. What about motives?"

She flashed her enormous brown eyes and shrugged.

We shut down for the evening, but even in the dim room, as I listened to Jane's restlessness ease, I kept wondering why Wendell had been murdered. Just as readily, recalling how the short time I'd spent with him in the national forest instilled anger, I wondered why not?

TWENTY-SIX

The team wisely chose Lorelei and Carlee as our representatives, our event captains, and from thirty feet away, by the looks of delight on their faces, Brock correctly discerned they drew plaintiff for our first match. Lorelei's bearing—straight back, raised chin, and the bright gleam in her eye—shouted confidence. "Watch out, world. Here comes winning team EsqChoir," Brock said, as he gleefully pounded on his chest Tarzan-style.

Felipe's dancing friend, Rocky, arrived in time to give Galen a knuckle bump and Kindra a hip check. She pointed first at her own eyes and then swung her two fingers over the team in an 'I'm watching you' gesture. With their assignment in hand, Dorene huddled our team together for a few final words of inspiration before she led the procession to their room.

Mitchell and CJ had picked up Drew and Pete, and Jane's phone pinged repeatedly, reporting a delayed ETA. Jane said, "Traffic is a bear. Let's wait here a few more minutes. It's not quite time, but I've texted the location of our trial, so they'll find us."

Sixty seconds later, the revolving door spit Drew into the foyer, followed by the other three in successive beats. They quickly checked through security and hustled to join Jane and me.

"I'm glad you made it," I said, striding through the multitude of parents, friends, and student fans.

Drew smiled. "I wanted the extra protection to start this morning, but I was told our coverage won't begin until after today's proceedings, and it's not guaranteed because we're not a priority. Their reasoning? There is no imminent threat, and this place is packed with people and loaded with law enforcement who are here for everyone. They've been made aware of our perceived—" Drew's air quotes came with a smirk, "—special circumstances." His blue eyes directed our attention to Jane's dad. "However, this morning on our drive here, Mitchell arranged private protection for the duration of our stay in Atlanta. His team reported they're already onsite."

I released a breath I'd been holding. "Good. When will we meet this detail?" I rubbernecked around the room, assuming I'd somehow be able to identify them.

"My dear, if they do their job correctly, you'll never know they're here," said Mitchell. "But I assure you, they're well-trained and discreet. You might see some familiar faces as well. I recruited extra personnel. Dianne felt like she let you down. She volunteered her services, and I thought it was a great idea. Richard and Noah are taking a break from flying to give their systems time to heal, but they are still on my payroll, and they will be in attendance as well." He winked.

I encouraged haste, but by the time we snaked through the crowds lining the hallowed halls and entered the courtroom at the end of the corridor, the only seats remaining in the gallery lined the back wall. We filed onto the hard wooden bench. I cast a glance around the room trying to spot Mitchell's security personnel and came up empty, but sure enough, the flight crew sat in the third row among the spectators.

Dianne seemed the happiest to see us. She turned around and waved a greeting. She nudged Richard, seated next to her. He fiddled with his phone and gave the impression he had better things to do but attended at the behest of his boss. He caught me staring and, without smiling, mouthed the words "Good luck," before looking back at his screen. Noah gawked at the surroundings, watching everyone. He gave an approving nod when, with one minute remaining on the clock, the courtroom door opened. ZaZa made her appearance, dressed to the nines in a cherry red skirt suit and matching high heels. I scooted closer to Pete to clear some space for her, but she took one look at what little elbow room she'd have and turned up her nose. She paraded to the front row and waited impatiently for the audience to stand so she could proceed to the sole empty seat, only to stop abruptly when she realized she'd been aiming for a spot between her favorite attorney (*not*), Dorene, and Leo.

Rather than awkwardly skulk back the way she'd come, she plopped into the narrow space Dorene provided. She crossed her long legs and wriggled, squirming a few inches loose from Leo, who seemed to relish his stepsister's discomfort.

Lorelei's opening statement laid out the case. "The executor of the estate of twenty-three-year-old Connor Robert Mitchell is claiming negligence by the White Star Line in its operation of the R.M.S. *Titanic*. Maggie Murphy is seeking damages for the breach of duty of care and the causation of fatal injuries, having suffered loss of life, loss of wages, pain, and mental anguish."

Her voice captivated me, and I already knew the words she'd use. "Maggie Murphy will give us an account of the fateful night when her fiancé perished and the losses she sustained. Captain Rostron of the *Carpathia* has first-hand expert knowledge of navigation and the results of the illustrious ship speeding to make up perceived time lost. Another famed survivor, Margaret Brown, will weave together the catastrophic threads of both the privileged and disadvantaged."

Observing the well-rehearsed trial drew me into the scene, and our tight surroundings melted away. All of the young attorneys-to-be knew the case inside and out. I thought our kids executed their parts with panache, but so did the opposition. With the high caliber of performances, my heart rate ramped up, but our kids didn't miss a trick.

If I didn't know Patricia was deaf, I wouldn't have noticed the one time she asked for a question to be repeated. The cross-examining attorney turned his back to check his notes, and she couldn't read his lips. The head judge missed a few words too, so when Patricia, aka Maggie Murphy, asked, "Would you repeat your question, please?" the judge cocked his head and waited. Felipe portrayed a believable Captain Rostron, straight-backed, intense, and deeply distressed. Carlee's Molly Brown came right out of the history books. Their solid performances drew the audience to the events and emotions of 1912.

Lorelei, Galen, and Kindra concentrated their efforts, asking appropriate questions and dispensing spot-on motions. They allocated their time wisely.

Because thinking on her feet came so easily, Dorene instructed Kindra to use only four of the five minutes in her closing statement, leaving time for rebuttal if needed. It wasn't.

The opposing attorney exceeded the time allotted in an unsuccessful bid to disrupt Team EsqChoir's easy flow. I'm not sure the seconds overtime served as the only detractor, but it lowered the overall performance score. Our kids secured a win and three first place ballots. In the power matching, points given to each performer are totaled, and the combination garnered a favorable placement for our second pairing.

Rocky bounced from foot to foot, her excitement palpable. "They can't be merely promising attorneys. They've got some magic going on. I believed every word Captain Rostron, I mean Felipe uttered, even purposely stumbling over the words about the *Carpathia* rushing to aid the *Titanic* at the expense of their own safety." She exaggerated shivering. "Gave me chills." With her eloquence, I couldn't imagine why she doubted her ability in speech.

To say our kids walked on air wouldn't do justice to the elation they felt. Who would've believed a team from west central rural Minnesota could compete at the national level against big city schools with years of experience, let alone win their first head-to-head court proceeding?

With the subsequent round scheduled after lunch, the next ninety minutes dragged on.

Lorelei paced. Her mother delivered a ham and cheese sandwich, and she shook her head. "I can't eat. I'm too nervous."

Carlee skipped to keep up with her pacing. She put a hand on her friend's shoulder to slow her down. "You need energy.

Sit. Drink some water. Eat chocolate. Order Galen around." Lorelei's shoulders relaxed a tad. "Laugh at Brock."

She dropped into a seat and sat so close to the edge, she appeared to be floating. When her jitters became so pronounced she could only nibble at the fixings on her plate, Dorene whispered something into her ear. Lorelei wriggled against the chair back and smiled.

"Did you give her one of those instructions to imagine someone in the room with red hair and a clown nose? Or anything like that?" I said, "Dare I ask?"

"You do not. It is between Lorelei and me." A Cheshire cat grin crept onto Dorene's face.

With fifteen minutes to go, they rose in a pack and hustled after Dorene and Leo to try their second case.

The gallery sat in rapt attention while Kindra gave the defense's opening statement for the less popular side of the case, at least in our estimation. "Good afternoon, Your Honor, members of the jury. Negligence is a legal term that means failing to act with the care a reasonable person would exercise in a similar situation. We are here to decide whether the plaintiff can prove by a preponderance of evidence that the White Star Line was negligent the night the *Titanic* tragically struck an iceberg and went down. Over fifteen hundred souls perished, and sadly, Mr. O'Conner was among them."

Brock led our witnesses, taking the stand convincingly as the professional, yet devastated, Second Officer Herbert Lightoller, the most senior officer to survive the sinking of the Titanic. Galen used his relatively massive athletic presence to set the stage for military attaché Mauritz Björnström-Steffansson. He testified to aiding the crew in marshaling women and children to safety while readily admitting he took the opportunity to jump from the rails of the flooded deck into an empty space at the bow of the last lifeboat to leave the ship.

Our acting ringer, lookout Reginald Lee, aka Felipe, wowed us again. Rocky silently applauded his proficiency in extemporaneous speaking, and mouthed, "He's so good." He sounded and acted just as I would have imagined Lee, and his performance provided the icing on the competitive cake.

Rocky gave the performers an ovation and looked at her watch. "I've got a rehearsal and competitive routine tonight. You're all invited. Felipe has the details. I hope you can come." She dashed out the door before I could ask any questions.

Dianne weaved through the bodies in the room and drew alongside Jane and her dad. "That was fantastic. I'm so glad I was able to see first-hand how great your team is. I can't be around tomorrow, but I wanted to wish you good luck."

"Thanks, Dianne." Dianne shook Jane's hand before getting lost in the crowd.

We moved forward with another win and three ballots as well. I threw my shoulders back and puffed out my chest. Mitchell squeezed Jane's shoulder and nodded. After Dorene and Leo gave the team time to cheer, they packed up, intending to visit with their Atlanta attorney friends for a brief tête-à-tête.

All I could think of was, *Yay, team.*

Carlee beamed at her dad who promised to check in after we attended the dance competition. Drew and Jane took a cab and the rest of us waltzed back to the hotel.

Before we ducked inside, a chill ran up my arms, and I peered from side to side to see if we'd been followed. Anyone could have hidden in plain sight on the busy street.

TWENTY-SEVEN

The brats, sauerkraut, and beans served by the attentive waitstaff in the hotel restaurant went down with less difficulty at the end of the day. Not a morsel remained on our plates. And even Lorelei had room for dessert—a scrumptious chocolate chip cheesecake.

Felipe gave us the details and easily sold us on attending Rocky's dance competition. "Here I thought I'd have to employ my tremendous powers of persuasion, but you're all pushovers."

"And you're smitten." Brock teased, but his eyes gleamed, acknowledging his own besottedness.

"Aren't we all?" Eddie chuckled, as he looked lovingly at Marietta.

I had to admit, I might've felt a few yips of my own when

I took in the tall, dark, and handsome Dr. Erickson. I sighed.

Drew arranged transportation across town to the Center for the Arts. Dancing occurred all day long, morning until night, tots to teenagers, jazz, ballet, tap, ballroom, modern, and hip-hop, but Felipe steered us through the venue with ease. "Some of our large speech meets were like this. If you didn't learn the map quickly, you might miss your cue."

"And we wouldn't want that to happen," Galen chided.

Rocky's distinguished team held court in the giant auditorium with other well-established sizeable programs. The Duluth troupe shone with artistry and skill, dancing to *Breath of Life* recorded by Florence and the Machine for *Snow White and the Huntsman*. Rocky performed her part at the forefront of her company as the evil queen, leaping, stretching, arching, bending, and spinning. Her villainous, animated facial expressions captivated the spectators as they transformed from powerful beauty to sinister collapse and disappearance. If I hadn't recognized her, I never would have figured out she rigged her costume to magically convert and match the others on her dance team. She melted seamlessly into the chorus line. We gave them a well-deserved standing ovation augmented by almost everyone in the audience. During the lengthy applause, Rocky failed to maintain her stolid comportment and winked at Felipe. Then the ensemble marched from the stage in perfect synchronicity.

We hadn't seen the entire registry of competitors, but we didn't need to. The yelping and shrieking girls from Duluth acquired a three-foot tall first place trophy, and when their excitement died down to a dull roar, Rocky bolted from her team.

"Thank you for coming." Her voice sang out as she slid off the edge of the stage. "What did you think?"

"Beyond awesome," said Brock, who rocked back and forth after receiving a tiny, friendly shove, first from Lorelei and then from Felipe.

A frown took over her face, and her bottom lip protruded in an exaggerated pout. "Our ballet gig is tomorrow morning, so I won't be able to attend your trial. But please make sure someone texts to tell me how well it goes. You were tremendous today, so I know you'll be amazing." A few of her friends shouted from the stage. "I gotta go. We're eating at this fancy restaurant tonight, but good luck tomorrow." Felipe reddened as she drew her index finger along his jawline.

Rocky blew in and out like a whirlwind. "Good luck to you too," we yelled to her retreating back. She tossed a wave of acknowledgment.

We navigated the colorful costumed and multi-sized participants to the front doors, beyond which our bus parked. Lester sat behind the wheel. He hadn't expected to transport us from this venue, and I didn't know who was more flabbergasted. I thought he was going to put the vehicle in gear and drive away. I read his face with its second or maybe third thoughts, and while he debated the best course of action, the kids tramped up the steps, oblivious to his consternation and my hesitation.

The bus bounced down the streets, and Kindra raised her hand. "Could we get together for a debriefing of the day? We got to play the defendant and plaintiff parts and won both, but if you have any suggestions, feelings, or ideas, we'd certainly give them serious consideration."

All the kids nodded.

"We know we have a good thing and want to make sure we're prepared for tomorrow."

Lester's eyes flicked from the rearview mirror to the side

mirror and the GPS all the way to the hotel. The boisterous kids didn't notice the obvious relief in his face when he drove off.

"Good evening, folks. Sounds like you had a great day." The doorman's cherubic cheeks barely contained his smile. "Welcome back."

We split up to ride the elevators. The rapid climb to our floor ended in a tie, and the lurch to a stop made my excited stomach flip.

The doors slid to the side, and Pete asked quietly, "Are you alright?"

"Big day." I giggled to hide my embarrassment. "And Maverick and Renegade are due shortly." I could use some steadying canine care.

"Let's convene in the Mackey/Wilk war room in ten minutes," said Drew, looking protectively at Jane.

He supported her calculated pace to our room where we met Samara exiting.

"All has been quiet today. No new husbands," she said. She smiled broadly and set her fists on her curvy hips. "If you need anything at all, give me a call." Her smooth, warm voice soothed my nervousness.

"Thanks, Samara," said Jane, entering and oohing in admiration of the towel elephant on her bed and the crab on mine. I wondered if Samara had a subliminal intent.

I called, but neither Dorene nor Leo picked up their phones. Leo texted.

Out with friends. What do you need?

Any advice for the kids? We're meeting in ten minutes for an impromptu pep talk.

Tell them I think they're wonderful and to get some sleep. Tomorrow will be another big day. If Dorene has any advice she wants to impart, we'll connect.

Ten minutes to the dot later, Drew opened the door to the heavy rap, and the kids charged inside, dropping cross-legged onto the floor like a room full of kindergarteners.

"What do you have for us, Ms. Wilk?" asked Carlee.

I didn't want to give away my utter satisfaction with today's outcomes right away, so I focused on my shoes.

"That bad, huh?" said Galen.

I looked into his eyes, and he couldn't miss my delight. He had a habit of punching the air over his head, a quiet hurrah. "Yessss," he said, appeased.

"You need to get impressions from Mr. Kidd and Dr. Erickson. They watched your presentation, and they'll give you fair and unbiased observations. I've witnessed your growth, but you've become so much more eloquent. I'm predisposed to think you're the best team at this tournament."

My phone buzzed. I took too long studying the screen, and Galen said, "You gonna get that?"

I accepted the FaceTime communication and flashed Dorene's visage around the room.

"Whoot. Whoot," she yelled, and dropped into her serious mode immediately. "But for tomorrow …"

Before I could drown in a sea of anxious teens, I passed my phone to Galen so the kids could get a better view. Dorene was nothing if not thorough, and I had a few minutes to think about Wendell.

Pete sidled next to me and whispered, "Why so intense?"

He had an uncanny ability to read my mind, so I told him. "Lester hadn't really been a contender for Wendell's murder, at least in my book, until the ride tonight. He looked guilty. I don't know of what, but when we need a driver again, I'll definitely ask for someone else."

"I noticed his discomfort too. You do what you have to do." Pete's charming brown eyes caught mine, and I swallowed hard. "What else are you thinking?"

Jane leaned close. "I'm curious too."

"Do you think we should go home? Do you think the kids are still safe?"

"I took two more days off," Pete said. "You have at least one adult per student. We'll take care of them."

"And we have Dad's security detail keeping track of us," Jane added.

Galen returned my phone, singing, "Goodnight, Ms. Dvorak, goodnight."

"Hang up already," Dorene said, and ended the call.

Another phone rang. All eyes turned toward Jane. She read the screen and smiled brightly. "Hi, Dad."

My phone barked with the easily identifiable ring tone for CJ Bluestone, and I accepted the call. My face crinkled. I hoped Maverick behaved today. He usually minded CJ, but one never knew how a dog might act. I turned toward the window and cupped my hand over my ear to hear better and not interrupt Jane and her dad. "Hello, Dr. Bluestone. Is everything okay? Are you on your way?"

"Katie," he said. "The police are here."

I heard a gasp, spun on my heels, and watched the color drain from Jane's face. Her hand dropped into her lap. "Katie, we have to stay. They've arrested Dad for Wendell's murder."

TWENTY-EIGHT

Mitchell's first phone call had been to his daughter, so Drew and Jane helped make the necessary legal arrangements.

Marietta, Eddie, Pete and I shepherded the solemn kids to their rooms with instructions to update their parents. The four of us gravitated to the lounge. Marietta cast her eyes out the picture windows over the nightscape dotted with varied colors and hues, and Eddie's hand rested on her shoulder. Pete used his wise doctor sense and kept his own counsel.

Minutes passed. A soft ringing broke the silence. After a short, quiet conversation, Marietta pocketed her phone and turned to me, her brow etched in concern. "The unanimous parental consensus is we should stay and compete, Katie. I hope we will." She worked up a small smile. "We're confident our children will be as safe with you as anywhere else."

"Please," came the appeals from the doorway, where seven faces peeked around the jamb. "We'll do whatever you tell us." Every voice had something else to say. "Promise." "No doubt." "Scout's honor."

Six faces revolved as one, checking the source of the last comment. Galen said, "You're not a Scout, Felipe," and Felipe had the wherewithal to screw up his face and blush.

Pete took my hand. "It's up to you."

"Let me talk to Dorene."

Fortunately, I didn't put my phone on speaker. After I explained what had happened, Dorene spouted all sorts of words I couldn't repeat in front of my kids but promised to assist in Mitchell's defense to the degree she'd be allowed.

Leo retrieved the receiver and picked up where she left off. "The kids will come first, but Dorene is a proficient multitasker. And she has me. See you tomorrow."

Sleep was elusive. Jane rolled and sighed. Her restlessness finally abated, but the last time I checked, the sky boasted too much red, yellow, and orange. The daunting adage, 'red in the morning, sailors take warning,' only made me want to duck under the pillow for the rest of the day.

Instead, I rose and crept around the room, getting ready as noiselessly as possible until Jane said, without opening her eyes, "I'm awake."

We began to talk at the same time, and I finally said, "You first."

"I know you're going to tell me to be with Dad, but I can't. His attorney won't let me anywhere near him. I need to keep busy, so I'm going to be at the courthouse with our successful mock trial team. No arguments."

"No arguments, but, Jane, what could've made them possibly believe your dad had anything to do with Wendell's death?" I resolved to do everything I could to help Jane prove Mitchell's innocence.

She breathed deeply. "The motives are apparent."

"Motives as in plural?"

She held up one finger. "The dissolution of the business partnership was fair, although not amicable. Over the years, Wendell accused my dad of many shenanigans. Did the charges affect the bottom line of Dad's business? I don't know. One of the accounts Dad manages for veterans is short, therefore, one motive is money."

"How much is it short?"

She scratched her chin and took her sweet time to answer. "A total of eleven million dollars over four years. He's been searching, but …" She hurriedly went on and raised a second finger. "Wendell allegedly stole some confidential plans, whatever they might be. If he was the reason our plane went down with us on board, Dad could have wanted revenge." She forcefully shook three fingers at me and spat angrily. "And to top it off, Felicity parroted the fabricated story of Wendell's mom's liaison with my dad. Anger. Three convincing motives, even if they are inadequate." Jane's jaw tightened. "Wendell," she hissed, clearly aggravated. "They can't hold him. They just can't. And we can't leave."

"But how does the dimethyl chemical connect with your dad?"

She breathed deeply. "Early in his flying career, Dad dusted crops with a pesticide that used that stuff. He doesn't use it now, but they are assuming he knows where to get it." Her sad eyes brightened for a second. "You look awful."

I had no comeback.

My search for appropriate clothing for the day yielded a power suit much like Dorene's. Since Jane always dressed to the nines, I found it mildly disturbing she put on blue jeans and a Columbia Cougars polo shirt, so I set out to dress accordingly. While rooting around in my drawers for alternate attire, I dislodged a familiar white card and froze. The waterlogged card had dried, taking on the soft curled look of papier-mâché, and the circles and lines had warped a bit, but it had completed the journey with me.

"We should go soon." My head said to listen to Jane, but my legs wouldn't move. I stared at the card. "What's that?" She held out her hand.

"I found it in the cockpit when you were saving my life, and I slipped it into my pocket. It just came along with everything else."

She examined one side of the card. "It's an analog flight checklist." She turned it over. "Are these circles on the back like the markings on the comic book?"

I pulled on my own jeans and polo, brushed my hair, and swiped my magic mascara wand over my lashes while Jane studied the card.

"You memorized the alphabetic substitutions, didn't you?"

I pointed out what I thought was obvious. "The decoder in the escape room displayed the symbols in alphabetic order, arranged in groups of four similar signs, except for the characters matched with e and f. I think it went like this." I recalled the alphabetic progression matching the symbols I'd memorized in the escape room, drawing the signs on the hotel notepad on the nightstand.

"Is there a message on the card? Can you make heads or tails of it?"

"The circles have the same general appearance, but there are more than twenty-six symbols here, and some are not at all the same." I buried my face in my hands and rubbed my temples. Another solution presented itself, and my eyes widened.

"What?" said Jane, watching my internal struggle.

I dug out the history of cryptology and paged past The Roaring 20s. "Listen to this. 'In the 1930s, Maxwell Grant, the pseudonym for Walter B. Gibson, often wrote curious codes for his popular radio show hero, the Shadow, and here are a few examples.'"

Jane peered at the page. "The symbols look the same."

"And the new symbols are right here."

"Does it work?"

The alarm on Jane's phone rang, her reminder for our breakfast meeting with the kids. "Later," I said. I searched for a good place to keep the card and opted to slide it inside the cover of the room service menu, securing it under the TV remote control.

Two behemoths in black suits and sunglasses materialized at the elevators and greeted us with a slight nod. "Security?" I whispered to Jane, unnerved.

She made a strange face. "Maybe."

"You don't know?" I yelped. "What if they're not from your dad? We can't even ask him." I could hear blood thrumming in my ears.

Our students streamed out of their rooms, and my fight-or-flight response readied itself to kick in. I rushed between our kids and the men in black. Three more doors released Drew and Pete, Marietta and Eddie, and Leo. Drew sauntered up to monster man one and said, "Morning, Timmy. How're you doing today?"

The incongruous, high pitch of his squeaky voice tickled my funny bone, and I tamped down my nervous laugh.

"Great, Mr. Kidd. Nothing to report this morning."

Drew pressed the call button. When the cars arrived, Timmy held one door for the first half of us to enter. The additional hulk stationed at the control panel inside gave me goosebumps on top of goosebumps, but if Drew trusted these guys, so did I.

We ate a scrumptious breakfast in the company of the giant protectors who accompanied us to the courthouse. With our power index rating, we remained in the upper half of our bracket. Lorelei drew the side we'd represent, and the team effervesced when it was revealed we'd offer the case for the plaintiff first again. The kids paraded confidently to their positions in the empty courtroom, and we had our choice of seats.

Of all our dramatizations, Mitchell's protection detail chose the best trial to watch and were duly impressed. Our team performed better than they did on the first day. Their jitters had evaporated. Every word uttered had meaning and fit the context of the case. Patricia had one instance of hesitancy when she glanced into the gallery. She might have missed part of a question, but she never halted her fluid performance. The moment was so fleeting, I could've imagined it.

After picking at lunch, our team posted another victory, winning all three votes and adding a huge number of points to their total, and they couldn't wait for the last round before finals. Jane smiled through her sadness and reminded me to contact *La Petite Salle de Manger* and up our reservation number to include Drew, Pete, CJ, her dad (fingers crossed), and the four members of the protection detail. Lorelei's calm demeanor allowed her classmates the luxury of imperturbability, confident in their skills. I relaxed until Felipe approached with a face full of worry.

"What's up, Felipe? You've done so well."

"It's Rocky."

I shook my head and smiled. Young love, I thought.

"She skipped the ballet performance this morning."

"That doesn't sound like Rocky. How did you find out?"

"Her roommate called. She's taken off a few times while she's been in Atlanta. She supposedly went early this morning to meet up with me, but she's always answered her texts. She's missing."

TWENTY-NINE

I'm sure she's all right." My skin crawled, not sure if I believed what I said. "She knows Atlanta like the back of her hand, and she has relatives here. Have they contacted her aunt?"

"I think they're too mad yet to be worried. She's kind of new to the dance troupe, and you saw her. She's a prima donna. Some of the other girls lost their place in the lineup because she's just that good, but I know she wouldn't disappoint them. She's always been a team player." Confusion masked the other emotions on his face.

The ten-minute warning gong sounded. "Go compete. Play your part. Be amazing. You're a team player too." He started to interrupt me. "I'll find her," I said, with much more assurance than I felt.

He tried to squelch his skepticism, maybe convincing himself by saying, "Okay, Ms. Wilk."

I texted a short message of excuse to Jane and Pete, but when I looked up, Felipe hadn't moved very far. "Go." I waved him in the direction of our courtroom. "I've got this." He spun on his heels, and the crowd swallowed him.

My phone buzzed. Thinking Jane or Pete wanted clarification, I answered before checking caller ID.

The awful, modulated voice said, "I'm watching. You're never alone." I immediately scanned the atrium, surrounded by a dizzying array of strangers. "If you want the kid to stay healthy, bring me the flash drive."

My heart jumped to my throat. "What are you talking about? Let me talk to Rocky." No response. How would they know Rocky was missing unless they'd taken her? "What flash drive?" I trembled. The only flash drive in my possession came from the Mock Trial America organization and contained files labeled Rules of the Competition and General Information. Before we'd arrived in Atlanta, I'd accessed them enough to memorize the contents.

"MJ Suites, Peachtree Place. Come alone. Fifteen minutes," the voice croaked.

I squeaked out, "I don't have—"

The voice clicked off. I punched the destination into my phone and exited the courthouse. I'd never make it to our hotel to collect my one USB, and hailing a nonexistent cab or calling a ride share would take time I didn't have. According to the GPS, walking could take eighteen minutes to get to the MJ. I broke into a run. Rocky's safety was more important than the flash drive.

My mind raced. Once I confirmed Rocky's location, I could explain the mix-up, ask for clarification, gain time—or offer myself in her place. She was just a kid.

I often walked my dog for long distances at a brisk pace but never considered myself a runner, so I channeled my inner Jane to keep putting one foot in front of the other, employing a speed I'd never tapped. With my face glued to the map on my phone screen, I nearly collided with a woman dressed in a red skirt suit and sky-high heels. The look she gave me could have frozen a bolt of lightning.

"Sorry." I tossed the word over my shoulder and continued along the route, though I paid more attention to my surroundings. I dodged customers exiting a coffee shop, unleashing the ambrosial aroma of java and bakery delicacies. No one spilled a savory drop on my account, but the group of tourists lined up in front of a fountain in one of the parks would be unpleasantly surprised by the frantic woman photobombing their landscape memories. A flock of pigeons, congregating on the sidewalk, scattered. My hands flew up to protect my face from the flapping wings and I skied through a whitewash of bird droppings I'd overlooked.

Eleven minutes remained.

Slow-moving cars honked when I scooted between them and tripped onto the curb. I darted between hustling executives and gawking visitors, some never even noticed. Red and yellow lights became merely suggestions of slowing. I trusted the GPS directions funneling me down the busy streets, though the tall commercial buildings lined my path and hid my destination.

Seven minutes.

The impact of the familiar building façade stopped me cold. I'd been here before. Shifting only my eyes, I recognized the storefront and the street. Bathed in cloudy daylight, the escape room lost a bit of its nighttime luster. Why so close to here, I wondered?

Six minutes.

My injured knee throbbed, a painful reminder of the trek through the Nantahala National Forest. I pushed off on the other leg, dashed the remaining distance, and skidded to a halt. The multi-story terminus loomed in front of me. I checked my watch. Four minutes remained. I bent over and my hands clenched my knees. My ragged breathing drowned out the sounds of the city. Precious seconds ticked by as I gasped.

"Now what?" I said to the empty space, loud enough to muffle the first ring of my phone. I cut off the second ring. "Where is she?" I hissed into the mouthpiece. Jostled from behind, my phone flew from my hands. I plucked it out of the air. Too late. The call dropped, and the silent phone gave up nothing.

I raced inside and scanned the open space, wondering where Rocky could be. Across the lobby at the bank of elevators, at least twenty people waited to purchase admission tickets for the upper floor destination. I skimmed the Chamber of Commerce tourist brochures filling the slots of the three-tiered display stretching along the wall. One pamphlet stuffed into the top row stood out.

The name 'Wilk' written in thick red marker arched across the top. I jerked it from the stand. It ripped. I dug my fingers into the opening and fished out the bottom half.

The folded paper crinkled as I opened the bottom half with shaking hands. Nothing. I flipped it over. Zilch. No instructions. No note. Opening the other half revealed an arrow, and I joined the line for the Brave's Observation Deck.

We slowly crawled ahead, and an impatient hand shoved me forward. My clumsy stumbling began a slow tumble of patrons, like meticulously lined up dominoes falling in precise rhythm. Before anyone held me accountable, a woman pointed out the culprit and shouted, "She did it. I saw her push you."

I looked behind me. Natalianna lifted her shoulders and raised her hands in a gesture of supplication. Perhaps she wanted forgiveness. My eyes narrowed as I climbed to standing. She looked up and pointed to the upper deck sign.

I could've gone after her, but I promised Felipe I'd find Rocky. I glanced at the ticket agent and when I looked back, Natalianna had vanished.

Nothing I did, or didn't do, sped up the process. Buying tickets seemed to take an hour, but according to my watch, it had only been fourteen minutes since the first phone call. I marched onto the elevator, realizing as the doors closed, this elevator had glass walls.

Once past floor eight, the elevator skipped the rest. Sandwiched between the clear view to the outside and a large man wearing blue jeans, a flannel shirt, and a cowboy hat, my knees gave out, but I couldn't go anywhere as we hurtled to the sixty-fifth floor. The car rose and the clouds descended. I couldn't wait for the haze to obscure the view of downtown Atlanta. Only then could I imagine I was back on terra firma.

The doors whooshed apart. Trapped by the shoulders of the other riders and swept out into the stream of excitement, I was deposited on the top level. With an unsteady gait, I inched along the wall at a snail's pace, scouring the faces of those admiring the breathtaking views. No one looked even a little like Rocky. Working up my courage, I inched closer to the short wall of an overhang. Almost paralyzed by the height, I clenched the top rail and leaned forward, peering into the restaurant below.

THIRTY

Rocky looked small, sitting alone with perfect posture, at a four-person table, staring out the gigantic window high, too high, above the city, unmoving.

My knees wobbled. I backed as far from the edge as I could and still keep her in my sights. I called Pete. The phone rang and rang. Of course, he didn't answer. The team was only twenty minutes into their fourth trial. I took a breath when I thought the call would go to voicemail. Instead, I heard his warm baritone. "Katie?"

"I found Rocky," I stammered. Ignoring everything else, I focused on her and carefully made my way to the restaurant.

"Where are you? Timmy followed Felipe. His partner assumed you wouldn't miss the trial and would be right behind them, so he followed Timmy too." A teensy bit of frustration crept in to his voice, replacing the initial tone of worry. "I've been calling since you sent that cryptic text."

One quick glance at my blank screen showed no record of calls missed. "They must have jammed my phone."

"Who jammed your phone?"

"I'm not sure. Felipe worried when Rocky didn't make her ballet performance this morning, and I got a call telling me I had to get to the MJ Suites within fifteen minutes if I wanted to see her safe. And hand over a flash drive. Rocky's here in the restaurant on the top floor. I'm going to her now."

"I'll be right there. Don't move."

"No problem. I don't think I can." I breathed deeply, lowering my voice as I closed the gap between Rocky and me. "Are our kids okay?"

He didn't answer right away, and I held my breath. "I left the room before the trial began, but Jane wasn't happy."

"That I can handle. See you soon."

I fumbled my way to the table, brushing by busy waitstaff and a figure wearing a Braves' sweatshirt and baseball cap. I knelt by her side and said softly, "Rocky? It's Ms. Wilk."

She turned her tear-streaked face to look at me. "Did you find Felipe? Is he okay?" She frantically scanned the room, collapsed in my arms, and squeezed an oomph from me.

"Felipe is fine. Why?"

"Where'd that other chaperone go?" Her voice quavered.

I held her a little away from me so I could read her body language; she conveyed fear in every muscle, every bone, every hair on her head, the very fiber of her being. "Who, Rocky?"

Her forehead scrunched with worry. "You must've just missed him."

"What did he want?"

"A guy called early this morning, and said Felipe wanted to get together for a bagel before we got too busy. I should've known better. I tried to check with Felipe, but our phones wouldn't connect. The guy didn't make me go with him or anything. He kept saying if it didn't work out, Felipe would understand and meet up with me soon. I really wanted to wish him good luck. When we landed up here, the guy took a call and told me Felipe had disappeared. He said, if Felipe was alright, he'd come here looking for me. Felipe's my friend, so I waited in case he needed me. I couldn't let anything happen to him. You're sure he's okay?"

"He was never in danger." But I didn't believe my own words. Timmy and his crew added an extra layer to the protective barrier surrounding my students, but it sounded like the *guy* was using Rocky to lure Felipe away until I came along.

She fumed, angry someone had used her. Her eyes opened wide. "You're missing the second trial today."

I shrugged and sat in the seat across from her. "My friend will come for us shortly. Are you ready to leave?" She nodded. "Are you hungry? Or thirsty?"

She shook her head. "I really have to use the restroom. I was afraid to move. The last thing he said was I might miss Felipe if I didn't stay right here. Now, I'm furious." She narrowed her eyes and gritted her teeth.

Rallying anger-wrapped fortitude from somewhere deep inside, I stood and shot a quick daring glance over the city. I scoped out the restrooms and led the way. "Felipe's with the team. He's fine. I don't know what's going on, Rocky, but you're safe now."

She scrubbed the fear from her face and pasted on the insouciant crooked smile I missed. "You're okay, Ms. Wilk."

While we waited for Pete, I asked, "Would you recognize the man who took you?"

She shook her head. "He had on baseball stuff and wore a disposable face mask." She shuddered. So did I. I think I bumped into him when I made my way through the tables in the restaurant while keeping my eyes on Rocky. "He said he'd take it off if I wanted, but he'd been sneezing up a storm. All I could think of was germs." She shivered. "I told him he could keep it on. It was kinda weird, but believable, too, you know."

A vision of Natalianna invaded my head. "And you're sure it was a man?"

Rocky nodded and looked down at her shoes. "I'm sorry."

"You have nothing to be sorry for. We'll straighten everything out with your dance instructors. I think they missed you too."

Rocky seemed at a loss for words and eyed me suspiciously.

"Your roommate is the one who called Felipe."

Rocky's brows shot up and her face seemed to shine. "She did? Really?"

I nodded, but before I could assure her, some hustling uniformed bodies caught Rocky's attention, and she stiffened. Pete led the way, with Knight and Day at his heels. Pete draped one arm around me and the other around Rocky. "How're we doing?"

Knight understood the trauma incurred by victims. Rocky answered Knight's few and gentle questions and finally said, "He scared me at first, but I'm so mad right now, I could spit tacks. I'll do everything I can so this will never happen to anyone I know." She hopped from the seat. "Do you think I could make my tap performance tonight?"

They finished talking, and Knight provided a list of resources along with her business card. "Call anytime, night or day."

Rocky pointed back and forth and chortled with half a grin. Day stood to escort Rocky to the dance venue, and indicated he'd stay with her through her final performance. Rocky took one step toward the exit and turned abruptly. She flew back into my arms, wrapping me in a huge embrace. "Thanks," she said, pulling away and wiping her eyes. "We leave on the red eye tonight. Cheap flight. Tell Felipe I'll keep in touch. And he owes me. Big time."

When they'd gone, Knight came at me, punching out her questions. "What were you thinking? Why didn't you notify someone? Anything could have happened. I should arrest you for obstruction of justice and hampering a police investigation. You're lucky the kid's unharmed."

The truth hurt. I looked down at my hands and murmured, "The kid's name is Rocky."

"Why did they go after her and call you for a flash drive?"

"I don't know." I shook my head. "She's a friend of one of my students. She must've been seen with our team, but ..." A thought occurred to me. "What if it's connected to Gromm? Doesn't this prove Mr. Mackey didn't kill Wendell?"

"Totally unconnected."

"How do you know?"

"Officer Knight," Pete said, closing his hand over mine. "This is neither the time nor the place. Katie did what she thought she had to do. I probably would have done the same. Do you have questions for her, or can I take her back to her team?"

Roused by his compassion, I lifted my head and tamped down my frustration. "I didn't have enough time to do everything I should've done. I apologize. The ... What do I call him?"

"I'd call him a kidnapper," Knight snarled. "But she

willingly went with him. Her coach said she has a track record of disappearing, and we don't have proof he threatened her," she lamented quietly.

"The kidnapper wanted a flash drive, but I only have one. On it are files for the mock trial competition. I had fifteen minutes to get to Rocky. I didn't waste time retrieving a worthless drive. The voice on the line said I was being watched. I think there was supposed to be a handoff, but I never received the final message. The call dropped. But," I locked eyes with Knight. "Kuznetsov was in the atrium and showed me where to go. Without her, I don't know if I would have found Rocky. Doesn't that prove it relates to Gromm?"

"Are you positive Kuznetsov was here?" Knight's hand went to her radio.

"She vanished right after she pointed to the observation deck sign. But remember, Rocky's sure it was a man who brought her. Maybe Kuznetsov's a partner in this. I don't know."

Knight's chest rose and fell as she sucked in a breath and said, "You're free to go, but don't leave Atlanta without talking to me first."

With Rocky's safe return and my eyes locked on Pete's dimple, the ride down wasn't nearly as terrifying as the ride up, until he said. "We have a dinner tonight, right?"

My breath caught and I raised my watch to check the time. "Graduation!"

"Relax." His set his chin on top of my head and tugged me close. Although I could no longer see the dimple, I knew it was there. I closed my eyes and breathed in the reassuring scent of his aftershave. "We still have time. Let's go back to the courthouse and join the kids. While you were talking to Officer Knight, Drew texted. The kids didn't win this round, but they're waiting for their final placement."

"They lost." I leaned away so I could see his face and make certain I understood his words about their placement.

"Ah, but power matching is fairly involved. They have ten out of twelve first place votes and they accumulated a sky-high point total for their performances." He looked as proud as I felt. "They're on the verge of making it to the finals."

THIRTY-ONE

Two teams brought forward a grievance to the committee in charge of the meet, and they suspended the announcement of the results. We had no control over the resolution and would be notified of the final decision by email, so we elected to walk back to the hotel and await the outcome.

"Was she okay, Ms. Wilk?" asked Felipe, matching me stride for stride. "Was Rocky okay?"

"She worries about you too, Felipe. Officer Knight talked to her. Officer Day won't leave her alone while she's in Atlanta, and her team will be on its way home tonight, but she said she'll keep in touch."

Relief washed over his face. "That's good. Why would anyone do that to her?" In my head I screamed, *somehow it was my fault.* He lifted his chin. "Ms. Wilk, it's my fault we didn't win the last trial."

I thought I misheard him. "What?"

"It was my fault. I couldn't concentrate. My performance was second rate."

"Oh, no you don't." I gave him a cheesy smile, thinking the words I said could easily apply to me. "Our team did much better than anyone expected. You can't hold yourself singularly responsible for the loss any more than you can take sole credit for the wins."

He stammered, "I didn't … I wouldn't …"

"Of course not. The bottom line is, did you have fun?" He almost rolled his eyes. "Discounting the scare that came with Rocky being spirited away, that is."

He conceded.

"And you're planning to continue to compete in mock trial next year?"

He nodded.

"Then everyone wins. It takes a whole team." I realized Rocky's abduction had more to do with the perpetrator than the fault of any one person, me included.

The walk across the hotel lobby taxed my aching muscles, put more pressure on my knee, and took extra effort. By the time the elevators gave us up, the subdued kids searched for guidance, eyeing one another. Giving direction was one of my jobs. I gathered what little energy I had left and said, "Let's meet in the lounge."

After each of them nestled into a comfortable position, I said, "First of all, I want you to know Rocky is safe and will be returning to Minnesota tonight after her dance." The kids hooted and applauded. "But we need to be diligent and watchful. Stay safe. Secondly, congratulations. What a super week. We're celebrating tonight with dinner at a French restaurant."

Lorelei knew the plan and gave Brock a knowing side-eye. She'd conspired with our principal to make it happen, and she'd never forgive me if I blew the surprise, so I plastered on a serious teacher look.

"We have a few hours before our transportation arrives, so rest up, change clothes, and call your parents. Timmy and his crew have stationed themselves at equal intervals down the hall. I trust them. You don't have to stay in your rooms, just don't leave the floor. If the mock trial results come, I'll be sure to let you know immediately. Questions?"

Lorelei yawned loudly, and it was contagious. "Sorry," she said, giggling—like tiny bells to my ears.

"Let's meet by the elevators at six forty-five." We gathered in the center of the room, punched our fists together in the circle, bounced to a count of three, tossed them up in the air, and shouted, "EsqChoir!"

Jane waited for the kids to disperse. As we walked down the corridor, she clenched my arm. "Katie, Drew and I are going to visit my dad. I'm sure we'll be back in plenty of time for the evening's event, but I have to know what's going on."

"Of course you do. We'll be fine even if you're late. Take your time and give your dad a hug from me." She released me in front of our room, and they hustled to the elevators, followed closely by one of our guardians.

Pete opened my door and put his considerate spin on the words Jane used hours earlier. "You look awfully tired." He led me in and handed me the keycard. "Rest up and I'll return in an hour."

I leaned back against the closing door and shut my eyes, humming in satisfaction. "Back in an hour." Sleep almost overtook me, but I peeled my eyelids open, one at a time, and lugged my tired bones to the closet. I toted my backpack into the room and opened the outside flap and searched. The mock trial flash drive wasn't there. Unzipping the pack, I shoved the books to one side, scraped the bottom, and frowned. I couldn't find my only drive there either, so I opened my drawers and shuffled the clothes from side to side. Dumping the contents of my purse didn't yield any results either. No flash drive. I remembered removing it from my backpack when Wendell and I supposedly went off for help and thought I'd seen it again, but with everything going on, I could've been mistaken. Maybe Jane had an idea where it might be, or maybe whoever wanted it had already nicked it.

Giving up, I hurtled myself onto the bed and nestled into the plush pillow. Wrapped in the thick comforter, I picked up the checklist card and tried to study the circle code on the back. I nodded off, but my tumultuous dreams didn't allow much rest.

The nightmare began with Wendell hunched over my backpack, piecing together a three-D puzzle. When finished, he inserted an oversized flash drive in the outside pocket and heaved it onto his shoulder, only to launch it off a ledge with me strapped to it. I soared through the air and landed in a perfume laboratory, squeezed into a beaker, unable to breathe past suffocating floral fumes.

When the effluvium cleared, Dianne appeared, dutifully distributing playing cards covered in circles to the confused passengers on Mitchell's plane. I imagined screaming as the plane dived again toward the forest floor. Jane slid the curtain to the side, but instead of uncovering Noah and Richard, Lester sat at the controls. In the midst of his cackling, he said, "I'm new. I don't know anything about this."

The plane spiraled and dropped from the sky. Rather than waking from the nightmare, I landed in roiling river water. The splash scrubbed the scene revealing Kuznetsov, exultantly hijacking our bus remotely from a cardboard box, steering it toward the escape room. The tire on the bus exploded and rhythmically whacked the pavement until the bus rolled to a stop.

I sat upright. Glad to be roused from the frightening images, I shook the fuzziness from my head and glanced at the clock. I'd only slept for fifteen minutes. I clenched my eyes and launched back onto the mattress, grasping at the fleeting straws in my dream before I forgot them all.

The exploded tire continued thumping, and the tenuous thoughts blasted out of reach. I reluctantly slithered from the bed and found Timmy's apologetic face on the other side of the peephole. I opened the door. "What is it, Timmy?" I whispered, afraid of his answer.

"A woman tried to get off on this floor. When I wouldn't allow her access, she scribbled a note and asked that I deliver it to Ms. Mackey, immediately. I know Ms. Mackey's with Agent Kidd, but if it's urgent, I thought maybe you should see it."

Remembering what happened to Rocky, I didn't want to leave anything to chance. I was in charge. "I'll take responsibility."

He handed over the tri-fold page. "Let me know if you need any help." He tipped his head and marched to the empty chair situated at the bank of elevators.

I pinched one tiny corner of the onion skin stationery between by thumb and forefinger, shook it open, and read the words beneath the embossed monogram, 'I was Wendell Gromm's fiancée, and I believe my life is in danger. Please come to room 220. If you have doubts, Google me.'

In order to mask the hollowness in our room, I read

aloud from the latest of many gossip resources populated by my query on the web. "The sole beneficiary of Dennis Diaz's gazillion dollar estate, daughter, Miranda, has dissuaded her multitude of suitors, saying, 'Heart of my heart, Wendell Gromm, has proposed and I've accepted. We expect to host a late fall wedding.'" Wendell would have married a classic beauty, but she certainly wasn't Felicity Williams.

A great puff of air escaped from my lips, and I knew I had to talk to Miranda. But I'd control the situation.

I plunged my face in a sink full of cold water and patted it dry, cataloging questions I'd need her to answer. In my haste to get the facts first, I had almost turned the door handle but stopped, stung by my recent reprimand, and wisely punched in the number for Officer Knight. Her voicemail kicked in. "This is Katie Wilk. A woman in room two twenty at our hotel is claiming to be Gromm's fiancée. I don't know if it's true, but I'm sharing the information I've been given. Call me. I'm going to ask Dr. Erickson to accompany me to meet this woman." As an afterthought, I said, "And Timmy."

THIRTY-TWO

Pete answered my soft knock. "That was the shortest cat nap I've ever seen."

"Don't tell Maverick. I call it a power nap." I handed him Miranda's note and stood quietly in the hall, growing uncomfortable as he read and reread it. What if he thought we should avoid this woman?

"Let's take Timmy," he said.

"I had the same idea."

We locked arms and approached Timmy, who argued against our plan to meet Miranda Diaz, having guaranteed Mitchell nothing would happen to our group. I'd already tested the limits of his coverage when I went after Rocky, and he looked wary.

"When Jane returns, you'll never be able to keep her from

Miranda. Wouldn't you rather we find out what she wants without bothering the boss's daughter?"

After huddling with the other two men, he relented and pressed the elevator button. "Let's get this done."

Never one to go empty-handed, I pocketed two pre-packaged, so-called gourmet brownies, which would have made my landlady cringe, and two bottles of water from the fridge in the meeting room. We rode the elevator in tense silence. I let Timmy lead the way down the comparatively dismal corridor and rap on the door of room two twenty. A cranky voice hollered from deep within the confines of the room, "Who is it?"

Timmy and Pete looked at me. "Katie Wilk. I'm a friend of Jane Mackey."

The door flew open, and a saucer-eyed, wild-haired brunette grabbed my arm and hauled me inside, slamming the door on Pete and Timmy, effectively locking them out. Their banging began in earnest. "Just a minute," she said in the same sing-song voice as Disney's cartoon Cinderella.

"Miranda, what do you want?"

She tossed her hair back and stuck her nose up in the air. She snatched one of the brownie packets, tore it open, and crammed a large bite in her mouth. She swallowed hard and wiped crumbs from her chin. "I want Jane Mackey to know if something happens to me, Felicity did it."

"Why would Felicity do anything to you?"

She scratched the backs of her hands, already red and scraped. "We've known each other for ages. I was her assistant fragrance chemist and confidant. When I deviated from her mother's magic formula and decided to go organic, we parted ways but remained friends. I just couldn't use those poisonous chemicals any longer and feel good about it."

Alarm bells clanged in my head. "Excuse me. What

poisonous chemicals?"

"Formaldehyde, benzene, DMS, phthalates, and the list goes on."

"Does DMS stand for dimethyl sulfate?" I cocked my head, trying to figure out if I believed her.

"Yes." She nodded. "It's used in synthesizing some pharmaceuticals and manufacturing dyes and perfumes, but my formulae are safe to use. Dad initially invested in my perfumes, and when they became successful, Wendell said he'd help me market them. I knew Wendell, of course. He'd been in and out of Felicity's life forever. They were like oil and water—a dangerous mix of personalities. After their last break up, they came to blows."

I cringed. Had Wendell been a carbon copy of his father? Did Felicity still wear a scar on her neck from an exchange with Wendell?

"Wendell continued to work with her, but I didn't realize she'd been expecting him to crawl back on his hands and knees again. He said he'd had enough. He'd fallen for me. I was the true love of his life." As Jane noted about Felicity, Miranda had looks and money as well. They traveled in an entirely different circle than mine.

With frenetic thoughts of DMS circulating in my head, I almost stopped listening. She sniffed, ignoring Pete and Timmy pounding on the door. "Felicity found receipts and read messages hinting he had something going on with someone else, and she threatened to kill the trollop. When she jumped to the conclusion Jane and Wendell had gotten together, I let her believe it. She's got quite a temper, and I didn't want her to blow up at me. Tell Jane I'm sorry." I had to stop myself from laughing at her fake contrition.

"Before I had a chance to talk to Felicity, to tell her my

side and smooth over any lingering anger, my bitter ex decided to stir the pot. He accessed one of my media accounts and announced my engagement Monday. But now Wendell's dead." She wiped imagined tears from her eyes. She appeared to have been more enamored with the idea of being engaged than with the person to whom she was engaged. "And she won't stop harassing me." She held up her phone, displaying eleven missed calls from Felicity.

"You should tell the police. They need to know."

Her brown waves shook. "I'm hiding out until the threat is terminated. Since no one can have Wendell now, don't you think she'll give up?"

I opened the door. "Miranda, I'm done here." Pete and Timmy flanked my sides. "I'm leaving. I'll give your message to Jane, but I still think you should talk to the Atlanta Police Department. Good luck."

As we rode to our floor, tension rolled off Timmy in sheets. "If anything happens to Miranda Diaz, she wants Jane to know Felicity did it. I wasn't ever in any danger."

"If you try anything like that again, you'll be in danger from me," Pete said in a throaty whisper, escorting me off the car. Timmy took up his position next to the elevator. His incensed façade promised he wouldn't be so generous with his time again.

I meant to apologize, but my phone pinged with a message from the Fulton County Courthouse. I read the text and then read it a second time before turning the screen so Pete could verify my interpretation. A small smile replaced his residual fear. "You'd better tell them," he said.

I composed a group text.

Believe it or not, YOU DID IT! There has never been a tie before. You are scheduled to face-off with your opponent

tomorrow at noon to determine who takes second place and will compete in the final trial on Saturday. YAY ESQCHOIR!

I hit send and waited. Seconds later, the air filled with yips and bravos and all kinds of acclamations. One by one the doors creaked open, and the inhabitants poured into the hall, hugging and high-fiving. Lorelei winked at her mother. Eddie puffed out his chest. Phones and faces cheered as they shared the news with families and friends. My phone pinged with emojis from Leo.

Still happily reveling in their success, they scattered, and I returned to my room to change for the evening's dinner. I curled my hair and donned a royal blue sheath and matching flats, applying a touch of makeup to hide the dark circles under my eyes. What looked back at me from the mirror could have been worse. With the remaining time, I extracted the journal and turned to the back pages where Jane and I kept track of our thoughts regarding the guilt or innocence of parties in the death of Wendell, penciling in DMS next to Felicity and adding Miranda Diaz's name to the suspect list.

A brisk knock on the door foiled my research into other curious uses of the chemical, and I stashed the book.

Pete wore a gray suit jacket over a black cashmere turtleneck and black jeans with mock oxfords. His damp, dark hair curled over his collar. I smiled coyly and interlaced my fingers so I wouldn't reach up and comb them through his thick hair, tucking it behind his ears. "You clean up well."

"And so do you." I laughed at his wiggling eyebrows. "Lorelei hinted at a secret plan for tonight. What can I help with?"

I stepped away from the entry. He ambled in and took a seat. He leaned back, securing his elbows on the chair rests, crossed his long legs, and tented his fingers in front of a sly grin. I removed the gift box from the top dresser drawer and handed it to him. "Brock chose the Mock Trial America competition over his graduation ceremony. His parents supported his choice; it's a great co-curricular activity to add to his already lengthy resumé. Immediately after Brock decided, Lorelei met with our principal, and since the rest of the seniors are graduating tonight, she got permission to hold a parallel ceremony here in Atlanta."

Pete carefully folded back the tissue paper. He caught my eye and winked, and my heart warmed. "This is a night he'll never forget." He repackaged the diploma. "Actually, make that a week he'll never forget."

Although I hoped he'd disregard some of the less than positive occurrences of the week, I agreed with Pete. "When Lorelei begins the evening's festivities, would you mind connecting with Brock's parents via your screen?" I tallied what remained on my to-do list and handed him my phone. "My juggling ability is limited to tennis balls. I was wondering how I'd manage all the details. The phone connection was Jane's assignment, but I haven't heard from her. I think her dad is foremost on her mind and that's the way it should be, but if you'll take care of—"

"Done," he said as he completed sharing the Isaacson's contact information and returned my phone.

"You haven't heard from Drew, have you?"

Pete's forehead creased. "Not yet. Mitchell appeared before a magistrate judge this afternoon who determined there was sufficient evidence to believe Mitchell committed the crime and the case is strong enough to proceed to trial. His bail hearing is scheduled for next week."

"But he didn't do it."

"Dorene said he has the best criminal defense attorney

in all Georgia." The crease softened. He stood and took my shoulders in his hands. He took a deep breath.

"What is it?"

"I have to go home tomorrow. Will you be okay?"

My shoulders dropped—just a teeny bit. I'd been expecting it. "I know they need you. The ER is always short staffed, and you took off to look for me. Thanks for staying as long as you did. So much has happened this week, it seems like a lifetime ago when you came to my rescue … Again."

Pete cupped my face in both hands. His dreamy eyes glittered roguishly. He bent down to touch his lips to mine, and someone pounded on the door.

"I know you're in there. We need to talk," a hard voice said.

THIRTY-THREE

"Hey, you can't be here," shouted Timmy's distant countertenor. "Get away from there."

The pounding continued, more insistent. "Open the door, Mackey. Hurry up."

Pete cocked his head, and we stood shoulder to shoulder. I inhaled, he nodded, and I pulled the handle. Caught off balance, Felicity fell forward. Pete arrested her dive just as Timmy grabbed her arm and dragged her back. She teetered in Timmy's vice grip.

"At least hear me out. Give me equal time," she said.

Timmy's lips flattened into a straight line, and his face took on an unhealthy purple sheen. "Sorry, Ms. Wilk," he spouted through gritted teeth. "While I broke up a commotion at the emergency exit, this one snuck off the elevator."

Felicity's self-satisfied smirk confirmed her participation in the ruse.

"Jane's not here, and I don't think we have anything to discuss. Take her away, Timmy."

"A little bird in Miranda's organization told me she's staying at this hotel and has already spoken to you," Felicity said hurriedly between fierce jerks from our antagonized watchman. "You owe me five minutes. You have what's mine."

I held up my hand to temporarily stop their progression down the hall. "What are you talking about?"

She tried to free her arm. "Wendel stole my inheritance, and I want it returned."

Irate, I stomped toward her. "What makes you think I have whatever that is?"

Felicity narrowed her eyes. "You have it. He hid the flash drive in your backpack."

Pete caught me as I staggered at the mention of a flash drive.

She shook her head of multi-colored hair and sneered, "Wendell confessed everything on our jaunt to Atlanta. He didn't have my drive with him. He'd stashed it in your backpack along with his insurance policies. That way he thought he'd be safe." She frowned.

Pete held me in place. "How do you know he wasn't lying?"

"I've known him for over ten years. He couldn't get anything past me."

Although he had a girlfriend you didn't know about, I thought uncharitably.

"I knew he was upset."

"Upset," Pete growled. "He was wanted in connection with Katie's kidnapping."

"Ha. He didn't even have a loaded gun."

"Who told you that?"

She disregarded Pete's menacing voice and focused her attention on me. "I found out about his engagement late Sunday, but Wendell was already going to call off his wedding. He'd found Miranda's attorney's draft of an iron-clad pre-nup among her work documents—he'd get nothing if they divorced. I don't have the deep pockets Miranda and Jane have, but I'm financially sound." Her lip curled. "I figured I'd lure him back, promising I wouldn't have him sign anything." Her voice hitched. "But it wasn't enough. He had bigger fish to fry. Wendell had procured a more lucrative prize and wanted to negotiate the safe return of the data from a position of strength. He'd know the location of the information desired, information he'd taken, and he could demand a huge return on his limited investment of time."

"What people? What information? The proprietary plans he stole from A.B.SEE?"

Felicity mimed zipping her lips and tossing an imaginary key.

"But you said he stole *your* inheritance."

Felicity flushed and rolled her eyes. "Before he left for Minnesota, he used my laptop to encrypt alternate storage devices. Safekeeping, he said. He trusted me, he said. I didn't trust anyone, and I kept a copy of my mother's perfume formula in the hidden zippered compartment of a laptop case I never let out of my sight," she bellowed. Timmy cringed.

"While he was in Minnesota, I uncovered evidence he had a girlfriend, and I decided to purge my computer, a metaphorical wiping of Wendell from my life." She sighed. "But when I went to reinstall my mother's formula, my flash drive was gone. I realize her perfume is no longer marketable, but it's all I have left of her. Wendell admitted he'd borrowed it." She emphasized the word borrowed. "When I dropped him downtown, he said he'd return the drive, and I could get on with my life."

Timmy dragged at her elbow.

"Was that reason enough for you to kill him?" I asked.

"I wouldn't kill him. And look who's talking? He dragged you all over the forest." She snickered, braced her feet and struggled to break free, wincing as Timmy tightened his hold.

My mind whirled. "Felicity, did you kidnap Rocky? Have you been threatening me?"

Pete tapped on his phone's keypad and raised the device to his ear.

"No, and what's a rocky?" She tsked, still unable to yank her arm free. "I need my formula returned."

"I don't have it." I hoped she believed me. "Where did Wendell find the pre-nup?"

"He used Miranda's computer for marketing and knew the ins and outs. He found a copy in an email." She wrinkled her nose. "I have to get on Miranda's good side again. Her memory is infallible, and she might share it with me. We wouldn't be in competition. Her recipe uses none of the same ingredients." For the first time since I'd met Felicity, she seemed at a loss. Her shoulders slumped, and she hid her face behind her curtain of hair. "I've been trying to call Miranda, but she won't pick up."

Pete said into his phone, "Officer Knight, Felicity Williams would like to talk to you."

Felicity wriggled, and Timmy latched onto her other arm. Steel gleamed in his eyes and in his white-knuckled grip.

"Fine," Felicity harrumphed. "Knight left some messages for me anyway."

Timmy passed her off to one of his henchmen. "Haul her down to the meeting room and keep her there for Officer Knight." He looked penitent and added, "Your transport will be here in five minutes."

Time flies.

"Do you believe her?" I asked.

"She wouldn't have had to tell us about her mother's formula, but she did. And she mentioned a possible second device containing Wendell's insurance." Pete wrapped his arms around me.

"But where are the drives? If Wendell hid them in my backpack, they would have been ruined when I took a dip in the river. Mitchell replaced that backpack." I nestled in closer. "He'd be the only one who might know if the drives were in there, and we can't even talk to him." I shuddered. "That makes three drives missing." Pete eyed me curiously. "Felicity's, the mock trial information, and insurance of special significance. We've also learned of another suspect." His brown eyes darkened. "If Wendell changed his mind about marrying Miranda, she might also have a motive."

Doors slammed and feet thundered down the corridor, punctuated by the happy sounds of youthful laughter. Pete, my lifeline, kissed my forehead. I looked into his dreamy eyes and my heart tap-danced. I wondered what would have happened if only we didn't have seven students waiting for us. "There's nothing for us to do but smile. Here come the kids. It'll be a great night. We have plenty of eyes on your students. There will be no talk of Wendell. No investigating. You will have a pleasant evening. Don't worry." We joined in the merriment.

Our students had settled on business casual, slightly more relaxed dress than when they competed, but they still looked impressive. The boys wore identical blue dress shirts with Columbia Cougar ties and pressed khakis—the attire they wore on wrestling or baseball game days throughout the year. The girls' dresses draped in soft, romantic pastels. Lorelei patted the large shoulder bag hanging at her side and lifted her eyebrows. I reciprocated her signal and tapped the satchel containing Brock's diploma.

"No Ms. Mackey tonight?" asked Brock.

"She thought she might be a little late. She'll meet us at the restaurant."

"She's checking on Mr. Mackey, isn't she?" I nodded. "He'll be okay, Ms. Wilk," Brock said. "He's innocent."

I wished I held his conviction. Dorene and Leo conversed quietly with Marietta and Eddie, surreptitiously glancing at Lorelei and Brock. I'm sure they were finalizing last minute tasks for our event. Timmy pressed the elevator button and loaded first one half of us, then the other. We congregated near the front of the lobby under the appraising gaze of our friendly doorman, who tipped his hat and said, "Have a fabulous evening."

Little did he know.

THIRTY-FOUR

Our bus pulled up, and the doors opened. Lester sat behind the wheel, and he did not look pleased. My heart hammered in my chest. I'd forgotten to request a different driver. I stepped onto the bus, intent on turning the tables. "We have time for you to arrange for someone else to drive if you find transporting us such a burden."

His face softened. "It's fine. If you don't mind."

I took my seat, smiling at each of the terrific kids as they mounted the steps. Pete brought up the rear and dropped into the seat next to me. His presence at my side augmented my courage.

"Lester, the other night you told Officer Day you're new to the area." I watched confusion take shape on Pete's face.

"That's right." Lester nodded, shifting the gears a few

times to get us moving forward.

"Are you from Minnesota?"

He glanced at my reflection in the rearview mirror. "How'd you guess?" he said in a measured tone.

"We're from Minnesota too, and you have the distinct Minnesota accent. Long o, doncha know."

Pete squeezed my shoulder. I felt his unspoken words, 'be careful.'

"Lester, do you know of the A.B.SEE company?"

"Yes, ma'am." His eyes narrowed to slits. "Guess you finally figured it out." His quick glances in the rearview mirror unnerved me. "I'm an investigator for A.B.SEE. I've been following the trail of a common thief that led right to you."

"Wendell Gromm."

Lester nodded. "He tried to rob the company last week. My job is to determine how he got as far as he did and come up with a plan to shut down future invasions."

"You said, 'tried.' What do you mean? Didn't he succeed?"

"Someone stole a set of plans earlier this year, and we thought we'd been able to rectify our security issue. But the method Gromm used was so rudimentary, he left the building, actually, the state, before we rallied. We thought he must've had help. It wasn't you. You've checked out." His eyes locked onto mine. "It looks like you're exactly who you say you are. But the thievery shouldn't have happened. Our security is tight. Fortunately, we knew something was off from our first encounter with Gromm. Just in case, we swapped in an encrypted copy of a worthless formula for making Viking purple dye, but he still escaped."

I sucked in a breath. Dyes. Perfumes. Pharmaceuticals. Chemical pesticides. How many more people, besides Mitchell, had access to the chemical killer?

"After all, we're better known as an electronics company." Lester snorted and stared at the road in front of him. "Funny thing. We expected a ransom call. It never came. In all likelihood, he'd broken the elementary encryption, a puzzle slide ordering the construction of the system used just for show, and dumped the worthless info. My job was to follow the file, determine how someone got in and out with the goods, and make recommendations to make certain it doesn't happen again."

"Unfortunately, your lead is dead."

"There is that. And I haven't found the drive."

Rapid-fire questions pummeled my mind for the rest of the ride. How many flash drives had Wendell stolen? Where were they—at the bottom of the river? Could Lester or Felicity or Miranda have done away with Wendell? Was Lester honest about the A.B.SEE formula for a dye? Or had Wendell made away with the real plans? What would they be worth? Were the plans his insurance? How did Natalianna figure into Wendell's death? Was she sent to recover the plans? Who kidnapped Rocky? Where were Jane and Drew? My head churned with worry.

"Lester, how did you get a job driving us around? What happened to our first driver?"

At least he had the decency to look sheepish. "The Sapphire Skyway's forced landing was all over the news. I followed the Mackey money trail and made your driver an offer he couldn't refuse." At another moment in time, his comment might have been considered funny.

The bus stopped. He dug a business card out of his pocket and held it out to me. "If you make any discoveries, here's my contact information."

I accepted the card, saluted, and spun away. The bus

emptied, and Lester pulled from the curb. We stood open-mouthed in front of the restaurant.

The multiple iterations of mullioned windows adorned with wrought iron, the dark cupolas, and the colonnades distinguished the beautiful baroque architecture of the golden-hued *La Petite Salle de Manger* from the surrounding commercial buildings. We stood at the front door, stunned.

Eddie gazed up at the entry and said, in a voice filled with awe, "This is reminiscent of Versailles, symbolizing the power and authority of the monarchy." He took Marietta's hand and dragged her inside.

The vivid vision that came to my mind was of the end of the French monarchy, and King Louis XVI and Marie Antoinette losing their heads.

I approached the reservation desk with my entourage and gave a hearty, "*Bonsoir*," one of the few French words I felt comfortable saying. The maître d' raised his chin and looked down his nose at our well dressed, yet diverse crew. He was the spitting image of Augustus.

"May I help you?"

"Reservation for Wilk, party of twenty-two." Lorelei edged next to me, leaning forward, smiling with all she was worth.

He ran his forefinger down the reservation list and tut tutted. "I do not have a reservation for Wilk."

The corners of my mouth dropped to my shoulders. "How can that be? I booked a special dinner a month ago. On Tuesday, I increased our number of guests and was told there wouldn't be an issue." I scrolled through the emails and landed on the confirmation.

"Ah." He matched a number on his list. "Cancelled," nodding his head, emphasizing his confirmation.

"How could that happen? I didn't cancel the reservation. We have a special celebration planned for this evening. Do you have any openings?"

"We do not. As you can see, we are an intimate venue and host singular events."

Lorelei burst into tears, and I almost joined her. Brock froze, not understanding her unexpected, implausible burst of emotion, but Pete calmly voiced his concern and wondered if there had been some mistake. "Do you have any reservation for twenty-two?"

"Yes, but it's under the name Lavigne."

THIRTY-FIVE

How …" I stammered. "Why? I mean, that must be our reservation. Ms. Lavigne is one of my associates." Some future day, I'd have a talk with her. Squelching my irritation, I relaxed my shoulders.

The maître d' raised one eyebrow as I described ZaZa in the best possible terms. He suspended his doubt—how could there be two different reservations for an unusually sized group and two French women with the same last name at his restaurant on the same evening?

His assistant gathered the large menu cards. "This way, please." She guided us to a paneled chamber set off from the main dining room by partitions in a forest-green velvet and a sheet of gold links and treated us to a room set formally with linen tablecloths and napkins and crystal water goblets. ZaZa sat at the head of the larger of two parallel tables, raising a glass of something bubbly.

"*Bienvenue aux étudiants, parents, amis, et collègues et felicitations. Ce soir, nous sommes ici pour célébrer la remise des diplômes de—*"

Harboring a residual annoyance, I didn't trust myself to speak, nor did I understand French without messing it up, but when Lorelei interrupted her, I slowly repeated the words in my head and attempted a Wilk interpretation. "Welcome students, parents, friends, and colleagues and congratulations. Tonight, we are here to celebrate the ceremony of graduation of ..." I debated whether she'd been unaware or if she'd planned to spoil Lorelei's surprise. Little did she know, Lorelei studied, in depth, everything she set her mind to, including French.

"*Merci*, Ms. Lavigne. We're so delighted to join you. I hope you'll help us translate the items on the menu and share your gastronomical insight."

ZaZa bowed her head, acting the part of hostess with the mostess. It was obvious she was pleased to be the center of attention. "But of course. The menu is *fantastique*. I have ordered cheese fondue to share. After salad or soup, the main courses are served, with *pommes et haricots verts*. And the dessert *carte* includes macarons, chocolate mousse, and the most delicious crème brûlée."

ZaZa winked at my boyfriend and patted the seat to her right. He yanked my hand, forcing me to accompany him to the table. After introducing himself, Timmy sat to her left, never taking his suspicious eyes off her.

Marietta and Eddie sat at the students' table and supplemented Lorelei's clarification on the use of each piece of cutlery, along with each of the plates and various glasses. The gentle teasing and contented laughter warmed the air in the room. Timmy's associates watched in fascination.

I sat on pins and needles, wondering how ZaZa would let this play out, but she was the perfect hostess. Dorene even sat back in her chair as ZaZa introduced the four choices of entrees. "*Pates au Fruita de mer* is linguini with bay scallops and prawns. *Entrecote Grille* may appeal to you, Dr. Erickson, or you, Timothy. It is a boneless aged ribeye. Those who prefer chicken might appreciate the *Poulet au Miel á la Moutard*, a chicken with mustard and honey, and they also serve an award-winning Beef Bourguignon."

While waiting for our first course, Carlee jumped from her seat and rushed to the entry. She caught CJ quietly observing the motley roomful. Nestling into his side, she said, "Dad, you're here." She towed him to our table. "Meet Mr. Timmy. He's part of our security detail."

By some magical body language, it didn't take long for them to discover the similarities in their backgrounds. Using facial expression, head tilts, a nod, and a blink, it seemed as though they'd been deployed to the same undisclosed location for part of their tours of duty. CJ hung his cane around the edge of the table and pulled out a chair.

Marietta made a move, but Eddie tugged her back into the chair and stood in her place. "Please bow your heads," he said. He closed his eyes, paused and then opened one eye, waiting for Galen and Brock to comply. "Bless us with good food, the gift of gab, and hearty laughter. May the love and joy we share be with us ever after. Amen."

We answered with a resounding, "Amen," and dug in.

Galen moaned indecently over his first bite, and between the elegantly plated courses of the lavish dinner, ZaZa told captivating stories I'd never heard. She'd led a fascinating life, of which I knew only a very small part. I pretended to listen intently—I really intended to, hoping, perhaps, to mend a fence or two—but my eyes kept circling the empty seats at the end of our table. I wondered what was keeping Jane and Drew. The leisurely evening would have been so much better if I'd known when they'd would arrive, if at all.

Although the portions were manageable, when I finished my chicken dish, I was happy to have worn a dress without a waistband. The resting time between courses wasn't nearly long enough.

Lorelei caught my attention, and when she excused herself, I volunteered to accompany her, ensuring her safety, of course.

As soon as we were out of earshot, she said, "Ms. Wilk, are we ready? Should we begin the ceremony without Ms. Mackey and Mr. Kidd here?"

"Go ahead. I'm not sure when they'll make it to the restaurant. And it's a good time to take a break before the desserts. Are you ready?"

She straightened her dress and tossed her hair back. "I'm ready if you are."

Her first words upon reentering the dining room were, "If I may have your attention, please." When Brock continued to laugh at something Galen had said, she gave him her laser stare until he quieted.

She stood at the end of the students' table. "There are only eighty-six thousand four hundred seconds in a day." Lorelei was already high on my list of bright students, but tonight she'd risen in my estimation. "That's not nearly enough time to finish everything you might be wanting to do, but we're going to make it work." She dug in her shoulder bag and shook out a long blue robe. "Brock, would you join me?"

He balked, a look of wonder on his face. His mouth opened to speak but formed no words. Galen gave him a friendly shove, and Brock nearly tipped out of his chair. He stuffed three olives into his mouth as if completing his last meal before meeting his executioner. Rising shakily from his seat, he lumbered next to Lorelei. He looked at his feet, his dark brown hair flopping over his eyes.

Lorelei helped him slip the blue gown over his head and handed him the mortarboard, which he held in his hands for a relatively long time, unable to contain his emotions. As the team comedian, he finally slapped the cap on his head. A solemn rendition of "Pomp and Circumstance" carried throughout the room, issuing from one of the phones in the middle of the kids' table. Brock tipped his head and swished the dangling tassel in front of his face in time to the music.

Pete stood and held his phone above the heads of the students. It looked like he'd successfully linked Brock's smiling parents to our event.

"If we were in Columbia, tonight you would've been awarded your diploma, but instead you supported our winning mock trial team. Thanks for being here with us." Lorelei beamed. "Ms. Wilk."

You could hear the tissue paper crinkle as I unwrapped the precious blue leatherette diploma cover and removed it from the gift box. I dismissed the solitary moment of unease, remembering its initial inspection at TSA. It seemed like a lifetime had passed instead of five days.

Lorelei had written my succinct script, knowing full well Brock wouldn't stand still for long. "In honor of the successful completion of all your graduation requirements—"

"And then some," shouted Galen.

I effectively quieted the tittering with my teacher glare. "I have been granted the power to confer the Columbia High School diploma on Brock Vincent Isaacson. Moving the tassel from right to left signifies a rite of passage. It marks your transition, moving on to college." I waited for him to flip the yellow cords. "May you be ever prosperous and happy in your future endeavors. Let me be the first to congratulate you."

I shook his hand, and his sudden bashfulness surprised me. He accepted the folder and opened it. His mouth formed an o, and he said, "It's the real thing." Brock slid the toe of his shoe across the ground in half circles, giving the impression he was contemplating a profound comment when I witnessed his brown eyes take on an impish gleam. Tapping his impersonation of Elle Woods in *Legally Blonde* he squealed, "I did it." He removed his cap and tossed it with a pitcher's arm. It collided with the ornate floral painting on the ceiling, knocking a few flakes of red and gold onto his beaming face. His eyes popped wide as he stared above. For a moment, everyone stilled, but he hadn't caused any damage, and our crew burst into applause. Felipe and Galen hefted him onto their shoulders and paraded him around the room.

I watched the doorway for a glimpse of the peevish face sure to tell us he could not tolerate our exuberance, but the waitstaff pulled the fabric across the entry, muffling the sounds, and stepped around the columns to join in our revelry. The joy overflowed, and we celebrated the amalgamation of Lorelei's successful surprise, Brock's graduation, a completed year of school, our trip to Atlanta, and our mock trial accomplishments. Privately, I thanked my lucky stars to be sitting in this room with people I cherished.

I snatched a macaron, and my mouth watered as the waitstaff torched the sugar on the crème brûlée.

Pete's phone pinged and he read the screen. "It's Drew." He turned away from the hoopla and answered. When he spun back around, his huge smile had faded and his face blanched. "He can't find Jane."

THIRTY-SIX

Marietta read trouble in a room faster than a cheetah. She whispered something to Dorene and CJ and maneuvered her way next to me. "Whatever it is," she said through a fixed smile, "the kids are outnumbered. We've got you covered. Go."

Pete and I raced out of the busy dining room. He called for transportation. I continually redialed Jane's number. She didn't pick up.

Pete directed the driver to Drew's location, mere blocks away. I kept my eyes peeled for the tall, white-blond, straight-backed man with blue eyes, speaking worriedly on his phone, or better yet, my mini-sized, blond bombshell of a friend. From what I could glean of their conversation through Pete's repetition of Drew's anxious words, they'd stopped at a convenience store for Jane to freshen up before they joined us. With her natural good looks, it never took her long, but when Drew sent a cashier in to check on her, she'd vanished.

I scrutinized every face we passed on the street, hoping to see her. We whizzed by a gas pump, and Pete said, "There he is." The driver slammed the car into park, and I dashed to Drew's side.

"What happened? How long has she been gone?"

"It's maybe been fifteen minutes, but the longest fifteen minutes of my life."

"Where could she be? Have you tried the app to find her?"

"Her phone is off—"

"Or it's jammed." Tears welled in my eyes. "How could you lose her?" He straightened as if he'd been struck. "I'm sorry. Why is this happening to us? What do we need to do?"

"Timmy's associate and I covered this street in both directions," Drew said, breathing heavily. "We need to expand our search parameters." He turned his fierce blue eyes on me. "I need you to stay here, Katie." When I started to protest, he said, "At least stay close. This is her last known location. Someone might have seen her. Maybe she's catching up with an old friend, and when she realizes we might be wondering where she is, she'll return." He swallowed hard. "She may be wandering around hurt ..."

I nodded and grabbed his forearm. "She'll be back." She had to come back. "I'll call Officer Knight."

Drew pulled his free hand down over his face, scrubbing away the fear and pain. "I've got to find her. I'd give her anything she'd want if only she'd pop up and say surprise."

"You'd give who anything she'd want?"

We all turned toward the familiar drawl.

"Jane, where've you been?" Drew raced to her side and

wrapped his arms around her. He took hold of her shoulders and held her at arm's length, examining her from tip to toe.

"Surprise," she said in a small voice with a hopeful expression.

"Don't ever do that to me again." Drew said with a sharpness I hadn't heard before. "What happened?"

She shrugged. "I did what I had to do." His eyebrows came together. "I walked in on Natalianna in the restroom."

I sucked in a breath and searched left and right in case Natalianna showed up again.

Jane shuddered. "Her grin gave me the willies, but when her incredulity wore off, she asked if *I* was following *her*. Then she laughed, as if that was the most unbelievable concept possible. I told her Drew and our bodyguard stood just outside, and we could all have a nice long conversation, but she blew me off. I didn't want to lose her. I know she plays a pivotal role in Wendell's death. Dad isn't guilty, and his attorney said there's no proof, only conjecture, but I'm sure she knows something that can help him."

"How could you be so irresponsible?" Drew said in a gravelly voice, thick with emotion.

Her brown eyes lit with fire. I'd witnessed it before. Drew didn't realize his choice of concerned words might provoke Jane, and in a contest of wills, I'm pretty sure she'd triumph. She inhaled twice, quelling her annoyance and postponing the inevitable diatribe. "When we stepped out of the restroom, I didn't see either of you anywhere. It took Natalianna only seconds to deactivate the alarm on the rear exit. I had to follow her. I wanted her to talk more. She was hired to test the guidance system—"

"So she says." Drew's shoulders sagged. I tried to warn him with a hard look and an intense thought, but my telepathic power fell flat. He said, "You can be so gullible."

"Why would she lie?" Jane stood taller, or so it seemed. "She said a very determined pilot took over—me—luckily wrenching control from the remote system, or the weather would certainly have taken the plane down with much more disastrous results."

I nodded in affirmation and momentarily lost my balance, tipping slightly, acutely remembering the sensation of our forced landing. Pete righted me.

"Who hired her?"

"She didn't say, but she did say to watch my back." Jane turned to face me. "She said to tell you she would never use a child, and I believed her. I think she was talking about Rocky. She said things about a leak I didn't understand, but she wouldn't elaborate."

"Do you know where she is now?" Pete said.

"No." Jane's blond curls fell in front of her face and hid her bright pink cheeks. "That woman has no fear. We were talking, and suddenly, she reacted as though she'd recognized someone. In the second it took me to check behind us, she leapt in front of a semi and scooted through the traffic. If I hadn't been hamstrung by this boot, I'd have followed—"

One of Drew's hands smacked against his forehead and the other supported his back.

"… maybe, but I lost her." Her remorse waned, replaced by rebellion. "It was an advantageous coincidence we ended up at this convenience store concurrently."

Drew pursed his lips. It was something he'd have said. For good or bad, Drew's erudite pronouncements were rubbing off on her.

"I apologize if I made you worry." Jane's eyes burned, and she said with defiance, "But I'd do it again in a heartbeat."

I sensed a storm brewing between them, but Pete's common sense prevailed, delaying the inevitable. "Let's get back to the kids."

The hired car dropped us off in front of the restaurant as the doors opened and the students emerged into the evening, laughing and slapping Brock on the back. When Jane stepped from the car, they rushed to exchange greetings with their Ms. Mackey and give her the longest possible list of highlights she'd missed.

"Congratulations, graduate." Jane removed an envelope from her bag and placed it on Brock's open palm. "This is from my dad and me. And by the way, I'm starved." She surveyed the kids, panning their cheerful countenances. "Anyone have any leftovers?"

Lorelei held up a heavy white paper bag with the restaurant logo embossed on the front. "No leftovers. We figured you and Mr. Kidd would need sustenance and ordered a ribeye, the seafood platter, and their award-winning crêpes."

"I can't believe my luck. You're the best, most thoughtful team ever."

Before she began to blubber, our transportation pulled up, minus Lester. I guessed now that his cover was blown, he didn't need to pretend to be our driver.

Dorene leaned close and whispered, though the boisterous students crowding onto the bus wouldn't have heard her anyway. "What happened? The kids were getting anxious."

I made a show of counting the heads of those climbing the bus stairs. "Kuznetsov appeared again."

Our unflappable leader said, "She didn't give you anything of substance, no proof of Mitchell's innocence."

"No such luck."

Before she stepped into the chaos, she said, "I lied and told the kids coaching their mock trial team is the third-best thing I've ever done in my life, so far."

I frowned. From the onset, she informed us her clients came first. We roped her into helping after the coach she'd recommended was arrested. Her thriving practice kept her busy, so we tried to keep her involvement to a minimum, but she was an all or nothing kind of participant. I hoped she didn't regret her time with us.

"Coaching is really the second-best thing I've ever done." She grinned. "Being a big sister is number one." She combed her fingers through her short black hair and followed Leo to the back of the bus.

ZaZa and CJ strolled out the main door, and I asked, "Do either of you need a ride?"

CJ clicked a key fob, and a chirp sounded. His smiling face was bathed in light from a cherry red sportscar parked under the light across the street. "If it is not too late, I think your dog might benefit from a short walk and to touch base. Twenty minutes?"

"Perfect." I took a step onto the bus, glancing back. "ZaZa?"

"I do not need transportation." ZaZa lowered her eyes and added quietly, "You chose the perfect venue, but as you do not need my expertise any longer, I have made plans."

"We compete at—"

"You will see me there." Her face brightened and she waved as a white SUV rolled to the curb. She gracefully slid into the front seat and leaned toward the driver before closing the door and shutting us outside the lightly tinted windows.

I climbed the stairs thinking a few of those words made up the nicest conversation ZaZa and I held in a long time.

The bus door clunked behind me, and when we pulled into traffic, I fell into the seat next to Pete.

"Susie called. They're having issues with the locum." His kind eyes shown with concern. "Mitchell has his hands full at the moment, so I've booked an early flight tomorrow … unless you want me to stay." He was torn.

"Of course, I want you to stay, but we'll be fine." As the words left my lips, goose bumps crawled down by spine, and I scanned the streets for someone watching us, but saw only an old man with long gray hair tipping back a bottle.

THIRTY-SEVEN

Nearing the end of a week filled with ultimate highs and dark lows, I paced our room trying to get rid of excess energy until my phone pinged. I peeked at the screen.

"Your face just lit up. Who is it?" Jane said, stifling a yawn.

"It's CJ. The dogs are a little rambunctious, and he's uncomfortable entering the lobby. I imagine Augustus is giving off negative vibes."

"I'm out. I've taken too many steps today. I can't drag that boot another inch."

"Are you up for a walk, Pete?"

He unfolded his long legs and stretched. "I'll stock up on steps in anticipation of sitting all day tomorrow. The dogs will be a healthy diversion."

Our dogs had a way of settling anxiety and calming

nerves, so I wasn't surprised Carlee and Galen took advantage of the opportunity to see Renegade.

In answer to the unbidden questions, as he pressed the call button and shook his head, Timmy said, "Until Mr. Mackey releases us, or you're out of the state, one of us will continue to accompany you just to be on the safe side. One never knows."

I stepped off the elevator, and Maverick saw me through the revolving door. He yanked at his leash and knocked CJ off balance. We hadn't quite mastered the art of listening to all cues, but CJ must have done or said something because, a moment later, Maverick sat, alert, and locked eyes with his trainer. I paused, in training as well, until CJ gave permission to join him.

CJ released the dogs. I didn't know whether Carlee or I giggled more as Renegade and Maverick brushed against our legs, nudged our hand for scratches and pets, and whimpered. When CJ whistled, however, the dogs stood rigidly at attention, and so did Carlee and I.

CJ handed me Maverick's leash and cued his release. Maverick took off at a fast clip. I jogged along behind.

Pete and I didn't realize how far ahead we'd gotten until we came upon a shiny green truck parked at the mouth of an alley and turned around to find an empty street. "We'd better wait for them, or I'll be treating Timmy for a coronary." Pete paraded around the front of the new vehicle for a better look. "This is awesome," he said approvingly. "By the time I need a new truck, maybe some of the extras will all be standard."

He bent to examine the chassis, at least I think it was the chassis, and a soft grunting sound drew my attention away from the vehicle and down the dark backstreet. It also drew Maverick's attention. He dug in his paws and jerked me away from the safety of the streetlights.

"Maverick." My admonition came out in spurts. "Stop." He didn't slow down. "Heel." He still didn't listen. "No."

As he gained traction, he picked up speed. I hung on and began to skid behind him down a cobbled lane slimed with damp and moss and garbage and who knows what else. My main concern was to stay upright until I could control my forward trajectory.

Maverick stopped abruptly, and I nearly flew over him. He barked. "Sh. Quiet." Coaxing with a sing-song voice sometimes lured him my way, but he barked more. "Come, Maverick." I tugged on the leash, turning to drag him, but his sixty-five pounds of fixated muscle wasn't going anywhere. It felt like I was trying to haul a freight train.

"Katie?" Pete called.

"Down here." A breeze stirred the trash on the ground and revealed what looked like a hand. "Pete," I squeaked. My insides coiled. More softly, I said to my dog, "I see it. Good boy."

His barking stopped. He'd communicated his find, and he sat.

Stepping closer, the tip of one finger moved. I tripped and fell backwards, catching myself, and prepared to crab walk in the opposite direction, but the accompanying groan drew me like a positive to a negative. I knelt beside the hand and said, "I'm here. Can you hear me?"

A dirty blond head rose like a specter materializing through the debris surrounding it. Green eyes tried to focus.

"You're hurt. Don't move. Help is on the way." I called out over my shoulder, "Pete, hurry."

She clenched my fingers and forced out a word in a throaty whisper. "Poison." Her pale face, red-rimmed eyes, and purple lips reminded me of Wendell.

"Who did this?"

Pete knelt next to me, already speaking into his phone with our location.

"Drive," she said, closed her eyes, and sagged into the pile of rubbish.

Pete held her wrist and bent his ear to her mouth. In a short time, sirens stopped abruptly at the end of the lane. I heard the clatter of a gurney trundling over the stones but kept my eyes on Natalianna. She didn't move, no rise and fall from breath, no flutter of eyelids, no fingers dancing.

The paramedics assumed charge of the patient.

Pete said, "I don't know if she'll make it, Katie. She has the same symptoms Wendell had."

Maverick and I backed up to the wall, as far as we could get away from the swarm of personnel intent on doing their job. I closed my eyes and slid down the cool bricks, wrapping my arms around my dog's neck, burying my head in his soft black fur. The voices melded with the other sounds while I concentrated on Maverick's steady breathing and the thump of his heart.

I felt Pete's presence and looked up at him through pools of unwept tears. He pulled me to standing and enfolded me protectively against his side. Maverick pranced close, glancing into my face, and we cleared the busy alley.

Quick steps shuffled toward us, and a familiar youthful voice said, "Dad, Renegade is really yanking." Maverick answered a familiar yip, and Carlee said, "Oh, no. Ms. Wilk, not again. What happened?"

"Maverick and Renegade are very good searchers, and Maverick found someone injured."

"Is there anything we can do?"

Pete said, "We can let them do their jobs."

Pete accepted a scratchy blue blanket from one of the EMTs and threw it over my shoulders. He led me past the ambulance, and we came face to face with Officer Knight. She gestured for me to sit in the back seat of her car.

"What can you tell me, Katie?"

I took a moment to figure out how I should answer. "After a lovely dinner at a French restaurant, celebrating the graduation of one of my students, CJ Bluestone brought Maverick and Renegade to see his daughter and me."

I knew I wouldn't tell her Jane might have been one of the last people to see Natalianna Kuznetsov because she had absolutely nothing to do with the attack. I had to figure out who set up Mitchell and Jane, but first I had to get Knight to start looking beyond the Mackeys.

"The dogs have been working hard and doing well, but they're in a new environment. And after my week, CJ thought I could use the visit. Maverick's in training for search and rescue, and as you can see, his nose is very good."

He sat primly at the mention of his name, smiling, tongue hanging out, rocking from paw to paw, tail brushing the pavement, just waiting for a hearty rub.

"There's someone still out there hurting people, Officer Knight. Doesn't it prove Mitchell Mackey didn't kill Gromm?" Hoping she'd come around to my way of thinking, I added, "Did you know dimethyl sulfate is used in making dyes and perfumes? Felicity Williams and Miranda Diaz are in the perfume industry." I was on a roll, and the words spewed from my mouth. "And the bus driver, Lester, is an investigator for a company who has a special recipe for dyes." She didn't let on if I'd told her anything she didn't already know.

"And pharmaceuticals and pesticides." She gritted her

teeth. "Stop doing our job."

"At least it has to provide reasonable doubt."

Rather than commit, she jerked her thumb and said, "Go, but—"

"We know the drill. Thank you." Pete pulled me from the back seat, and as we rounded the last police car, we headed back to the hotel.

With everything she'd dealt with this week, I couldn't bring myself to wake Jane when we returned and tell her about Natalianna. A morning conversation would have to do.

Too wound up to relax, I nabbed the remote from the nightstand and opened the room service menu, dislodging the flight checklist card with the weird back. I decided the light would wake Jane, so I carried the card to the conference table in the next room and began to decrypt the symbols. Walter Gibson's code in the cryptology book offered an explanation for four unique symbols. They oriented the page—up, right, left, and upside down. When I completed my unraveling, I noted my answer in the back of the journal, along with our murder musings. I moved the vase to the precise center of the table and slipped the card beneath it as a reminder to share my translation with Jane.

Only the Shadow would know for sure, but I came up with a curious solution.

THIRTY-EIGHT

By six a.m., the kids had begun to crawl the halls, talking in annoying whispers. I didn't think I'd ever observed as much angst among them at any other time of the year. When Jane woke, she tried to be so upbeat for the students, the time to tell her about Natalianna didn't present itself. Group text messages flew back and forth, deciding on times for breakfast, calling parents (including mine), rehearsing opening and closing statements, walking one of the lawyer paths, and even geocaching.

Gathering all her chipperness, Jane whipped open our door and jumped in front of five of the seven optimistic yet guarded faces. I didn't want to leave her hanging by herself, so I joined her with my take on a Ninja warrior. "Hi-ya. Ready to eat?"

With his distinctive eye roll, Galen said, "It's too early, Ms. Wilk."

"Nope. They begin serving at five-thirty during the week. All those businessmen and women need sustenance before taking on the day, and so do we. After breakfast, you can determine what you want to do with the rest of the time this morning. Are Felipe and Patricia up?"

Brock nodded, his face still shining from last night's fete. "Rocky's back in Minnesota and called to wish us luck, and Felipe got all googly eyed."

"Patricia's about ready too," said Kindra. "How are *you* doing this morning, Ms. Wilk?"

Carlee blushed. "I told them, you know," she stuttered. "Last night, you found—"

I cut Carlee off while Jane practiced her yoga flow nearby, lest she find out she was the last one to be informed. "Everything is great."

Timmy and his eagle-eyed crew immediately escorted our full complement to the restaurant. We filled our plates, but no matter how delicious the fare might have tasted, nervous energy filled the air. Although not much was eaten, they did succeed in organizing their day and returned to our floor to prepare.

My students had earned the right to be proud of themselves. They'd already performed so much better than anyone expected—except me. How could I assure them everything else was just icing on the cake?

I'd worked up my courage to talk to Jane when Pete stopped by our room to say goodbye. His morning flight would get him to Minnesota around noon, and the limo would arrive shortly to take him to the airport.

With a twinkle in her eye, Jane said, "Excuse me. Drew's

riding with Pete to the airport and on to the DOFS to see if they are willing to share any more information. Bon voyage." She waggled her eyebrows. "I'll see if Drew's ready."

"Right," I said, as if I could possibly believe her. I wasn't sure the panic causing my heart to race was Pete's departure or the conversation I needed to have with Jane. Pete wrapped his arms around me, and I held on tight. He cupped my jaw in his tender hands and asked again, "Do you want me to stay?"

"The hospital needs you, and I don't want to use up your vacation time. Jane will stay in Atlanta until her dad is cleared, but our return tickets are scheduled for Sunday, and I'll see you when I get back with the kids." I stuck out my lower lip and made a show of crossing multiple pairs of fingers on both hands, silently praying the return journey would go according to plan.

He kissed my forehead. "Good luck today and tomorrow too." He lifted his luggage in one hand and took mine in the other. We rode the elevator to the lobby, but he had no time to waste. Drew sat in the car idling at the curb. Pete's proper goodbye today would have to be a welcome home Sunday.

Carlee arranged for her dad to bring Renegade and Maverick for another visit after breakfast, and we all knew how well pet therapy worked. The Calders and kids emptied into the lobby where I distributed my copies of the curated walking paths provided by the bar association. The kids voted for a longer tour to allow some of their jittery butterflies time to escape, but tired of lugging around the extra weight, Jane couldn't wait to shed her heavy boot, and she chose to stay at the hotel. She dispelled my unease, promising not to move one inch until I came back for her, sitting where Timmy's associate could keep his eye on her. Thankfully, Augustus wasn't around to observe our traipsing through the lobby. I wasn't prepared to begin the day with another glower.

Eddie herded the kids together, gave them the daily reminder, and pointed at Timmy. Before passing through the revolving door to meet CJ and his pet team, our genial doorman bowed and wished us a successful day.

"Yours is the first face we see when coming in and the last face we see going out. It's a great face, but it's been the only one. Are you on twenty-four-seven, man?" Brock teased, bowling out into the warm, hazy day.

The doorman simply winked.

Maverick's backside wiggled eagerly, and he jabbed his nose into my palm, aching for a scratch. I braced myself and knelt, accepting the tickling tongue. CJ handed me Maverick's leash, and because he'd worn himself out the night before, we trailed the procession to locate the three mystery geocaches Brock and Galen had chosen along one of the two-mile routes around our hotel, a much-needed distraction.

Once again, I had the creepy feeling we were being watched, and I shivered, but the empty street was easy to survey, and no one seemed to take notice of us. Happily, my unease dissolved when we found the first geocache and was replaced by the enthusiasm the kids had when solving riddles. They gave their all in everything they put their minds to. We toured the sites noted on the map and found the second geocache as well.

Using Lord Bacon's centuries old cipher and translating "GreAtesT STatUe syMBOlizING aTLaNta RisiNG froM the AsHeS" by mapping the 'a' to lowercase letters and the 'b' to capital letters, the kids decoded the final hidden message. We stood in front of the statue of *The Phoenix*, snapped a few photos, marked the cache as found, and claimed it as a favorite.

The hour-long trek helped take the edge off, and we checked one more item off our Atlanta bucket list. Raring to go, we dashed to the hotel for last-minute prep for the afternoon trial. I grabbed one more minute of dog-time while the valet brought CJ's car around. Maverick barked, unusual, but not unheard of. CJ corralled the dogs and said, "I will be in the gallery today." He held his hand over his heart. "And remember, you always have Maverick here." My dog woofed again.

I stood on the curb as they drove away, content, but also wondering what Maverick could have been trying to tell me. I entered the lobby, and a moment of fear grabbed me by the throat and throttled me. I expected to find Jane, tell her about Natalianna, and ask her to contact Officer Knight, but her seat was vacant. I hustled through the lobby, searching.

Sensing my alarm, Martha called from the registration desk, "Ms. Wilk, Ms. Mackey has gone to her room with an old friend."

THIRTY-NINE

I bounded into the room with clenched fists, fully understanding we visited Jane's bailiwick, Atlanta, her hometown, and she knew people, but I felt the weight of our circumstances pressing in. The sight in front of me brought me up short.

Noah Lexington lounged on the sofa across from Jane drinking sparkling water, and my fingers relaxed.

He leaned forward, and not wanting to undergo another overly friendly greeting, I hastily said, "No need to get up, Noah. Welcome."

Jane's bright smile filled her face. "We've been talking over old times. You wouldn't believe the trouble we got into back then."

"Actually," I said, cocking my head, "I would."

"I suppose you would." Her head dropped back, and she said, "I can't believe we made it. We had as many questions for our teachers as they had for us, and we were shuffled among the instructors. They threatened to blacklist us, but we were never out of order."

"And we were only in the same program until I earned my private pilot's license."

"We did all that in less than six months?" She shook her head in dismay.

"Remember, we'd get together at the club after a hard day's work." Noah winked a tawny eye. "We'd talk about the skies."

"I'll admit, they made a pretty good tonic and lime, but what a classy place it was." Jane's eyes took on a faraway look. "They decorated the tables with seasonal flowers and made the best cream puffs in the world."

"You were always hungry, like you had a hollow leg. I never knew where you put it."

Jane sobered. "Did you know Wendell never completed his training?"

Noah whistled in disbelief. "I often wondered about him. I never saw him after that first year, although I haven't seen you either since we went our separate ways."

"Wendell was difficult to like, and I didn't follow up on him either." Jane eyed Noah with curiosity. "Do you like flying for my dad?"

He nodded. "Mitch has the best interest of his passengers and crew at the heart of all his decisions. Richard heard what happened and let me know about Mitch's arrest. I came to tell you how sorry I am and offer my support. He's true blue and wouldn't kill anyone, certainly not Wendell."

The room grew quiet as we pondered secrets and families.

"Why do you just teach?"

"I love the kids, and I love what I do." Jane sounded affronted.

"But you wouldn't have to. I know you love flying too."

"I wanted to make it on my own."

"Well." Noah slapped his knees and stood. "I won't keep you. Jane said you have another important trial today. I wasn't expecting to become so invested in the first one, but it was enthralling, and I'll try to attend." He hooked a fabric ring at the collar of his decades old jacket and slung it over his shoulder. "But if something comes up and I don't make it, good luck, and I hope I see you both again before you head north." The chaste peck on her cheek turned Jane a light pink. He paraded to the entry, turned, and said, "If you need anything …"

The door closed, and I said, "Jane …" I had so much to tell her.

She brought a hand up and read a text. "Not now, Wilk. We've got to feed the gang and win a trial. Jeeno's has been delivered to the conference room. They've got to be starving, and I'm positive they'll eat this lunch."

The aroma had enticed the kids into the hall, and by the time we entered the meeting room, half the boxes sat empty.

At the conclusion of the mouthwatering lunch, Lorelei and Dorene fired up the troops with uplifting words of wisdom. With adrenaline amped up, the team changed into performance duds and charged onto the bus ready to take on the world.

I almost didn't notice Lester in the driver's seat.

"Lester, you're here. I thought you'd gone back to Minnesota."

"I have a question for you."

"Ohhh. Kay," I said slowly.

"Rumor on the street says you acquired Wendell's flash drive. I'm trying to tie up loose ends to determine where he was going to unload his contraband. I haven't been able to close the circle, and I can't help but think, because you're merely a math teacher, you're out of his circle, and the gossip is wrong."

I bristled at what I ordinarily would've considered fighting words, but he mumbled, "Sorry."

"Lester, I've searched everything I have with me, and I have absolutely no flash drives at all. I think I lost the one that came with us from Minnesota along with any extraneous drive Wendell allegedly planted on me when I was swept down the river in the Nantahala National Forest."

He nodded. "That's what I will put in my report." We bumped along the street. "Katie, be careful."

We didn't have far to go, and before I could formulate a query as to why I needed to be careful, he stopped the bus, and the doors clacked open. "Good luck today." The students barreled off the bus and the adults followed. This tie-breaking trial would determine which teams met in the final scheduled for Saturday afternoon, and my team exuded confidence—until they met the opposition and stopped in their tracks.

The pompous brown-haired troublemaker and his blond toady from the competition's welcome event sat behind one table. The sneer on his face soured my stomach, but I took courage finding our supporters peppered among the spectators in the gallery.

The Calders, CJ, Timmy and crew, and even ZaZa watched in fascination as the kids donned their professional personae and prepared to conquer their tiny corner of the world. Noah entered, caught Jane's eye, and glided into a seat near the back.

At the very last moment, Drew coasted to the seat behind Noah, winked at Jane, and gave the team a thumbs up.

The bailiff exclaimed, "All rise. The Court of High School Mock Trial America is now in session. The Honorable Judge Truth is presiding."

A tall white-haired woman mounted the bench. "Welcome fellow Fulton County attorneys. You will serve in the capacity of an impartial jury. I needn't remind you to listen to the evidence and render a fair verdict."

"Counsel, approach the bench." One of the seemingly very young and green evaluating attorneys rose in the jury box, and the judge admonished, "Not you this time, Lloyd." He sat, red-faced. Lorelei and the brown-haired young man met in front of the judge. "Congratulations to both teams. Attaining an equal score is unprecedented, but we are here today to break that second-place tie and determine which of you will compete in this year's final trial. You have not met prior, so both teams may represent either side. Mr. John, heads or tails?"

The silver disk tumbled in the air, and he called, "Tails." The entire room hushed, and the coin landed with a thud. Three heads peered at the result, and Mr. John named their preferred side in a superior tone, "Plaintiff."

I would've hated to evaluate the trial. Both teams gave riveting performances and provided compelling arguments to support their claims. We'd never been better, nor had we met a worthier opponent. Our fierce attorneys landed solid declarations of presumptive innocence. Lorelei, Kindra and Carlee seemed untouchable. The plaintiff's attempts to trip up Brock, Galen, and Felipe failed, but the plaintiff delivered an equally talented production. When both sides rested at the conclusion of the case, the gallery, the attorneys—aka the jury, and the judge stood and applauded. When the judge and jury retired to chambers to deliberate the future of our team, the tension released as a collective sigh came from all quarters.

The opposing attorneys excitedly approached our defense table, and the blond giggled. "You were on fire. That was the most fun I've ever had. I'm Stephanie."

Her associate stood behind her and let her rant. When she finally took a breath, he stepped up to Lorelei and thrust out his hand. She examined it and when assured it wouldn't bite, she grasped it. He uttered, "I'm Greg. Dy-no-mite. You deserved to be here. Nice job. I guess now it's in the hands of the judges."

The entire slate of contestants praised each other. It was definitely a toss-up. What would be, would be.

Time dragged on and the gallery emptied of all but the teams' closest supporters. And we waited.

FORTY

Our kids claimed third place in a national competition, but the loss still stung. Wallowing was allowed for a bit, and no one yet had the enthusiasm to pack it away in the chest marked 'lessons learned'.

And if that wasn't bad enough, when we trudged into the lobby, our compassionate doorman said somberly, "Sorry, Ms. Katie. Hang in there for a bit. I've made a call."

As we made our way across the lobby, Augustus raised his voice. "Ms. Wilk, I need a word."

I urged the kids toward the elevator as I approached the desk. "What can I do for you, Augustus?"

He lifted his snooty nose and said, "I must ask you to find other accommodations." He turned the registration papers to face me, tapping on one highlighted paragraph detailing expectations. "You have violated hotel policy by bringing in unauthorized dogs to visit."

I narrowed my eyes. "What are you talking about? We asked permission to bring the pets to visit. They are better trained than some people, I might add."

Martha tiptoed near and extended a piece of paper with uncertainty. "This email came—"

Augustus slapped it away and continued, "You have engaged in disruptive behavior requiring police involvement. Your children have been noisy and unruly, unsettling our other guests, and you consort with criminals. I am not paid enough to supervise children. And on top of that, your benefactor is in jail."

A man with deep wrinkles creasing his face, a mop of messy gray hair, and wearing a worn suit backed up Augustus. "That's right."

Stubbornness was part of my makeup. "You can't do this."

"Sure, he can," the man said.

I inspected the face. "I know you. You've been following us."

"Augustus and I are old friends. He's been helping me keep tabs on you." He glowered. "I'm your worst nightmare."

Before I could summon help, Jane flew in the front door. "Lorelei texted there's a problem. What's happening?"

The older man replied with saccharine sweetness, "Augustus is tossing your teenaged critters and you out on your diamond-studded ear."

Jane softened. "Mr. Gromm, I'm sorry for your loss." My head swiveled between them. "I never thought I'd see you again."

"And yet here we are." He gulped hungrily from a stainless steel decanter and wiped his lips with the back of his hand.

"You always thought you were better than my boy. Not this time. He called me. He'd found a way for us to get all that was coming to us." He took another long swig. "And it was snatched from him. Janie, this is retribution."

"I don't know what Wendell told you, but he stole from a company in Minnesota and kidnapped my friend. What do you hope to accomplish by seeing us thrown out of the hotel?"

"Satisfaction."

Mitchell Mackey marched through the revolving door. I caught a fleeting moment of uncertainty in the raise of Augustus's eyebrows.

"Mr. Mackey. What are you doing here?" Augustus flattened his hands on the countertop.

Gromm said, "Don't back down now, Augustus. He killed my boy."

"I'm sorry about Wendell, Gromm, but I had absolutely nothing to do with his death," Mitchell said. Gromm glared.

"They released you?" Augustus stammered.

"Yes, Auggie. They've reexamined the evidence and found it insufficient. And I think we have a teensy problem." Mitchell's tone of voice brought Augustus's awareness back to their present discourse.

"I can't imagine what that might be." As if an afterthought, he added tartly, "Mr. Mackey."

Martha walked up behind Augustus and attempted to get his attention again. A piece of paper fluttered in her hand. "I think you'd better read—"

Augustus flicked his fingers and blew her off.

Mitchell said, "It seems you have tried to prematurely expel your guests. Guests, by the way, whose rooms and board have been duly paid for."

Augustus stiffened. "The policy of this hotel is quite explicit. Disruptive behavior is a violation of company policy, as is allowing pet visitors. These guests are no longer welcome."

"Well, Auggie, that's where you're mistaken. These students, their chaperones, and their coaches are eminent guests of this hotel, and you will reinstate their reservation immediately." Mitchell's lips slowly grew into a grin.

"I beg your pardon." Augustus stiffened. "I will not."

"Yes, you will."

"He doesn't have to do anything you say," shot Gromm, boosting Augustus's waning confidence. Augustus stood rigid and his lips formed a thin, straight line.

"What happened to you, Gromm?" Mitchell's eyes darkened, and he turned away from the men. "Martha, you're in charge."

Augustus's brows knit together. "You can't do that …" He waited a beat before relaxing his facial muscles and adding disdainfully, "… sir."

"I can, and I will. I recently purchased this hotel and you, Auggie, are fired."

Augustus sputtered. Martha smiled and waved the page. Gromm sneered in disbelief. "Mackey, you did it again." He guzzled from his flask, and staggered to the door, held wide by our friendly doorman.

Mitchell shook his head ruefully.

"He's a sad, bitter man, Dad." Jane hugged Mitchell tightly. "You're out?"

"It was Katie's doing. She helped Officer Knight conclude the flimsy evidence against me was circumstantial."

"Do they know who killed Wendell?"

"Not yet, Jane." Mitchell eyed the revolving door. "First

things first. A little birdie told me I was needed here, but my attorney and I still have some paperwork to finish." Mitchell gently moved Jane's hands and squeezed them. "I'll catch up with you later," he said and strode purposely to the fairy-godfather-like doorman. They shook hands like old friends, which they probably were, and Mitchell disappeared.

Seconds later, Dorene marched in and scrutinized our motley crew. "I've scheduled an appointment we need to keep."

Our kids groaned. They hadn't had time to recover from their latest defeat, but I trusted Dorene knew best. Her raised eyebrow silenced the entire group.

"I've arranged for you to meet my favorite Georgia State Supreme Court Justice in his chambers, and he will give you a private tour of the Supreme Court of Georgia. He can't wait to meet you." Dorene had stunned her charges. "He's an old friend and I don't want to be late, so shake a leg. You have five minutes to be out on that bus."

The students glanced back and forth to gauge her veracity.

CJ entered the lobby, and Carlee's face lit up. "Can my dad come with us?"

Dorene nodded. "You're all invited."

The kids quickly dispersed.

As the adults headed for the bus, Dorene, uncharacteristically, approached me with caution. "Katie, I hope you won't take this the wrong way, but the judge has a rancid taste in his mouth when it comes to high school math teachers." A guffaw escaped from my lips. I'd certainly heard that before. "I told him about you, but his calc instructor gave him a grade that kept him from getting into his top school. I pointed out the teacher obviously didn't prevent him from excelling in law, noting his success, but he'd appreciate your absence.

We've got the kids covered, and in place of the visit, I've scheduled a hot stone massage treatment and aromatherapy with the spa. I'm paying, of course."

My bones warmed in anticipation of the luxurious pampering and alone time. "You'll have your hands full, but you won't need me. I'll gladly stay."

She exhaled. "Thanks. You don't know what that will mean."

Unfortunately, she was correct.

FORTY-ONE

The blessed peace and quiet lasted for less than a heartbeat. Before I could revel in my mandated solitude, I heard a quick, hard rap on my door. I peered through the peephole and stared into another eye. It had to be one of my students. Tempting fate, I opened the door.

Lorelei's words rushed out. "We've got the best coaches in the world. I can't believe we're going to take a tour of the Supreme Court. It's a dream come true." I guarded my face, grinning inside at her youthful passion for the law. "I just wanted you to know how much I appreciate this entire experience." She wrapped me in a hug, and something in her hand thumped against my back.

Her friends standing behind her did not exude the same level of ardor. Their mumbles would hardly be considered a rousing endorsement, but she attempted to elicit a more enthusiastic confirmation. "All of us appreciate it," and received a few uh-huhs in response.

"Sorry, I forgot to give these back." She held a resealable bag out in front of her. "I know you said you had extras, but I didn't mean to keep them, and Mom doesn't need the old agenda any longer." She winked. "We're on a new, uncharted course. Have fun at the spa."

She and her friends raced to the elevator.

I closed the door and leaned against it, drinking in Lorelei's earnest approbation. When I'd basked long enough in the rare sunshine of a student's sincere thank you, I entered the bedroom and flopped onto the bed, breathing in and out. I unzipped the bag and dumped the contents onto the top of the dresser: a plastic folder containing the week's matchups and schedule of events and ... My heart nearly stopped. Lorelei must have grabbed the folder containing the flash drives when she retrieved a copy of our schedule for her mom and had it all this time. I stared at four red rectangles and quickly shot a glance around the room before pocketing them, so as not to get caught holding something clearly important to law enforcement. Wendell must have secured them in the closeable bag and when I went under water, they survived. I didn't realize they'd been transferred along to the new backpack with the rest of my belongings.

I mulled over what to do and who I could call. Everyone from Columbia in Atlanta was on the bus in transit to the Supreme Court. No one in Columbia was in a position to help and would simply worry. Mitchell and his attorney had important paperwork to complete. I could contact Officer Knight, but these drives might mean nothing at all.

I removed one drive from my pocket and turned it over in my fingers. Caught up in the activities of the week, I had no reason to open my laptop before, but the plastic cases were figuratively burning a hole in my pocket.

I lifted the lid on the laptop at the conference table, and it seemed to take its sweet time booting up. I itched to insert the device but waited until I logged in. The first drive opened to beautiful, soothing piano music, light and quick arpeggios playing as waves rolled onto a narrow strip of sandy beach under a picturesque moonlit sky. I clicked the small square icon at the top of the page, and the video dissolved into a million pixels, uncovering the photo of a handwritten chemical formula under the heading 'Williams' Magic Scent.' I didn't need to know anything about the formula to determine it belonged to Felicity—the drive Wendell had taken. Snapping a photo, I ejected the drive and searched for a marker to annotate my findings with an F.

I wriggled the second device out of my pocket, and my heart felt like it wanted to pound its way out of my chest. I installed the information and discovered the Mock Trial America Schedule of events. I even clicked out of the mock trial catalog to see if something might have been hidden, but there was nothing unexpected on the drive. It received the notation MTA.

An unexpected knock on my door startled me. None of our team should be in the hotel. If it wasn't Jane, whoever was at the door wouldn't have a keycard unless they were staff, and they'd be able to enter anyway.

Jane would accuse me of being paranoid, but as quietly as I could, I picked up the laptop, closed the lid, and snuck into the bedroom to hide the drives in the safe.

With more pounding on the door, I realized how alone I was. No one would hear the noise and come to my rescue. There weren't many options, but a call to Officer Knight might be in order—until I remembered my phone sat in the middle of the conference table next to the flowers. I pressed my fingers to the space between my brows and prayed the visitor would go away.

The rapping stopped, followed by muffled words spoken in two different octaves. When it became quiet, I waited, wondering what could be happening. My curiosity got the better of me. I tiptoed to the door and forced myself to peer out. I'd put her out of my mind, but clearly relieved, I exhaled and yanked on the knob. "ZaZa, thank goodness, it's you."

ZaZa stood with her hands on her hips and eyed me with suspicion. "What are you doing here? I thought you would be on the legal tour."

"The judge has a bad history with a math teacher, so I was uninvited."

"It's his loss."

Her sudden and short commiseration confounded me. I didn't know why it brought tears to my eyes. It seemed there were few things we agreed upon since we lost Charles, but we both taught math and encountered students with a paralyzing fear of numbers, employing similar tactics to ease students' apprehension.

"What are you doing instead?"

I swiped at my face. "I just … ah …woke up." The yawn I started to fake turned real, and she gave me a withering glance. "Did you need something?"

She glared at me. "I wanted nothing, but I sent away the visitor pounding on your door."

Too earnestly I said, "What did he look like?"

"Some guy in workout clothes carrying towels and a robe."

My spa treatment? With more to do than lounge around and

indulge myself, I said, disguising my regret, "How'd you like a massage? My treat." Her jaw dropped. "This week would never have been the same without you." That was too true.

"That would be ..."

I tilted my head, prompting a reply.

"Acceptable." She glanced away from me, saying softly, "You should be proud of the work your students have done." If I'd had enough time, I'd have worked up the courage to give her a hug. Two accolades in one day? Before I could puff out my chest, she said, "I never thought you could pull it off." She stared at me for a beat. "You do not look so good, Katie." A strange smile crept across her face. "Even worse than usual. I suggest you go back to sleep."

The ZaZa I knew, and worked hard to ignore, had returned.

"I'll do that. What'll you be doing this evening?"

"This trip has been a traumatic ordeal. I need a break. After the massage…" It seemed to me she'd taken a sabbatical the entire week. She let out an exaggerated sigh and gazed dreamily at some vague spot on the ceiling. "I have a date."

"Do I know him?"

Her gaze turned scornful. "I doubt that very much."

"Have fun, and ZaZa, thanks for being here."

Reassigning the spa time was much simpler than summoning the courage to examine the deadly drives. I set everything on the table, and picked up the third one, threading it over and under my fingertips, trying to center my scattered thoughts as the device climbed up and down the four-step ladder until it tumbled from my fingers and onto the floor. I scooped it up and examined it carefully before inserting it. It whirred for a relatively long time, but just before I conceded it was a bust, a rectangle popped up requesting a username.

From past integrations with passwords, I knew when too many were offered, a device could lock out the user, so my choice had to be considered with care. After pacing back and forth through the two rooms and interlacing my fingers, hoping for inspiration, and finding none, I decided on a diversion.

Our trip journal needed updating. I opened to the first empty page and jotted a few notes, then flipped to the back pages and the multiple meanderings of curious minds. Mitchell was out of jail, but not necessarily out of law enforcement's line of sight. I wanted to make certain he was cleared and no one else in our party came under scrutiny, so that meant finding out who had killed Wendell.

So much had happened, I delayed telling Jane about Natalianna and still hadn't found the right time. Maybe the right time didn't exist. Poor Natalianna might've been guilty, but we had no way of knowing. Maybe she had been an assassin and maybe she hadn't, but she was in the right places until she wasn't. She had the opportunity to do away with Wendell, but she, too, was a victim.

Felicity topped our viable suspect list of those with realized access to dimethyl sulfate. I'd be able to talk to her again when I returned the formula. Of course, I'd have to explain how I came to have the drive, but I had witnesses. Miranda Diaz, Wendell's now known girlfriend, didn't seem to have a strong motive, but love can make people do strange things. Lester was a conundrum. The company he worked for was out a supposedly worthless recipe for purple dye, and although he could work for Mr. X and be the culprit, he'd taken me into his confidence after letting me know I was not among *his* suspects—classic misdirection.

I turned to Jane's list of suspects who didn't seem to

have any connection to the murder poison and included our primary driver who was never seen again. We'd discussed Junior and didn't believe he had it in him to kill someone. Adding our names hadn't been even the least bit funny. Jane had penciled in the others to fill out the list, but we hadn't uncovered possible motives. I trailed the names with my finger, lingering on the flight crew, which reminded me of the coded card I'd found in the cockpit.

I lifted the vase. The checklist card was gone. I searched the floor, the chairs, the closets, all the drawers in both rooms, under the beds, and even in the trash cans. The card had vanished.

FORTY-TWO

I slumped in front of my laptop, staring at the pulsing rectangle, frustrated. I thrust the glass vase back into its more tolerable position, dead center in the middle of the table. A shower of petals dropped from among the stems, and something clattered noisily against the polished black walnut surface. I dusted away the buttery yellow flowers and uncovered a flat, gun-metal gray, rectangular plastic box measuring about one and a half by one half by two inches. I searched my tired, muddled mind, and realized it looked a little like Wendell's dictating recorder. I took a photo and let google describe the unobtrusive nanny cam in my hand.

I bolted upright. What if the man Samara believed to be my husband hadn't originally been here to take something, but rather to leave something behind? I trusted Samara hadn't allowed him to enter, but she may have inadvertently accepted the daisies and the surveillance device nestled innocuously amid the blooms.

If someone was monitoring Jane and me, it wouldn't have been for a perfume recipe or a mock trial schedule. There must have been something else. I rewound all the conversations we'd had in this room. At the same time, I flipped open the journal and fanned the pages to my decryption of the code on the card. My translation looked more and more like a username and password.

I had no time to lose. I dropped the nanny cam in a glass of water next to the vase (Jane couldn't miss it) and turned the lens to the cloudy view outside in case it continued to emit a signal.

The laptop, drives, and journal fit snugly in my backpack along with my keycard and my billfold. I raced to the elevator. Watching the numbers light up on their way toward our floor, I imagined coming face to face with Wendell's murderer. The thought forced me to dash to the stairs. Why take a chance? Just before I gently closed the exit door, the elevator dinged, and someone exited.

Descending the stairs softly, but as quickly as possible, I tripped. Catching myself, I halted just long enough to punch in Drew's number. It went to voicemail. If he'd turned off his phone, I was certain they all did in deference to the Supreme Court of Georgia.

I raced down another flight and called Officer Knight. Her phone also went to voicemail. "This is Katie Wilk. I've come into possession of four flash drives, which might have been what Samara's assailant was after."

The air pressure in the stairwell changed ever so slightly, and I heard the small click of a door closing.

I blundered down the last few flights and slammed into the push bar on the door at the end of the stairs, but instead of ending up surrounded by people in the lobby, I spilled out into the vacant alley behind the hotel. Try as I might, my keycard didn't readmit me.

A thousand thoughts clouded my head and matched the sky as I hustled out of the gloomy, dismal backstreet. Where should I go? Library? Coffee shop? Courthouse? What would be open? How could I find the nearest police station? Encountering too little foot traffic early on Friday evening to feel protected, I decided I needed a crowd. As I ran, I called Pete.

Nothing. No connection. Or maybe my phone had been jammed again.

I raced to the location where I knew lots of people congregated. When I stopped running, I gasped. The immense MJ loomed in front of me.

I dragged my feet to the admission counter where I gathered my inner strength, bought a ticket, and squeezed my eyes shut for the entire ride up. The door opened and I stumbled onto the observation deck. My eyes didn't stray, but I sought a table with a clear line of sight to the entry at a seat right next to the monstrous window. I'd either have to look over the city or take a different seat and jeopardize my safety.

I placed the journal next to my laptop and studied my solution before reinserting the third drive. My server set down a glass of iced tea I ordered and retreated.

A pair of quotation marks set off the first thirteen upper and lower-case alphanumeric characters, "WbWolm1b9e1r6." The string that followed contained punctuation marks and special characters in the rest of my decryption.

I confidently entered the characters into the username

field. The screen dinged, and a message popped up, flashing red in case I missed it.

Two more attempts before access denied

I'd been wrong before, but not often. Between measured glances at the door, I chewed on my thumbnail, a nervous habit I thought I'd conquered years ago, and carefully considered my options before making a second attempt. After another chastising ding, angry at myself, I wondered what I'd done incorrectly. What would be kept on a flash drive requiring such a level of security? And how did I get it wrong?

Examining the list of suspect names again, the solution took my breath away. Again, I took a moment to observe diners entering the door and upbraided myself. My transcription had been imprecise, but the numeral '1' could look an awful lot like the letter 'I.' I breathed deeply, typing with accuracy befitting a neurosurgeon, and was rewarded with a new screen.

My brow furrowed. The page opened to a dialog box with seven input rectangles.

Admittance requires password and account number.

My arithmetic mind kept interfering. With twenty-six letters in the alphabet, ten numerical digits, an asterisk, a dash, an ampersand, and dollar sign, there were over a hundred billion possible combinations. Would my decryption be correct?

Swallowing my own momentary math anxiety, I trusted I'd discerned the correct combination for the characters needed. I pecked at the keyboard, entering one character after another and hit return.

Permission granted

The short menu in the upper left-hand corner offered a range of tasks, including the options to make payments, read year-to-date invoices, change password, access account information, deposit money, and transfer assets. I didn't take the time to open the amended file added to the drive. I had too much to do.

For my first task, I changed the username and password and wrote BA, my shorthand for bank account, on the side of the drive.

To make sure there were no other surprises, I inserted the fourth device. Much like the first flash drive, it opened with a video. Unfortunately, the video was a collection of fifteen still shots of what looked like a sophisticated guidance system. I shook my head, smarting from Lester's lie. He'd easily led me to an erroneous conclusion. The puzzle on the final screen required sliding twenty-three tiles into some semblance of a blueprint. The puzzle lines disappeared with the lilting music to indicate a correct placement of all the pieces, and when complete, I clicked the enter icon, but instead of super-secret guidance plans, a recipe filled the screen, using crushed snail shells and potash to create Imperial Purple dye. I fell back into the chair in fascination and took a breath before scribbling IP on the drive.

I took a moment to glance out the window. The merest hint of orange backlit a sky filled with beautiful architecture, and the night swallowed everything at a lower elevation except the white dots of city lights. My harried reflection indicated I still didn't like heights, but I feared the consequences of my discovery more.

Returning to the disturbing account information on drive three, the balance grabbed my attention and shook it. I knew it wasn't true, but if I let Jane tell Officer Knight she'd seen Kuznetsov on Thursday evening, and Knight discovered the notation of monies paid to Natalianna Kuznetsov for service rendered, the Mackeys would likely slide back into first place among the murder suspects.

In order to gain access to the drive, someone needed the username, password, and physical storage device. I possessed all three, but what would I do with eleven million dollars and change belonging to Sapphire Skyway Trust? The missing money.

The username was key. I understood what was behind Wendell's death and I had a pretty solid idea who'd stolen the money, but I needed irrefutable proof. If I didn't get it right, Jane and her dad could both be facing criminal charges, and I might be considered an accessory. I slid the BA drive into my pocket, patting it to make certain it stayed where I put it. The strain of the week weighed heavily on my heart. My head drooped into my hands. I closed my eyes for what seemed like only a few seconds and entirely missed Jane's approach. The critical tone of her greeting surprised me.

"Katie, what are you doing here?"

I clutched my chest, tossing everything from the table into my backpack. "You scared me. How did you find me?" I leaned forward and planted my hands on the table. "Never mind. I've got so much to tell you. I found the drives."

"We guessed right this time." Jane tilted her head at the figure behind her. My stomach lurched and I clenched the edge of the table with both hands to steady them when I glanced over her head. I knew, without a doubt, the eyes of the killer hid behind those dark glasses.

FORTY-THREE

I first questioned what kind of person wore sunglasses at night. My second question was how would we make it out of this alive?

I hoped the need to be with the team would speed us along. "Sorry. We should get back to the kids. I suppose they're expecting us." I stood up too fast. My chair flew out behind me and crashed to the floor.

Noah Lexington chivalrously lifted it, set it on its legs, and said to the startled restaurant patrons nearby, "It's all good." He hooked his thumbs on the front of his bomber jacket, but I didn't want to find out what gave the pocket its heavy, ponderous, sinister swing, and I worried about our safety.

"Drew said to take our time. He ordered Jeeno's. Again," Jane said.

My hope was dashed. If they weren't expecting us, they wouldn't know we were in trouble or worse. We would be at the mercy of a murderer. I tried to think of a way to keep us in the crowd where we might be protected until I figured out what to do. "I'm a little light-headed and could use a quick bite first, if that's okay. Have you eaten, Jane?"

I wanted nothing better than to be wrong about Noah, but he said with a mischievous lilt, "I know this great speakeasy." His smirk gave me the willies. "Can I talk you into stopping for a unique adult beverage?"

"Noah has frequented the best places, Katie. He always knew where they made a mean—"

"Aviation? You know the gin drink?" I encouraged her to think about the tenuous connection with our escape room fiasco and finding Wendell.

"Never heard of an Aviation." Noah gestured toward the elevator. Before I could say I wasn't in the mood for a drink, he added, "But they have an entire menu of delicious food, anything you could possibly dream up." He slid his glasses to the top of his head, and the piercing cold gleam in his eyes told me he knew I'd worked out at least some of his involvement in the nefarious incidents, and Jane was at a distinct disadvantage. He reached for my bag. "Let me carry that for you. You look like you're going to crash."

"No, I'm alright." I winched it onto my shoulder in one fluid motion. "I can carry it."

"Nonsense. I insist." He latched onto the strap and yanked hard, relieving me of my burden. "Mama taught me to be considerate, to always help a lady," he said with an ominous glint in his eyes. "Sorry."

Not sorry.

Jane snaked her arm through mine. "Katie, the tour at

the Georgia Supreme Court was inspiring. Dorene's friend entertained us with stories of outlandish criminal cases tried before him, on the public record, of course, and he said he can always detect the guilt or innocence of the defendant."

"I wonder if he'd have the same success rate if he had to determine the innocence or guilt of a friend or family member." When the word guilt came out a little louder than anticipated, Noah gave me a not-so-subtle nudge toward the exit.

Jane continued, "And you should have heard what he had to say about Dorene."

I listened but with only one ear. I had to let Jane know we were in trouble. We'd studied Morse code with the kids when we began our preparation for the *Titanic* trial. I gave her three short squeezes and three more separated by a moment of time, but Jane rolled out of my grasp and toward the terrifying mile-high windows before I could complete my message.

She sighed. "Just one more look."

I gritted my teeth to keep them from chattering and took my place next to her, pretending to admire the view. My head pounded with questions. *What could I do to keep her safe? How would we get away from Noah without anyone else getting hurt? Would Jane understand?* I took another shot and repeated signing 'escape' to my reflection as Noah slithered next to me and said, "If you want to relieve your parent volunteers some time tonight, we'd better get going."

"Marietta and Eddie have been wonderful, but they've got to be exhausted. Maybe we *should* get back to the kids now," said Jane. "There's bound to be extra pizza."

"After all you've been through, I'm sure they'll understand a short respite." Noah edged us into the glass tube of doom.

I wasn't smashed against the outside and I didn't have to

look out, but I realized Noah was trapped in the space with us. Someone would notice if he tried something, wouldn't they? "This has been a week of reunions, Felipe and Rocky, you two and Wendell."

"Poor Wendell," Jane said. "Every once in a while, he awarded us a good moment. I think he was at his finest when we started our pilot's training."

"Wendell was a crucible. You realize he did everything for money, Jane." Noah continued to stare at me, and I tried to hide the thought, *so would you.*

The door hadn't quite closed when someone yelled, "Wait," and pressed the call button. The doors retracted. A group of four adults and two youth crammed onto the car and shunted the three of us to the rear, forcing Jane away from me and Noah. I caught Noah's irritated image in the glass.

"I couldn't tolerate Wendell much, but he was broken," Jane said quietly and shook her head. "His dad really did a number on him. He had a rough life."

"Didn't we all?"

"Genes can certainly make an impact." I swallowed, working up the courage to accelerate our conversation. "Wendell said you are a direct descendant of a World War I bomber, and that's his jacket?"

"All the first-born males in our family have worn this jacket. But no others are named after the ace like me."

Jane's forehead creased. The other passengers quieted, listening intently.

"What made him an ace?" I asked. If I could keep him talking, maybe he'd let something slip.

He shrugged. "He flew a mission for the United States Navy in January 1916. I have his papers and his Medal of Honor."

"Navy, wow. How come I didn't know that?" Jane's eyes feverishly circled the small space. "I'd love to see those artifacts, Noah."

His gaze skated to Jane.

"What a legacy," I said, eager to draw his attention back to me. "And what a family heirloom. He made it through the war, I hope."

"Not without lung damage, I'm afraid. On one of his sorties, he crashed and was gassed." His audience gasped. "The lingering effects lasted for the rest of his life."

Jane chewed on her lower lip.

"Have there been other pilots in your family?"

His eyebrows knit together, as if curious to see if I had an agenda, and although I did, he couldn't understand, could he? "No." He raised his chin. "I'm only the second."

I read a hard resolution in Jane's eyes. She'd known Noah a long time, and if I read Jane correctly, I was ninety percent certain she understood Noah was not exactly the person she remembered.

The cityscape rose to greet us, and my eyes locked on the spots of light as they grew larger. I acted as if I'd lost my balance, teetered a bit, jostled the man next to me, and knocked against the car operating panel, clumsily depressing the three remaining selection buttons.

"Oops." I sagged, creating as much deadweight as possible.

Noah dug his iron fingers into my arm and jerked me upright. When we stopped on the eighth floor, Jane used the diversion to slip behind some of the passengers.

Noah's voice grew hard. "Jane."

Bubbly Jane answered, materializing on his other side. "Right beside you, big guy."

"Wouldn't want you to get lost."

He sounded exactly like poor Wendell. More importantly, poor us.

"Look at those flashing lights," said one of the passengers, leaning over to look out the glass. "What's going on?"

Police cars converged on the base of the hotel, and Noah's fingers tightened around my arm even more. He tensed. We slowed for the next stop, and he shoved me toward the opening. I struggled. Jane grabbed at the backpack, and he used his free arm to knock her to the floor.

The jaw of a gray-haired woman, standing in the middle of the car, dropped open. She wound up and swatted Noah with her colossal purse. "What is wrong with you, little man?" He ducked when she swung again.

The elevator stopped. Avoiding another attack, he pushed me aside. I tumbled into our savior while he escaped onto the dimly lit floor.

The door closed. I lent Jane a hand up and turned to hug my rescuer. She lifted her purse, looking ready to smack someone again, and I retreated, but my champion's eyes lit up, and she opened her arms. "Come here, girl. Tell me all about it."

She rocked me back and forth. I decided only Ida gave a better hug, but she was twelve hundred miles away.

FORTY-FOUR

I think our rescuer almost whacked someone again when the elevator finally made it to the lobby level. The doors slid wide, and we stared into the muzzles of a half dozen police guns. Knight immediately dropped her weapon and cleared the car. "You okay?"

"How did you get here so fast?"

She hung her head. "When I finally listened to your voicemail, we went to your hotel. Jane and Noah had already gone to retrieve you, but your students were more than happy to rat out your location."

"Ohhhhh," I groaned. I was so thankful, but we were going to have to deactivate the Find Me feature soon, certainly when we returned to Minnesota.

Drew pushed through the bodies and embraced Jane like

there'd be no tomorrow. "I got your SOS."

"He got away." She looked up into his face and pounded his chest.

"We'll find him."

She turned to me with fire in her eyes. "You let him take the drives."

I wriggled my finger into my pocket, extracted the device marked BA, and handed it to Knight. "He has my computer, which I will miss, and three other drives, but we have what we need."

My eyes met Jane's. "How did you know?"

She sniffed. "If he hadn't gone on and on about his ancestor in World War I, I might not have thought much about your ASL signs. Not bad, using a reference to escape twice. You do everything with a purpose. Patricia will be proud. But more to the point, the United States entered the war to end all wars on April 6, 1917, a year after Noah's supposed ancestor flew, and the first and only naval ace, which by the way requires downing more than one enemy aircraft, was Lieutenant JG David Ingalls. How did you know?"

The disciplined entry of the rest of our team, marched together by Timmy and his crew, interrupted my explanation. My students appeared unusually ill at ease, but the worry on their faces dissolved when I raised my hands, lifting them in a question, and said, "What does it take to get a minute alone around here?"

Relaxed and surrounded by good wishes, I began, again, writing out the disk's username and my explanation.

Obnoxious noise from a malcontent burst from the front of the hotel. Officer Day wrestled Noah Lexington inside, hands cuffed behind his back. "Let me go." He shook his entire being and the jacket front flapped heavily. My arms flew out like a mother hen's protective wings, shielding my chicks.

"Look out. There's something in his pocket," I cried.

Day pulled up on Lexington's arms. Lexington wriggled as Knight fished a canister out of his pocket, bagged, and tagged it. If it was more dimethyl sulfate, he'd have a host of new charges brought against him.

"How did you catch him?" I asked.

Day threw a glance over his shoulder as Mitchell stormed in the doors carrying my backpack. "Mr. Mackey air tagged your bag."

Mitchell lifted one of the outside flaps, revealing a small, shiny circle clipped to the zipper. He grinned awkwardly. Jane lowered her head and shook it from side to side. "Oh, Dad. What next?"

Lexington thundered, "Let me go."

"You'll go away for a long time," Day said.

Lexington bristled.

I couldn't wait to hit him with another jarring realization. "Your username and passwords weren't very secure." I wrote out the first seven letters and filled in between with the next six— WWI1916bomber.

I passed the digital keys to their rightful owner, and Lexington squawked and struggled as Officer Day hauled him away.

Officer Knight promised to return the perfume recipe to Felicity Williams and the Imperial Purple formula to Lester and allowed us to return to our hotel.

While waiting for more pizza in the conference room, the kids scolded Jane and me without mercy, complaining about being left out again, explaining what we should have done, and pointing out how they never trusted the guy with the red hair.

CJ brought the dogs. Maverick curled up next to me, and I rubbed my fingers over his silky ears until our fabulous bellboy made a late night, special delivery to Marietta Calder. After the day's happenings, she and Eddie were a bit leery, so the bellboy took it upon himself to open the box for them as we looked on. He ripped the center tape and peeled back one flap at a time. Inside were a dozen gorgeous, black, linen-covered photo books with text highlighting our week away.

"We made one especially for you, Mr. Mackey, in appreciation for providing this wonderful opportunity to participate in Mock Trial America." Lorelei presented the gift with nearly the same pomp and circumstance she'd dedicated to Brock's graduation. "It turned out so well, we printed one for everyone."

With tears in her eyes, Marietta hugged her photo book to her chest and ordered everyone to take the books to their rooms to get some rest. I wasn't sure Eddie would be able to strip it from her until she was fast asleep.

* * *

Morning sunlight streamed through the windows. I sat up straight, thinking I'd missed half the day, but checked the time and flopped back onto the fluffy pillows.

The kids wanted to watch the mock trial championship scheduled for midafternoon, so we booked morning spa treatments for those who wished or a walking tour searching for the local Tiny Doors—the seven-inch artistic visions to enhance community engagement.

We attended the Mock Trial America final and came away more satisfied with our own performances because the team led by Greg and Stephanie won. Their congratulatory salutations included a promise to compete again next year. Galen assured them there would be a different outcome.

The only tasks yet to be checked off the to-do list for the day included supper and packing, but when I counted heads for a trip to the special extraordinary dinner Jane and Mitchell had planned, two students had vanished. My heart boomed like timpani. I checked all the rooms twice. It seemed Brock and Galen finally made good on the subversive look they'd given each other after Eddie had promised everyone would do what they were told.

They hadn't shared plans with the Calders. I checked with the desk, and they hadn't left a message. I'd been lax, and now there were missing.

"Timmy, did you see two of the boys take off?"

Timmy repeated my room checks. He helped parade the five remaining students into the meeting room for interrogation.

"Kids, this is serious. If you know where they might be, you have to tell me. Their lives may depend on it."

"I know nothing," Lorelei said.

Carlee added, "I know less than nothing."

Felipe said, "Ms. Wilk, you caught the bad guy. They'll be fine."

I sputtered. "But what if they're not."

Poised to connect with Officer Knight, my call was halted by the forced earnest look on Timmy's face and the giggling from the girls.

"They're on their way up," said Felipe.

I fumed. My face grew so hot my ears could have been steaming. They would get more than a piece of my mind. What if? What if? *What if* was all I could think of.

The elevator numbers moved in our direction, and I planted myself in front of the doors. In the few seconds it had taken to rise to our floor, I composed my castigation.

The elevator stopped, and I filled my lungs to support my passionate admonishment.

The doors swished to the side, and Jane and Drew stepped out first (I hadn't even noticed their absence), followed immediately by Brock and Galen. I began with, "Jane, how could you leave and not tell me what was happening?"

I spun on Galen and Brock. "Where have you been? How could you go off like that? Don't you know …" Then my ability to speak disappeared.

Galen held out a bouquet of a dozen yellow roses. "Thanks Ms. Wilk. This is from all of us. We had an incredible year."

Stunned, I burst into heartfelt tears and spent most of the ride to the restaurant Mitchell had selected holding back my emotions. However, my eyes popped when I read the serendipitous name of the establishment, and after the delectable shakes and personalized sandwiches, Grindhouse Killer Burgers would certainly be my go-to on our next visit.

FORTY-FIVE

The eventful week came to a delightful end. Texts and calls from family and friends rained in on the students, bestowing kudos for their extraordinary performance and toting home a whopping third-place trophy, and mining for information regarding our return flight and times. A reporter from the *Columbia Sentinel* interviewed each of the students and arranged to have a group photo taken later in the week. She said newspapers from the Twin Cities had requested permission to reprint her article in their weekend variety pages, and local bloggers wanted in on the news.

Jane had spent time with her dad, although quite a bit less time than originally planned, and he understood the importance of her role teaching young adults.

Mitchell met us for breakfast and released Timmy and

his friends from duty, but even after eating, they seemed reluctant to leave. After milling about for an inordinate amount of time, Lorelei laughed and pulled out her deck of cards. "Okay, here's how it's done." The four huge men eagerly pulled chairs around her table and stared at her hands. Timmy even videotaped the routine.

"I can't wait to astound my girlfriend." He screwed up his face and finally said, "We had a great week with you, and don't take this the wrong way, but we'll be very happy never to see any of you again."

Lorelei tossed the deck of cards at him, and he pretended to duck before snatching them out of the air. "Thanks."

ZaZa booked an earlier flight back to Minnesota and left for the airport immediately after breakfast. Leo and Dorene delayed their return for one day, planning to spend the time our adventure had usurped to catch up with old friends, and Mitchell arranged for Drew, CJ, Maverick, and Renegade to fly home in style. The rest of us were scheduled to head home together on the same commercial flight—a blessing.

Mitchell took care of the smallest detail. He set us up in comfortable seats on the airplane, purchased snacks, and provided Atlanta gear, all for the pledge of a return visit. For our final Atlanta experience, he arranged transport to the airport by taking MARTA, the Metropolitan Atlanta Rapid Transit Authority, public transportation without the hassle of driving. After landing and collecting the school van, the two-hour drive to Columbia would get us home in time for supper, and Pete promised me a late-night walk with Maverick.

To placate me, we arrived early, not too early, and ZaZa's flight had been delayed just long enough for us to hear the call for first-class passengers at her gate.

Jane left her boot at the hotel, but mobility required

careful thought so she wouldn't reinjure herself, and she decided she'd be safer sitting. She had her choice of seats on our side of the concourse.

"Don't you love watching people, Katie?" Jane said, scanning passing faces.

"But we have all these people to watch." I let the swish of my hand extend over our fabulous team. "Actually." My hand fell to my side, and I said with a grin, "Aren't you exhausted?"

The kids quietly settled into seats behind us. Although smiling, weariness was visible in the set of their shoulders and their soft gazes. Marietta told no stories. Eddie reclined, extending his legs crossed at his ankles, closing his eyes, and letting his head drop back in a most uncomfortable pose.

"So that's where she always disappeared to," Jane said, with whimsy in her voice.

"Who?"

"ZaZa."

I glanced at the opposite gate. Poised to enter the jetway, ZaZa hoisted the strap of her purse over her shoulder. I attempted to catch her eye, but my wave halted in midair when I recognized the man laughing with her. I slid down in my seat.

"What's wrong girlfriend?" Jane said.

"The man with ZaZa is someone I knew a long time ago." My fingertips thrummed across the armrest. "He isn't … wasn't a nice man."

I watched them move together toward the agent scanning tickets at the boarding desk. My blood turned to ice when his eyes met mine, and he made a show of putting an arm around ZaZa. She snuggled close. It wasn't a casual movement or a chance encounter. ZaZa was much too staid. But if I tried to tell her about him, she'd accuse me of trying to screw up her life again. I hope he'd changed, or their meeting was fleeting. My breath came back when they disappeared down the boarding bridge.

I caught Carlee's hearty laugh and listened as she and Lorelei debated the best places to use their vouchers. As I considered how to donate mine, Jane said, "I'll always wonder what Natalianna's up to."

I'd been remiss. I hadn't found the time to tell Jane about Natalianna's poisoning. A guilty bead of sweat dribbled down my back.

"I wonder where she's going now."

"Jane, there's something I have to tell you."

Jane flicked two fingers, acknowledging someone across the concourse. "When Drew's deep undercover, I pray every day he'll come home safely. It's a good thing her handler came forward, and they knew how to treat her exposure to dimethyl sulfate. She's an irreplaceable asset. In addition, Drew said, she filled in all the blanks."

"Blanks?" I couldn't make heads or tails of Jane's words. "Handler?"

"For years, Noah funneled money from Dad's charity account for veterans into a private account he named Sapphire Skyway Trust. It was always about the money, for both Noah and Wendell. They resented anyone's good fortune. Wendell took what he could, but Noah stole from Dad every chance he got. He was actually in on a conversation Dad had with an A.B.SEE exec about a possible test run of the remote guidance system. Noah stole an earlier set of the plans. He wanted to sell them on the black market to the highest bidder but needed proof of their worth. Drew said they found a file containing a copy of the plans added to that bank account drive."

"Noah's never been happy it seems."

The corners of Jane's mouth turned down as if she found something unsavory. "Natalianna works undercover for one of our government alphabet agencies. Because of the account holder designation, she thought Dad had hired her to determine how well the remote system functioned before he sold it to the highest bidder. But then she discovered it was really Noah who needed the results. Unfortunately, Noah didn't realize the fentanyl he dispensed would affect him right along with Richard, and he hadn't expected the inclement weather to get in his way."

"And one determined blond pilot."

"There was that. It was bad luck Wendell had a habit of taking things that didn't belong to him. I don't think he ever figured out what he'd stolen, only that if the drive belonged to Noah, it was valuable. Apparently, Wendell found the drive while digging around in the luggage before he took off with you and attempted to ransom it. Wendell planted the camera in the flowers so he could keep tabs on you. When he informed Noah, he became a liability, and Noah cut out the middleman."

She waved again, but more of a goodbye. "Without Natalianna, it could have ended so differently."

I turned to see who else she knew in the airport. Natalianna returned her wave and winked at me.

1917 AVIATION

INGREDIENTS:
2 ounces gin
½ ounce maraschino liqueur
¼ ounce crème de violette
¾ ounce freshly squeezed lemon juice
Brandied cherry garnish

INSTRUCTIONS:
Add the gin, maraschino liqueur, crème de violette, and lemon juice to a shaker with ice. Shake until well chilled.

Strain into a cocktail glass — Nick and Nora glass preferred.

Garnish with a brandied cherry on a stick/skewer.

ZAZA'S CREPES

2 large eggs
1 C whole milk
6 T water
1 C flour
½ tsp salt
1 T sugar
½ tsp vanilla
3 T melted butter

Heat flat pan to medium. Whisk ingredients until smooth. Melt a small amount of butter in the pan. Pour a thin layer of batter onto the pan and swirl to the edges. Cook until the edges begin to brown. Flip and cook on the other side. Each stove is a little different, so watch for your time.

Slide out of pan. Fill with your favorite: berries with sugar, lemon with sugar, Nutella, butter, jam, and fold or roll.

Thank you for taking the time to read *Airplanes, Atlanta, and an Assassin*. If you enjoyed it please tell your friends, and I would be so grateful if you would consider posting a review.

Word of mouth is an author's best friend, and very much appreciated.

Thank you,
Mary Seifert

WHAT'S NEXT FOR KATIE AND MAVERICK?

What happens during summer break should stay on summer break. Free time abounds. Katie hopes to enjoy more time to bike, take longer walks with Maverick, and spend precious time with Pete, but bored by day two, her packed school schedule sounds enticing. To chase away her ennui, she takes on a part-time job, a hobby or two, and promises to help her landlady host a June festival. Then she uncovers more mayhem when ZaZa introduces her new beau.

ACKNOWLEDGMENTS

I had so much fun writing this book because so much of it really happened. This one's for you, John, and your walking canine companion. Thank you for your continued love and support. And for Thomas—fair skies always.

But it takes a village, and I had immense help making the words in this story as true as possible. Rest assured; the mistakes are all mine.

I am grateful for the invaluable help of my editors: Stephanie Dewey and Lee Ellison. You catch so much and make the words shine. I can't thank you enough for your continued encouragement and words of wisdom. I couldn't do it without you.

Of course, those who volunteered to check the continuity and polish the rougher edges include Brenna Gehlen, who helped point out inconsistencies and missing information, and dear friends, Colleen and Dennis Okland, who always make my words flow better and aren't afraid to give their honest opinions. I also appreciate help from my wonderful Guppy Group, Kate Michaelson and Judy Jones. The beta readers, given the task of catching something that doesn't quite sit right or is missing, are instrumental in helping get my stories to the finish line. Thank you Sandra Anderson, Paula Webb, Marcia Koopmann, Susan Gross, and Eve Osborne.

The information regarding flight and aviation came from my brilliant pilot sources: Forrest Lovley, Patrick Sullivan, Thomas Seifert, and Daniel Rogers, and I can't thank you all enough.

Dianne, Richard, Karly, and Stephanie Krizmanich lent

their beautiful names to my characters. And let it be known, I absolutely couldn't do without their friendship.

In my youth, I spent a lot of time with tremendous family friends, Marietta and Eddie Sharkey, and their names fit my story perfectly. Eddie gave me my first plane ride.

Pharmacists know the right questions to ask and Matthew Smith, PharmD, and Anne Bruckner, PharmD, helped refine my understanding and fill in the blanks.

Tourists don't always see what locals see. Help in discovering the flora and fauna found in Nantahala National Forest came from Ruth Neely (as well as the correct pronunciation of the national forest). Jim and Amy Ellingson humored me by attempting their first escape room. We succeeded with seconds to spare, and they checked to make sure my recollection of our intense experience was honest.

The first-rate Barbara Hall tour of Atlanta helped bring the city alive from an insider's perspective. Downtown, Midtown, Buckhead, and Cumberland provided the sights, sounds, smells, and tastes of the locations and brought the action so much closer to mind. I did my best to use that reality. I recreated the iconic The Westin Peachtree Plaza. It's a wonder to visit, but I gave mine a different name. We visited the house where Margaret Mitchell wrote *Gone With the Wind*, walked the streets near the Fulton County Courthouse, toured Truist Stadium and the World of Coca-Cola, and searched for some Tiny Doors. Minnesota has excellent eating establishments, but as of the date this story was completed, none of them have been included in the list of Michelin restaurants, so partaking of such highly rated fare was truly a treat. In addition, thanks, Elaine, for an all-encompassing first-class education of the Atlanta Braves baseball stadium.

In addition, I don't think Luke and Kathy Seifert minded

much being guinea pigs for the Aviation cocktail—they survived. Thanks for joining me on this journey.

Sincerest thanks to my family and friends and everyone who has read my stories. Your comments and notes make it all worthwhile.

* * *

Get all the books in the Katie & Maverick Series!

Maverick, Movies, & Murder
Rescues, Rogues, & Renegade
Tinsel, Trials, & Traitors
Santa, Snowflakes, & Strychnine
Fishing, Festivities, & Fatalities
Diamonds, Diesel, & Doom
Creeps, Cache, & Corpses
Pranks, Payback, & Poison
Juleps, Jockeys & Justice
Airplanes, Atlanta & an Assassin

Get a free short story from Mary—click here to find out how!

Visit Mary's website: MarySeifertAuthor.com/
Facebook: facebook.com/MarySeifertAuthor
Twitter: twitter.com/mary_seifert
Instagram: instagram.com/maryseifert/
Follow Mary on BookBub and Goodreads too!

- **2024 Chanticleer International Book Awards**
  - Semi-Finalist - Mystery & Mayhem category
- **2024 Killer Nashville Silver Falchion Award**
  - Top Pick - Cozy Mysteries
- **2024 International Impact Awards**
  - Winner - Books in a Series

Mary Seifert has always loved a good mystery, a brain teaser, or a challenge. As a former mathematics teacher, she ties numbers and logic to the mayhem game. The Katie & Maverick Mysteries allow her to share those stories, as well as puzzles, riddles, and a few taste-tested recipes.

When she's not writing, she's making wonderful memories with family, exchanging thoughtful ideas with friends, walking her dog whose only speed is faster, dabbling in needlecrafts, and pretending to cook. You can also find her sneaking bites of chocolate and sipping wine, both of which sometimes occur while writing. Mary is a member of Mystery Writers of America, Sisters in Crime, American Cryptogram Association, Dog Writers of America, and PEO.